Unanimous Praise for
Lynn S. Hightower's ELAKI Novels . . .

"ONE OF THE BEST NEW SERIES IN THE GENRE!"
—*Science Fiction Chronicle*

ALIEN BLUES

The smash debut novel—introducing homicide detective David Silver and String, the partner from another planet . . .

"An exciting, science-fictional police procedural with truly alien aliens . . . an absorbing, well-written book." —*Aboriginal Science Fiction*

"Hightower takes the setup and delivers a grittily realistic and down-and-dirty serial killer novel . . . impressive . . . a very promising first novel."
—*Locus*

"Not only are Hightower's aliens truly alien—her cops are actually human! A high-spirited and spooky new *The Silence of the Lambs* with otherworldly overtones."
—Terry Bisson, author of *Voyage to the Red Planet*

"I recommend it highly. A crackerjack novel of police detection and an evocative glimpse of a possible future."
—Nancy Pickard, bestselling author of *IOU*

Turn the page for more rave reviews . . .

"Her cast of characters is interesting and diverse, the setting credible, and the pacing rapid-fire and gripping." —*Science Fiction Chronicle*

"Truly special . . . original characters, plot twists galore, in a book that can be enjoyed for its mystery aspects as well as its sf . . . a real treat." —Arlene Garcia

"Hightower shows both humans and Elaki as individuals with foibles and problems. *Alien Blues* provides plenty of fast-paced action . . . an effective police drama." —SF *Commentary*

"Hightower tells her story with the cool efficiency of a Mafia hit man . . . With its lean, matter-of-fact style, cliff-hanger chapter endings and plentiful (and often comic) dialogue, *Alien Blues* moves forward at warp speed!" —*Lexington Herald-Leader*

"A great story . . . fast and violent . . . difficult to put down!" —*Kliatt*

"An intriguing world!" —*Analog*

ALIEN EYES

The exciting return of homicide detective David Silver and his Elaki partner, String—a shocking case of interstellar violence brought to a new battleground: Earth . . .

"Alien Eyes is a page-turner . . . fun, fast-moving . . . a police procedural in a day-after-tomorrow world." —Lexington Herald-Leader

"Hightower takes elements of cyberpunk and novels about a benevolent alien invasion and combines them with the gritty realism of a police procedural to make stories that are completely her own . . . a believable future with a believable alien culture . . . interesting settings, intriguing ideas, fascinating characters [and] a high level of suspense!" —Fort Knox Turret

"Complex . . . snappy . . . original." —Asimov's Science Fiction

"The sequel to the excellent Alien Blues [is] a very fine sf novel . . . I'm looking forward to the next installment!" —Science Fiction Chronicle

Ace Books by Lynn S. Hightower

ALIEN BLUES
ALIEN EYES
ALIEN HEAT

Alien Heat

Lynn S. Hightower

ACE BOOKS, NEW YORK

If you purchased this book without a cover, you should be aware that this book is stolen property. It was reported as "unsold and destroyed" to the publisher, and neither the author nor the publisher has received any payment for this "stripped book."

This book is an Ace original edition,
and has never been previously published.

ALIEN HEAT

An Ace Book / published by arrangement with
the author

PRINTING HISTORY
Ace edition / July 1994

All rights reserved.
Copyright © 1994 by Lynn S. Hightower.
Cover art by Duane O. Myers.
This book may not be reproduced in whole or in part,
by mimeograph or any other means, without permission.
For information address: The Berkley Publishing Group,
200 Madison Avenue, New York, NY 10016.

ISBN: 0-441-00072-X

ACE®
Ace Books are published by The Berkley Publishing Group,
200 Madison Avenue, New York, NY 10016.
ACE and the "A" design are trademarks
belonging to Charter Communications, Inc.

PRINTED IN THE UNITED STATES OF AMERICA

10 9 8 7 6 5 4 3 2 1

This book is dedicated to my parents, Joyce and Clyde Simmons, who were right not to let me hop a freight train the summer I was fourteen. I still haven't figured out how you knew what I was up to. Psychic, I guess.

Acknowledgments

My thanks to Rachel, for discussions on psychic phenomena, and for all the help during the summer while I worked. Thanks for the doorbells you answered, and the Sno-Cones you brought me.

My thanks to Laurel, who finds things in dreams, and takes it in stride. Thanks for the discussions and insight on psychic phenomena, and for fielding the phone like a pro.

My thanks to Alan, for discussions on the future of basketball, and pickup games—though never again for money. Thanks for the food you brought to my desk, and for screening the interruptions.

To Walls, who knew I needed to talk to him to research this book before I did. Your insights and your honesty were thought-provoking and illuminating. Take care of yourself.

My gratitude to Gary Nolan, top-notch arson investigator. Thanks very much for your time, which is so much in demand, and for the loan of research materials. Your experiences and insights were fascinating and a big help.

ONE

THE QUIET WAS ODD—THE HUSHED SILENCE OF A HOUSE WITH-out utilities, a home without life. The windows were shattered and full of darkness. David flashed his light, saw the clean outline on the soot-blackened floor where they'd found the family dog.

Water dripped somewhere down the hallway. David skirted a pile of blackened rubbish that was still smoking, and walked up the stairs, hoping they'd hold. Wood creaked underfoot.

A soft intermittent chirp made the hair stir on the back of his neck. He flashed his light along the charred walls, saw the red glow of an overloaded detector. He stood on tiptoe to disconnect the chip.

"Seven occupants in the house," came a raspy metallic voice.

David jumped back.

"Two adults, four children. One adult visitor present."

David reached up to loosen the connection.

"Occupants are Celia, age thirty-two—"

He yanked and the voice stopped. Sweat filmed the back of his neck. Wrong, of course, to tamper with the alarm system, but he did not want this litany of the dead. Not when four of them were children.

David heard the wail of sirens—more fire jeeps, late arri-vals, too many and too late. A bomb threat had been called in just as the fire started and the square block of tenements had been sealed off, while the bomb squad looked for explosives that had not been there.

The order for grid release had come a good fifteen minutes after the fire was called in—an eternity under the hot lick of flame. The death toll from the supper club would be astro-nomical, and three houses had burned along with it.

The families had escaped from the other two. This one had ignited early.

David headed down the hallway, shining his light in the master bedroom.

The fire had burned hot and heavy here, lit from below by a burning ember from the supper club next door. David's light caught the charred remains of the bed, where one of the women had been found, her body covering two children, all blackened beyond recognition, fused to a mattress that was nothing more than ashes and springs.

David moved back down the hallway to the baby's room, where another female, Caucasian, adult, had been found outside the door.

Very little damage here. Soot smeared the sheet in the battered old crib where a fire fighter had found the baby. David had seen her tiny nightgowned body laid on a sheet on the pavement next to the charred remains of her mother, her aunt, and her two siblings. She had died of smoke inhalation; there had not been a mark on her. The fireman who had carried her out had crouched at her tiny feet, his eyes red with smoke and tears.

One child and one adult unaccounted for.

David heard shouts, a scream, a muted voice on a bullhorn. He went to the window, careful of broken glass.

The scene below was going from very bad to worse. People pressed against men and women in riot gear, moving in a mass toward the carnage of the supper club.

"Where's Harry?" A woman's voice, hysterical. "I got to know if he's okay. Harry? Where's Harry?"

A man's voice cut her off. "I don't believe there was no fucking bomb."

Anguish and rage were palpable in the heat of the night.

A bottle flew, caught a woman on the lip. Her face blossomed in blood. Someone screamed and the press of bodies surged forward. David heard a crash, saw an ambulance go over in a splatter of broken glass and crumpled metal. The riot was born.

He headed down the hallway at a dead run, thundering toward the stairs.

When the third step broke beneath his feet, his momentum

pitched him headfirst. His ankle twisted and he grabbed the bannister. It held, just for a moment, then the staircase collapsed, and the bannister tore away from the wall. David's stomach lurched as he swung sideways.

"*Shit*," he said, and fell.

It was a quick drop, eight feet and two eternal seconds, and then he was on his back, trying to breathe, the wind knocked out of his lungs.

He lay still in the close, sweltering darkness, the smell of smoke like a hand on his chest. He wondered where his light had landed. He sat up, tried to catch his breath. His chest ached and he rubbed the scar where he'd taken a bullet in the lung, a good six months ago.

Everywhere he turned he felt or sensed a conglomeration of shapes, things, pressing close all around. It was hot here, incredibly hot, and he wondered if there were live embers close by.

He squeezed his eyes shut, fighting the old sick claustrophobia.

And then miraculously, he heard voices. He checked the urge to call out—if there were locals wandering in, he wasn't sure he wanted to be found. A homicide detective would make a prime target.

"The human is a law officer, Yo Free. He would hear the trouble and join in."

"Shut up, will you? I heard something." A woman's voice, sounding exasperated. "Now look at that, will you? Some shithead's disconnected the alarm. These guys go charging around a fire scene with their thumbs up their ass, don't think twice about messing up the scene, and no idea how dangerous it is. First the fire fighters, tramping through with their big boots and gel grenades, then all of a sudden now we got these prima donnas from *homicide* who . . . See that, Wart? I see a light. Hello?"

David wondered if he wanted this irritable woman to find him. "*Down here!*" he shouted. Silence. "Hello? *Hey!*"

"I hear you, baby, hang on."

The shaft of light was a welcome thing, coming through the well of blackness above him. The light hit him in the face, and he covered his eyes with a soot- and sweat-grimed hand.

"Sorry, baby. You Silver?"

David coughed. "Yeah, I'm Silver."

"You hurt?"

"No, but I'm not real comfortable."

"I hear you, baby. Have some patience, I'm a get you. If you don't mind, I'm coming down there an easier way." The woman's voice dropped an octave. "Get his flash and shine it down there, Wart. Keep him talking. He doesn't sound too good."

The light came back.

"Hello, the Detective Silver of homicide. I am Arson Investigator Detective Warden."

David squinted, eyes aching. "An Elaki?" Stupid question; people didn't talk like that.

"Yes, Elaki am me." The tone seemed stiff, though it was hard to tell with Elaki. "You work with Elaki too, I know this. Homicide Detective String? He does the magic tricks?"

David grimaced. "He tries."

He listened to the woman's footsteps, marking her progress. She was close. Something crashed, just a few feet away, then he heard a creak, and saw a stream of light to one side.

"Silver? You in here?"

"Wherever here is." He squinted, aware of her shape, vague and dark, behind the halo of brightness.

"You're in a closet, baby, under the stairwell."

A closet. It made sense. He kept moving, felt himself in open space, felt air circulation, felt the claustrophobia easing away. He could not see the woman in the darkness, but he felt her near him.

"So you're Silver from homicide, huh?" She played the light up and down his chest.

"Yeah. And you?"

She shone the flashlight on her face. "Detective Yolanda Free Clements, Arson Squad. You the turkey disconnected the alarm up there?"

She gave him a half smile, hand on one hip. She was black, high cheekbones, big brown eyes, lush lips. Her face was interesting. Her hair was long, fanning out in the plaited wedge that was all the rage.

She flashed the light at his feet, then let it sweep sideways and behind him. David heard her intake of breath.

He looked over his shoulder. "What is it, Clements?"

"You want to come out of there first?"

And then he saw it, the two of them huddled close, a hand's breath from the spot where he'd fallen.

The missing woman and child.

TWO

THE LIGHT FLICKED ACROSS A BLACKENED TENNIS SHOE, A small one, child's size. David studied the huddled bodies, twined and fused in death. Had they waited under the staircase for rescue, listening for sirens that came way too late?

Outside, voices rose and fell, and David heard a boom that resonated like the beat of a drum.

"You hear that?" Clements said.

David nodded. "Hologram troops. Must be bad out there."

Clements led him back through the burned-out house. The Elaki was waiting by the splintered remains of the front door. He was tall even for an Elaki, eight feet to the usual seven, and so thin David wondered how he stayed erect. Like all Elaki, he was fine-boned and flippy, covered in scales, and balanced on a bottom fringe that rippled like the belly of a snake.

His colors were muted, as if he'd been bleached in the sun. The tender inner area was pale ivory-pink, the outer a soft pearl-grey. His eye prongs were very pronounced, and he skittered sideways when he noticed David staring.

Elaki had arrived on Earth with attitudes reminiscent of the British colonials who had invaded India in the far distant past. They loved to meddle in politics, health care, and anything else that caught their fancy. These days, it seemed almost every aspect of human enterprise had an Elaki element— taint, was how some people put it. The Elaki strength was in social sciences; they were able to cure an array of human mental illness that had overwhelmed psychologists for years.

They were fascinated and bewildered by the human psyche. They made excellent cops, and formidable criminals. They were also racist, arrogant, and prickly. People were fast becoming second-class citizens on their own planet.

6

Warden waved a fin. "Hologram troop, hear this? My other officers in need of the assist."

Clements shook her head. "Wart, baby, they'll tear you apart."

"I will be like flea on hamster—"

Hamster? David thought.

"I will hide in hologram. I can be of the help."

Clements looked at David. "Your Elaki this stubborn?"

"Worse."

It was hot out—still in the eighties, here after dark, the humidity one hundred percent. David didn't feel the heat, he didn't feel anything, but sweat drenched his clothes, and Clements's face glistened.

The scene was lit well enough to pass for high noon, though the light had a bluish cast. Emergency lights from ambulances and police cars flicked across the holograms, making the troops—except the real ones—go green with every pulse. The holographic troops flickered around the edges, the stuff of nightmares for the living-breathing cops interspersed inside. The real cops wore riot gear and carried stun clubs—weapons that sent a cone of voltage capable of knocking ten people off their feet with one sweep.

The worst was over. The troops, backed up where it counted by real officers, had cut through the crowd, separating them into smaller and smaller bunches. People had been herded down the street and away from the scene, and the riot cops had them on the run, wearing them down.

Bodies lay side by side away from the road. Even blackened, the human corpses had bulk and form. The Elaki remains were like deflated balloons, long and shriveled and black. David saw two fire fighters carrying a dead Elaki out of the supper club, saw the body break apart in the middle, streaming black-streaked yellow juice.

Supper club was a misnomer for what had once been someone's cherished brownstone, years ago when the neighborhood had been good. Up until tonight, it was a place where Elaki and humans could come together in vice and mingled bad habits. It was a dark, Elaki-style maze of rooms with loud music, cheap drinks, varietal smokes. Upstairs cubbies were available for anything from gambling to group sex. The club was frequented by just enough of the fringe criminal element to attract young, fun-loving humans and Elaki, the poor and the slumming wealthy, and anyone else who imagined they were up for a walk on the wild side. The club gave them a little taste of down and dirty ambience, and the bad guys liked dropping in to be admired.

The smell of smoke and burnt flesh was heavy in the night air. David looked up, saw press choppers, though he could not hear them over the boom of the holographic generator. He wondered if anyone had tried to reassure the residents, organize them into helping units. It would have gone differently on the other side of town.

A woman in a tight white dress sat sideways on the tracks in the middle of the road. Her dress was soot-stained; one of the fragile shoulder straps had broken loose and peeled away from burned and blistered flesh. Tears ran down her cheeks, and she opened and closed her fist.

Her temple was bleeding thickly. David knelt beside her, unfolded his handkerchief, and pressed it to the side of her head.

Her fist opened and closed, opened and closed. "I had his hand."

"It's all right," David told her, his voice a soft, reassuring murmur.

She clutched his arm, fingernails breaking the flesh. "I climbed out the window, he was right behind me, *right* behind me. I tried not to let go. I pulled him so hard. I knew if I let go he would die."

"Can you stand up?"

She opened her palm and David saw that she held a class ring. It looked very new. David saw from her eyes that she was sliding into shock. He put an arm beneath her shoulders.

"Let's get you up and out of here."

She didn't react, except for the convulsive opening and closing of her fist. David heard an engine, looked over his shoulder, saw a police wagon headed their way.

He bent down and picked her up. She was small, for which David was grateful. Her leg was red where the track had left an impression in the skin. She smelled like smoke, sweat, and lilacs. She wrapped her arms around his sweaty neck, and hid her face in his shoulder. His shirt grew wet with her blood and his sweat.

He went to the closest medic wagon. The overturned ambulance still lay on its side. A woman in a Red Cross jumpsuit had crawled through the smashed windshield and was rooting around for supplies.

A black man with a Red Cross patch on his shirtsleeve gave David a look of annoyance. "Triage, man. If she's yours, you'd do better to take her to a hospital yourself."

David frowned at him. "I'm a police officer. I found her in the middle of the road. She's shocky, you got a blanket?"

"You mind getting it? Right there in the truck. Then set her over there, I'll get to her when I can."

David found a stack of slivery thermal blankets, disposable. They felt like old-fashioned gum wrappers. He set the woman in the dirt beside the ambulance, wrapped her in the blanket, squeezed her hand. She opened and closed her fist.

David walked away.

A man in a fireman's hard hat and a business suit shouted for more light. The fire was licked, but the fire fighters were still hauling people out of the supper club. David looked at the growing stack of bodies. He felt a hand on his shoulder.

"If you're through gawking there, they need us to go upstairs and pull crispy critters out."

David turned, saw the sweaty, soot-stained face of his partner, Mel Burnett.

"I see you survived the riots," David said.

"Hell, yes, it's you had me worried, what took you so long? Had to send a cute little mouth from arson in after you, and she was none too pleased."

"Arson Detective Yolanda Free Clements?"

"Her Elaki calls her Yo Free." Mel sniffed. "Smells like a fish fry, with the Elaki in there."

David glanced at the Elaki bystanders and winced. As usual, their backs were turned on the carnage, out of consideration for the privacy of the victims. David followed Mel around the side of the building. His shirt stuck to his back, soaked in sweat. The streets ran with water and garbage.

"You hear anything on the bomb threat?" David asked.

"Just rumors, nothing confirmed. Looks like it got called in just as the fire got started. The grids froze traffic for miles, and of course they did a search before they'd release. Then the fire vans got caught up in the middle of the evacuation, so we get this piece of shit circus here."

A surge of intense light flooded the streets, as if the sun had come up. The holographic troops faded, the power siphoned to the light generator.

In better parts of town, this wouldn't have happened. In better parts of town, a foamy syrup would have dripped from ceiling spigots and quelled the first wisp of smoke.

David coughed, chest hurting. Technology was a wonderful thing, if you could afford it.

THREE

DAVID SET THE PHONE DOWN AND LEANED BACK IN HIS CHAIR, wondering who it was he'd been planning to call. He smelled bad, clothes stiff with dried sweat, smoke grime, and blood. He wanted a shower. He wanted a nap. The body was weary, but the mind was jazzed.

He'd like to be clean.

He glanced up at the captain's glassed-in cubicle. The people were still in there—an old man, his young teenage son, and a woman whom they all seemed to watch and defer to. They had trooped through the squad room, ducking their heads, too polite to stare, but bewildered by the sweaty, smoke-stained cops, every desk occupied, every printer going, all computers alive and talking.

No one paid them any attention, except the captain, who paid them too much.

David took a covert look at the woman. She sat separately from all of them, looking preoccupied and saying little. She cocked her head to one side as if listening to something, turned and looked at David.

She was pretty, from a distance, and David was aware how bad he looked. He smiled, embarrassed, and she smiled back. Captain Halliday craned his neck to see who she was looking at. The man and the boy turned, and Halliday motioned David into the room.

"Shit," he muttered.

Della looked up at him as he went by. Her expression caught him—he was seeing that unhappy look on her face more and more often. A sandwich sat untouched on her desk. Her hair was bound tightly back, as if she could not be bothered with it. For once in her life, she was not drinking a Coke. The joke around the department was that if she ever needed a

11

transfusion, they would put the IV in the Coke machine.

"You'll have to excuse my staff," Halliday was saying. "We had a bad fire last night."

The death toll had been over one hundred sixty, the last David had heard. He did not like being apologized for to these suburban well-feds who ought to have more sense than to be bothering them right now.

"Dr. Jenks, this is Detective Silver, he handled your wife's file when it came through our office."

David frowned, shook the man's hand, thinking Jenks was a name he recognized. The man's grip was firm, but his bones felt frail. His hair was white, tufty, his eyes pale blue, with heavy bags underneath. His suit was expensive, and David knew from his days in bunco that the man's watch was worth more than a year of his own wages. The man's air of sad fatigue quelled any flutter of envy.

"My son, Arthur," Jenks said softly.

The boy was overweight, mannerly, and serious. His hands were soft and childish, but his grip was firm.

"How are you?" David said.

The boy blushed, ducked his head, and looked at the floor.

"Teddy Blake," Halliday said, looking over his reading glasses at the woman.

Unusual name, David thought, shaking her hand. For some reason her cheeks turned pink when he met her eyes—brown eyes, large, gentle, and tired. Her hair was thick and full, and had been plaited carelessly. Likely it had been neat and elegant some hours ago, but now strands of soft straight hair hung down the back and sides.

She wore loose khakis and a stark white shirt that was too large and slid down off one tanned shoulder. She pulled it up absently, giving David a glimpse of an ivory satin bra strap.

David remembered the case now. Theresa Jenks had disappeared in Chicago three months ago. She'd been seen in Saigo City by a friend, and the Chicago PD had contacted their office, asking them to follow up.

It was a courtesy thing, a not very likely lead that had petered out. David had done what he could, which wasn't much, considering the workload.

"Any news from Chicago?" he asked gently.

"Cold trail," she said, low and soft.

Halliday was nodding. "Detective Silver will pull the file, answer your questions, anything else you need." He seemed to be talking to Blake, who nodded. "Any problems, concerns, questions, he's your man. David, I think conference room C is open."

David gave him a thoughtful look. Conference room C—reserved for top brass and special occasions. It actually had carpet, and almost-fresh paint on the walls. No windows, of course. That would have been too much.

Halliday gave David a careful look. "Ms. Blake was called in to help by the family. She's been working with Bruer in Chicago."

She didn't look like a private investigator, David thought. Which would probably make her a good one.

"I'm a psychic, Detective Silver." Blake lifted her chin and narrowed her eyes.

David's smile faded. He looked at Halliday, making it intense, then cleared his throat. "The conference room is this way."

Teddy Blake's smile had faded with David's. She raised an eyebrow at him and headed out.

David waited till everyone was clear before he spoke. Halliday was still standing, his tie knotted neatly, pointed chin clean shaven. He didn't show the fatigue he surely must feel. He'd gone home and had a shower, David thought, wishing he'd done the same, wishing he was there now.

"Any chance we can reschedule this, Captain? Under the circumstances?"

Halliday sank into his chair and rubbed his forehead, eyes shut tight. "These people are wealthy, David, they have influence. I have orders, which means you have orders. *Go.*"

David went, pulling Halliday's door softly shut. String, the Elaki David and Mel often partnered with, was holding up a fan of cards to Della. David noticed the boy, Arthur, edging close.

"Please to choose," String said.

Della glared at him. "String, I am *not* in the mood."

Arthur took a small step forward. "I'll choose."

Dr. Jenks shook his head. "No, no, Arthur, don't—"

"It's okay," David said.

String's left eye prong swiveled and he slid close to Arthur, who swallowed, but stood his ground. David had the impression Arthur had never been quite so close to an Elaki before.

String was fascinated by human children; he would be kind with this boy. David had the feeling that Arthur needed kindness.

He looked at Teddy Blake. "I'll call the file up and print it out. Be just a minute."

"There's physical evidence, isn't there?" She was civil with him, but the warmth was gone. "The detective in Chicago, Bruer. He said there was a sweater. I'd like to see it, please."

"Picture do?"

She looked at him like he was stupid. "I need the actual sweater."

"It's in a warehouse, all the way across town. May take a while."

Her chin lowered and she looked away. Evidently she wanted it now. Had she expected him to keep it in the bottom drawer of his desk?

David sat down at his computer and keyed in a command, bringing up the Jenks's file. Theresa Jenks had been content to marry a mere plastic surgeon, but she was the niece of Bianca Jenks, who had turned the Jenks's family money into a hefty fortune. Theresa had numerous assets, and there would be more when Bianca died. David glanced at the husband. He stood to inherit a nice sum, but most of it, if Theresa followed family tradition, would go to her child. David looked at Arthur. The serious look was gone from his face, and he was laughing and talking too loud, as boys of that age did when their defenses were down. David felt a twinge, thinking how vulnerable children were. He glanced back at Jenks, then to the computer screen. He had precious little to report. These people were wasting their time. They were also wasting his.

The phone rang.

"Silver, homicide."

"Daddy?"

"Kendra?"

"No, *Mattie*."

He should have known, but all of his girls sounded like babies when they called.

"Daddy, you know how you told me to leave Elliot's food bowl out near the garden? I looked in there and I think he ate something!"

"Really?"

"Really, Daddy."

"That's wonderful, Mattie. Did you look around, see if you could find him?"

"Yep, a long long time, but it's so hot. I had to come in."

He pictured his daughter, sturdy tan legs pocked with scabbed over bug bites, wandering through cornstalks which were almost over her head, rampaging through bean plants and tomato vines, looking for the large, fat, ill-natured iguana who had been missing over a week.

"Is Mommy there?"

"She's outside with Haas. They're looking for Elliot too."

David set his teeth. He didn't just want to find the iguana, he wanted to find it before Haas did. Rose's very good friend, Haas.

"Bye, Daddy."

Mattie sounded hopeful and happy. He felt ashamed to resent Haas's efforts to find the iguana. Likely Haas was reacting to the same thing he was—the look in his little girl's eyes when she stood outside and called the lizard home.

"Bye, sweet," David said. He looked up, saw that the woman, Teddy Blake, was watching him. He looked back to his screen, hitting the print file command.

What kind of a woman called herself Teddy, anyway? The kind of woman who set herself up to take advantage of a bereaved family, with the willing and able cooperation of the Chicago and Saigo City PD. Money gave wealthy people large pockets of vulnerability.

Something he'd never have to worry about.

He felt a hand on his shoulder. Mel leaned down, eyes on Blake.

"What you got here, David?" Mel had just had a haircut, leaving the brown hair short and curly. His skin was sun-bronzed, his shoulders solid and muscular under the worn suit.

"She's a psychic, Mel. Working on a missing person. Remember Theresa Jenks?"

"The red sweater we found? Next to the book on reincarnation?"

"That's the one."

A lazy smile spread across Mel's face. "No kidding? So we're baby-sitting them when we got a death toll over two hundred in this supper club fire?"

"Two hundred now?"

"And counting. Captain wants 'em in conference room C, I bet."

"Very good, Mel."

"Maybe I'm psychic. Look here, David, why don't I help you out? No point leaving them standing around in the squad room. I'll get 'em settled down in C, do the pretty for you." He squeezed David's shoulder. "Feel free not to show up."

FOUR

DAVID CHECKED HIS WATCH AS HE WALKED DOWN THE HALL-way. He hadn't meant to leave them alone so long, but three calls had come through on the fire, Detective Clements was keeping him informed to the minute on special interest groups who took credit for the arson, and he'd taken a moment to wash up and change his shirt.

He heard Mel laugh, and opened the door to the conference room.

No one noticed him, printout clutched in one hand, clean white shirt neatly tucked into filthy trousers, hair damp where he'd sluiced it with water in the sink of the men's room. Mel was bent over Teddy Blake, refilling her coffee cup. Jenks was smiling benevolently at Arthur, who was holding a deck of cards and listening to String.

Maybe he should let Mel handle it, after all.

He went in quietly, laid the printout in the center of the table. The walls were beige here, instead of green, the carpet tan and freshly vacuumed, the table fake wood grain. There was an actual art print on one of the walls, instead of a wanted poster.

No one seemed impressed.

Blake set her coffee cup down and picked up the printout. David tried to remember what Bruer had told him.

Theresa Jenks had packed a small bag and left in her Mercedes—no, not Mercedes. Some kind of a sports car, which had been abandoned right outside of the city. The navigator chip showed that she'd been to and from the airport, and had programmed a route to First City, though she hadn't followed it.

She'd taken large sums of money from her personal bank account. Nobody liked the sound of that, not David, not Bruer.

She had called her lawyer, but he'd been unable to talk, and she hadn't called back.

Her plane had landed in Pittsburgh, and she hadn't been seen since, had made no charges on any accounts. She'd been gone a week when she was spotted coming out of a Saigo City instant laundromat. It had been a fluke—a man she knew in town on business. He had not been sure it was her.

None of it smelled good to David, and Bruer hadn't liked it either. David had gone to the laundromat and found a battered paperback book on reincarnation, and a sweater hanging from the back of a chair. The book had Theresa Jenks's prints.

Arthur dropped the cards and bent down to pick them up, murmuring apologies.

Teddy Blake frowned as she went through the printout. Either she was skimming, or a very fast reader. She handled the file with a familiar ease, which made David think that for her, working with police investigations was nothing new.

"There's not much there, Ms. Blake, and what is there is pretty straightforward. But I'll be glad to answer questions, if you have any." David stayed on his feet. Making it clear he wanted to leave.

"I might in a minute." She kept reading, and picked up the coffee cup, taking a sip. Making it clear she would take her time.

The wall phone rang. Mel held the pot of coffee up. "David?"

"No, thanks." David grabbed the phone. Listened, hung up. "What's that all about, Mel, some kind of messenger?"

Mel set the coffeepot down. "There we go, Ted, I told you we'd have it down. I'll be right back."

Teddy Blake gave David a smug smile. "The sweater and the book on reincarnation. From the warehouse. I reckon Detective Burnett is more resourceful than others."

She gave herself away when she was rubbing things in. The Southern inflection got thick then.

"You need the actual items?" David said.

She shoved the printout to one side with an air of rejection and disappointment. "I'm a remote reader, Detective. Do you know what that means?"

David shrugged, shifted his weight.

"Why don't you sit down? You can always jump back up again. I promise not to take it as a commitment."

String twitched an eye prong. Dr. Jenks looked from David to Teddy Blake.

David pulled up a chair. "Tell me about your wife, Dr. Jenks."

Arthur looked up. Jenks touched the boy's shoulder. "Sit still, Arthur."

David held his tongue. Jenks had no gift for children, even his own.

"She's outdoorsy, Detective Silver."

David liked the word, outdoorsy. He liked it that Jenks used that word, instead of saying "outdoors woman." If Jenks had said outdoors woman, David would have been positive, for no particular logical reason, that Jenks had killed her himself.

Jenks was staring at a spot on the wall. Even in conference room C, there was a spot on the wall.

"She was a very good swimmer. She liked boating, waterskiing. Fishing."

David smiled at Arthur. "Your mom take you fishing a lot?"

"No, sir."

Arthur did not look like a boy anyone took fishing. David realized he had blundered into painful territory.

The door opened and Mel came in, a parcel crinkling in his hands. David could see the red sweater through the clear package.

"Here we go." Mel unwrapped the plastic and set the neatly folded sweater on the table. Next, he unwrapped a worn paperback that had golden thunderbolts on a black cover, and the word REINCARNATION in large white letters.

Hokey, David thought. Arthur was rubbing a fist in his eyes. The boy should not be here. Someone should be gentling the child through this, not throwing things at him with no warning or care. Blake was a con, but Jenks should have had better judgment.

David leaned across the table, his voice gentle. "Arthur, do you recognize the sweater? Does it belong to your mom?"

Arthur stared at the soft red knit. "Can I pick it up?"

"Sure."

The room was stone quiet. Everyone watched the boy paw through the sweater, clutch it close to his chest.

"It's hers," Arthur said. His voice was steady, though he was at the age where it changed on him without warning. David caught the telltale tremble of the lower lip.

"You sure, kiddo?" Mel's voice was kind.

Arthur held up a sleeve and poked a finger through a hole in the shoulder where the yarn had unraveled.

"She wore it all the time, even with the hole."

Jenks leaned forward, fingering the worn red knit. "It was hers."

David flicked a finger at the book. "You recognize this?"

Arthur was nodding his head. "She read lots of stuff like that, before she left."

"Like this? On reincarnation?"

"With thunderbolts on the cover."

David flipped the book open, and Teddy Blake frowned at him. David had the feeling she didn't like him touching it. He looked inside the front cover. Small press publisher. The Mind Institute.

David nudged the book toward Teddy Blake. She looked white around the lips, and he wondered if she was ill.

"Can I get you a glass of water?" David asked.

She nodded at him, looked over her shoulder at Jenks and the boy. Out of the corner of his eye, David saw that Arthur was holding the sweater up close to his face, smelling it.

He headed into the hall, then filled someone's clean mug with water from the dispenser. He had the strong feeling that Teddy Blake did not want to talk in front of Jenks and the boy. Which meant that she thought Theresa Jenks was dead.

David went back to his desk and picked up the phone, asking for the extension to conference room C. It rang twice. Mel answered.

"Mel? David."

"So good to hear from you after all this time."

"Get the boy and his father out of there, okay? Send String and Arthur for a candy bar, and futz Jenks with some bureaucratic red tape that looks like progress and attention."

"Yeah, yeah, Mrs. Miller, I'm glad they found your cat. I didn't realize Elaki liked cats."

David waited till he saw Arthur trailing behind String, then
scooted back down the hallway to the conference room. An
Elaki slid by him in the hallway, her eye prong twitching.

David raised a hand. "Hello, Walker."

"Yes, yes, the constant greeting all day long. I say hello to
you at beginning of week, Detective Sssilver, do I keep the
greet up for all the times in between?"

"Not you," David said. He slid into the conference room,
easing the door shut behind him.

Teddy Blake dropped the red sweater and pushed away from
the table, a puzzled look on her face.

"Interrupt something?" David sat down and set the glass of
water next to the book.

She tapped a finger on the table. "So what's the problem, Detective? Some fortune-teller drop you on your head
when you were a baby? I tell you what. I've worked with
police departments in New Orleans, Wichita, Chicago, and
New York. I've worked in LA, for God's sake, where everyone
and their brother is psychic. I've even worked in Alabama, and
I've never met anybody hostile as you."

"I should be flattered?"

She snatched his hand, and the contact startled him. He
started to pull away, then changed his mind, letting her keep
it.

"How about I read your palm?" She touched the sensitive
skin beneath his wrist, then traced the life line across his palm.
"Looks like you lost something. Somebody named Elliot? Yes,
Elliot. But not someone, it's a lizard, right?" She looked at him
steadily, eyes big and brown.

He nodded, wondered how she knew.

"I heard you talking on the phone, that's all. Confirms your
opinion, right, Silver? Psychics are nothing but cheats."

David thought of Mattie, sobbing into his shoulder the night
Elliot ran away. He reached across the table and took Blake's
wrist, turning her palm up. He felt the resistance of her muscles, the weight of her hand when she relaxed.

He looked into her eyes, not bothering to glance down at
the palm he pressed with his thick rough thumb.

"Let me tell your fortune, Ms. Blake. You take advantage
of people. People who are hurting and vulnerable and sad.

People who have money. Little boys who miss their mothers. Fathers who don't know how to be comfortable around their own sons, who want their wives back to make them a family again. You do it because you like the money, and because you like the attention. My guess is you were a lonely little girl."

She bit her lip, then lifted her chin. "You done? Had your say?"

"For now, anyway."

She stood up. "Okay, Detective. I got better things to do than fight with you. You're a very perceptive man, for all your faults. Thank you for clearing the room."

"The boy shouldn't be here."

"No. He's upset. Jenks says he cries himself to sleep at night."

David nodded, thinking this was a mental image he could do without.

"Anyway, I've done my reading. I have no questions for you and I'm ready to go."

"That's it?"

"Did you expect me to wrap myself in a shawl and pull out a crystal ball?"

"What do you think's going on, then?"

She leaned back against the table and rubbed her temples. "She's dead."

David nodded. He thought the same, but he was only a cop. A homicide prima donna, at that.

"Up till now, I thought she was alive."

"The sweater changed your mind?" David asked.

"Yeah, right, there was a message on the label."

"You told Jenks and the boy you thought she was alive."

"I thought she was, till you brought the sweater in. When I saw it, I knew that the person who wore it was gone."

"Too bad, since you've been keeping their hopes up."

"Look, Detective, I didn't create this situation, and Jenks came to me for help. I do my best, but I don't guarantee happy endings."

"Just endings," David said.

"There's plenty of comfort to be had from just knowing. You should know that."

His voice was sharp, clipped. "Why should I know that?"

She flipped her braid off her shoulder. "Because you're a cop. You've been through this stuff with families. You must know the hardest thing is never knowing what happened."

David nodded, unsmiling. "Yes. That's the hardest part."

"I'd be embarrassed to tell you what else I saw."

"Why?"

"It shoots the hell out of my credibility." She looked at him and laughed. "Not that it matters, where you're concerned."

"What did you see?"

She stood up, shoved her hands in the pockets of the khaki pants. "Saw a hallway, what's left of it. There's been a fire; it's still smoking, still hot. Water's dripping somewhere."

David frowned, folded his arms.

Teddy Blake rested a knee on the plastic chair. "I think . . . I heard a noise, kind of a beep. And there's something on the floor. A dog, some kind of spaniel. I thought it was sick, but now I think it's dead. And I think there was a baby crying."

David felt the hair stir on the back of his neck. He wondered how Teddy Blake was able to describe with such detail the fire scene of the night before.

FIVE

DAVID CLOSED HIS EYES, BREATHED IN STEAM, LET THE HOT water run over his head and aching shoulders.

He did not believe in psychics, not now, but there were always cops who went for readings—it was an addiction for some of them, a natural response to a job that involved sudden danger and constant tedium. He recognized the need to control what could not be controlled, but he hated to see fellow officers waste their money because they were worried and vulnerable. He hated to see police departments waste man-hours following vague and useless whims.

How do you find a body "near water" when "the number four" is significant?

David soaped his hair. Ridiculous.

Teddy Blake had precisely described the fire scene he'd walked through hours ago. Why was she seeing the fire, when she was tracking Theresa Jenks?

She was a good con, that was all. She'd had him going about the iguana, and he knew better. She was an intelligent, good-looking, manipulative, evil woman with honest brown eyes and a reassuring air that made you want to please her. And she was very much beside the point.

The combined human/Elaki death toll from the supper club was over two hundred and thirty now.

David stepped out of the shower and wrapped a thick yellow towel around his waist. Water ran down his chest. He rubbed his hair dry, then combed it with his fingers. He put on a clean pair of jeans and a white shirt. Rose had left the bed unmade, as usual, and the twisted mass of sheets and blankets did not beckon. He'd skip the nap.

He went out of the bedroom, barefooted, rubbing the livid red scar on his chest. He would grab something to eat and go.

He paused in the doorway of the kitchen.

Mattie had the cat, Alex, by the head and front paws. His hind legs dangled, little pink pads visible as he swung from side to side in Mattie's tight grip.

Kendra wore an apron and stirred something in an iron skillet. She looked tense and focused, cooking dinner from scratch all by herself. Rose stood nearby, chopping an onion.

"Is this enough, Mama?" Kendra asked.

"Stir it till all the pink turns brown." Rose sounded absent, faraway.

Lisa sat in a corner, sketching. She looked up at David and smiled.

"Hi, Daddy."

His wild child, the middle girl, very like Rose—even though she was there, she wasn't *there*. Her hair was tangled, her face smudged. For some reason David thought of Teddy Blake.

Dead Meat, the dog, was scratching at the back door, whining. Rose looked up over her shoulder at David.

"Look who's here. Mattie, let the dog in."

David bent close to Rose. Her shoulders tensed at his approach, and he gave her a polite kiss on the cheek. She smelled of fresh cut onions and the outdoors. He noticed that her hair had been cut a few inches, shoulder length now, black, thick, and curly. He wondered when she'd had the cut.

Mattie hugged his knees. "Hi, Daddy."

He rubbed the top of her head, his one daughter who didn't mind having her hair messed up. The phone rang. Rose gave him a polite look. She used to get tense when the phone rang at suppertime, worried another family dinner would be interrupted.

"David, why don't you pick that up? Likely, it'll be for you."

Any number of his colleagues would have given their right arm for such a pleasant, understanding spouse. David wondered how you got them to the polite part without hitting the uncaring stage.

"Hello?"

"I figured you'd be home."

"Hi, Mel."

"I assume you've had a shower, a rest, something to eat, and quality time with the fam?"

"I've been here twenty minutes, Mel."

"You shouldn't live so far out." Somewhere in the background someone laughed and sang loudly. Mel raised his voice. "I been talking to Detective Yo."

"You mean Clements?"

"Yeah, Detective Yo. She wants to take us over the supper club. Looks like they finally got all the bodies out."

"What's the toll?"

"Two hundred forty-three."

David knew the number would rise as people waited for the clogged medical system to decide how much they'd be helped.

"So when's a good time to set this up?" Mel asked.

David glanced over his shoulder. "How long till supper?"

Kendra dropped her wooden spoon, trailing grease from the stove to the floor. "I'm doing my best, okay, Dad? You can zap a package in the mike if you don't want to wait for the real thing."

David made a mental note to strangle his daughter. "Give me a couple hours, Mel."

"Okeydoke. Tell my sister hello. Tell the kids I'll take them out for ice cream next week."

David hung up the phone. "Uncle Mel says hello."

Mattie took his hand. "Come on, Daddy, let me show you Elliot's food bowl."

She led him out the door, into the backyard and the tall grass. How would it be for the girls if he and Rose split? Did he really want to pull the security out from under this little girl who looked at him with eyes that reminded him so much of his father?

He had been naive at the birth of his children, vowing to be a perfect parent, sure he could shield them from all the hard edges, and give them picture perfect childhoods.

What was it in his marriage that held him? Did he love Rose, or was he just afraid to let go of the fairy tale? Some days the rest of his life seemed like a very long time.

The garden was choking under a waist-high tangle of weeds. The leaves of the plum tree had been stripped by Japanese beetles and were brown, dead, and dry. The plums that had survived the final freeze were just now showing hints of purple. It would be a race to see who got them first, the birds or the kids.

Mattie led him to the grape arbor, another example of good intentions gone to hell. He looked into the blue plastic food bowl. The bits of broccoli had dried and been bleached almost white by the sun. The lettuce had dehydrated and lined the sides of the bowl like a layer of paper. The fruity iguana mix was dried and crumbling.

"See?" Mattie said. "Something ate some of the iguana mix. So Elliot's been here, he's okay."

David knelt down till he was eye level with his youngest. "It looks to me more like birds have been at it."

Mattie tucked her chin close to her chest. "That's what Mommy said."

"Why don't we look in the garden? Maybe Elliot's in there."

Mattie shook her head. "Me and Haas already looked there." She kissed his cheek, then turned away, heading back into the house. Her shoulders slumped and she walked slowly. She had given up.

SIX

THE SIDEWALKS WERE EMPTY NOW, THE CHARRED BODIES bagged and waiting in the morgue. The scorched shell of brick was stark against purple twilight.

David heard a car engine. He stepped off the track and out of the way of a battered white van—police issue, Elaki-adapted. The driver's door opened and String slid out.

"Good of the evening, Detective David." The Elaki was bedraggled-looking, as Elaki went, one eye stalk crumpled, bare patches where scales were missing. He was black on the outer parts, his tender inner belly warm pink.

"Hello, String."

"Is the lizard friend of your pouchlings still being loose?"

The passenger door opened and Mel climbed out, grimacing. He did not like riding in the van, did not like being forced to stand. He slammed the door.

"Say 'on the lam,' Gumby. That's the way people say it."

"Why would this lizard be on a lamb?"

"He's hiding out." Mel scratched his left armpit and looked at David. "No sign of the little sucker yet, huh?"

David shook his head and headed for the line of sensors.

The Elaki skittered sideways. "Little ones sad?"

"They're missing him," David said.

Mel nodded. "He was a great little pet. What's that you said about him just last month, David? You were going to wring his little green—"

"He bit me," David said.

"Yeah, what an endearing little guy. Bit the kids, whipped them with his tail, ate like a pig."

David tried not to laugh. "Come on, Mel. The *kids* miss him."

"I guess 'cause he was so affectionate."

28

"The whipping of small girls with the tail. This does not to me seem the affectionate." String rolled toward the sensor control box.

Mel shrugged. "That's just females, String. They like you more when you treat them bad, even when they're little bitty."

"I do not believe this, Detective Mel. Why do you have such a pet? Is it the Rose Silver who has brought him? It is another animal rescue, like the ostrich?"

David looked over his shoulder at String. "The less said about that ostrich the better. Rose is still suspicious as hell."

String skittered backward. "You will not tell?"

Mel grinned. "He will not. Or he will be in as much trouble as you."

"And you," David said.

The supper club was roped off, sensors up. David passed his ID into the control slot and waited for the green light. The sensors had been known to malfunction, zapping officers with enough volts to knock them off their feet.

David looked at his partner. "After you, Mel."

"Nah, David, you go ahead, you got seniority."

"I will go." String rolled toward the glowing crime-scene tape.

Mel put an arm out, catching him across the fin. "Nah, we don't need a fish fry, Gumby."

"Please to explain?" String said.

"Too much voltage for a little twerp like you."

"I am one foot taller than the average height male human, Detective Mel. Though many inches thinner."

"Don't get nasty." Mel pushed through the barrier.

The screech of brakes caught their attention. String surged back toward the sensor line.

"That van has hit itself into my van!"

Mel craned his neck, looking back over his shoulder. "It's okay, String, I don't think it connected."

David turned, saw another white van, police issue. The passenger door opened violently and Detective Clements climbed out, hair swinging, hands pawing the air.

"I *don't* care, you keep it on the track, Wart, and watch those sudden stops, or I'm not letting you drive anymore. Scare my baby to death."

Detective Warden slid out of the driver's side ramp. "Pouchling seems happy to sudden stop."

Clements leaned into the back of the car. "Come on, sweetheart, we got to move, Mama needs to work."

Mel and David exchanged looks.

"Is little baby one," String said. He scooted back and forth, moving around David, trying to get a better look.

The boy looked about eight years old, and wore bright red shorts and a grey tank top that said SAIGO CITY ANGELS. David looked at the high-top tennis shoes. Chippers, he thought, the kind Mattie was wanting, the kind that told stories and sang songs.

An expensive brand.

The boy's movements were jerky and restless, and David watched, thinking there was something different about him. Clements took the child by the hand, and passed her ID through the sensor. She hummed softly, under her breath. She wore heavy rubber boots. She glanced down at her son, looked at his feet.

"Watch where you step, Calib. You hear Mama?"

The boy was looking at String. An experienced father, David knew quite well Calib had not registered a word that Clements had said.

"Detective Yo," Mel said loudly.

She acknowledged them for the first time, not breaking stride as she passed through the sensor. David was impressed. It took a tough cop not to flinch. Or a distracted one.

"I told you, didn't I, Burnett? You can't say Yolanda all the way out, call me Detective Clements."

"Call me Mel," he said.

She put a hand on her hip. "Introduce me to your Elaki."

String was standing next to the vans, looking between them. He waved a fin. "I am String."

"You know Wart over there?"

"Warden, yes, I know him. He has hit my van."

Wart moved close to the vans and String. "I did not make metal to metal contact."

Clements looked at them over her shoulder, lips tight. "Boys,

I got work to do, and laundry waiting at home, so let's get along."

Ever the mother, David thought.

Detective Yolanda Free Clements led them into the ravaged supper club.

SEVEN

THE ORB OF LIGHT STAYED WITH THEM, BOBBING OVERHEAD, giving off a harsh, blue-white light that hurt David's eyes, and washed them all in a cone of illumination that dispelled every shadow and made them look ill and exhausted.

"Fire started here," Clements said. Calib tugged her blouse and she hugged him, then pulled her handcuffs out of her pocket, securing his small bony wrists. "Play, Calib."

The boy smiled beatifically. David raised an eyebrow.

"It's not as bad as it looks. Calib loves locks, and it keeps him busy."

"He's awful quiet," Mel said.

Clements smiled at her son, ran her hand over the tight nap of his hair. "He doesn't talk, one of many things Calib doesn't do. They made a mistake with some minor in-utero surgery. These things do happen."

David watched the boy with the handcuffs. "They could use him in technics."

Clements grinned. "They won't let me take him down there anymore. He dismantled a padlock that was supposed to be pick proof, and they haven't forgiven him yet." She looked over her shoulder. "Where are the damn—'scuse me, Calib— the Elaki?"

"Still arguing over the vans," Mel said.

"Hang 'em, let's get on with this." She picked her way through the lumps of charred debris. "We haven't got a lot. I've talked to three people and one Elaki who made it out alive. Not a one of them have any idea what happened. Fire seemed to be all over the room before they noticed. Looks like it started in several places at once."

"Arson?" David asked.

"I say so. We got three alligators—".

"Three what?" David asked.

"Come here and look, behind the bar, see that? See the ragged way it's burned, like the skin of an—"

"Crocodile?" Mel said.

"God, the *mind* on this man. Anyway, it's a matter of where the charring goes the deepest, where the most damage is. That'll be where the fire starts. Looks like we got three points of origin here, and it didn't smolder long anywhere before everything else went up. So what it looks like we got is some kind of delayed action, set up in three places, so this place would really burn. There, behind the bar." She pointed to one side of the room, then waved an arm. "Over here, where they had the music, and there beside the kitchen."

David looked at the gel-saturated lumps of incinerated garbage, thinking that Clements saw the room as it had been, instead of as it was now.

"That means that likely the bomb threat was tied up with the arson," David said.

She was nodding. "Could well be. Get the grids tied and locked so the fire department can't get through. No safety system in this building, thanks to yet another fifty-year extension on the grandfather clauses."

David grimaced. "Whoever it was, wanted to make sure it went all the way down."

"Somebody hiding something?" Mel asked.

Clements glanced at her son. "More likely insurance scam. We look into this, we're going to find the owner's got money trouble, big time."

"Why do it when it's full of people, then?" David said.

Clements frowned. "That's a sticking point. But if they were hiding something, they hid it."

David glanced at the ceiling. "Anything from the emergency sensors?"

"Not much more than a head count. We got one strip of carbonized disc, and it's in the lab. If they can bring up just one segment, we'll get all the compressed images. Be blurry, but we'll have it. Be nice to see it as it happened. If nothing else, we may confirm ID on some of the bodies. Make sure we don't match wrong DNA to the right person. The death claims are pouring in, and we already got two hundred more requests for benefits than there are bodies."

Calib pulled a short plastic flute from the pocket of his shorts and blew hard, making squeaky noises.

Clements waved at him absently. "You already got those cuffs off?"

David saw that the boy's hands were free. Clements bent down and clipped his wrists back together. Calib smiled sweetly and dropped the tiny flute.

"Anything else you can tell us?" Mel asked.

She was nodding. "Sensor dogs got traces of sulfuric acid and sugar, right there near the kitchen."

"Which means?"

"Which means it was there innocently, or it was used to set the fire. Either case, we just got the barest trace—not enough to present in court."

"But *you* think it's arson? It's enough to convince you?" Mel asked.

"That's not what convinced me," Clements said. "Come on into the kitchen here, and I'll show you what I mean."

They took her word for it, that the small cramped room, knee-high in sheets and wads of burned lumps, was a kitchen. She pointed to a blackened rectangle, said "Stove," then went to a waist-high crumple of melted metal.

"Food storage. See those ashes, there?"

Mel looked over her shoulder. "See what? I don't see anything."

"Exactly right, baby. No food. Should be some packages, some cans, some residue of something. Instead, somebody's carted it out of here. Beforehand. Some little tightwad who didn't want to see all that food go to waste. Somebody who knew the place was going up."

Mel pulled his ear. "Sounds like management to me."

A thin trail of music came from the next room. The melody was unfamiliar, and it made David think of darkness, and full moons, and being alone.

Clements looked at him. "That's Calib."

"You kidding?"

The music stopped.

"No, Burnett, I'm not kidding. He usually can't play worth a damn, just makes those squeaky noises that make you want to scream. Then, every now and then, you get this."

"He had lessons?"

"No, he hasn't had lessons. Boy has no attention span for anything except locks, music, and those story-telling tennis shoes—been through three pair in the last six months, but it keeps him interested. He doesn't talk, can't read, hates vids. But he loves that little flute. Comes by it naturally, his daddy was a musician."

David knew he shouldn't ask, but he wanted to know. "Where is his daddy?"

"Left me when Calib was a few months old, soon as we knew the boy wasn't right." Clements turned her head sideways, listening. She frowned and went to the edge of the kitchen, sticking her head into the bar. "Calib?"

David heard the edge of panic in her voice, parent-familiar. "He'll be close."

"Silver, you're a prime example of a man who doesn't understand fire scenes. Close does not mean safe."

David went to the window and looked out. It was dark and hard to see. "String?"

"Yesss, please?"

"The boy out there?"

"He has unlocked your car and is playing with this radio." String flowed to one side. "We have had message. Must go to morgue, Detective David."

"Got you. Keep track of the boy." David pulled his head back in. String was a fine homicide cop, but he'd be a hell of an au pair. He saw Detective Clements in the doorway. "He's okay, he's with String."

Clements took a deep breath. "Good. Thanks."

Mel looked over her shoulder. "Find him?"

"Outside with String," David said.

"Figures. Here, Yo, here are your cuffs. And the little flute." Mel held the small ivory cylinder up to the light. "I never seen one like this."

"Besides Calib, that's the only thing his daddy left behind."

"His loss," David said.

EIGHT

THE COLORED LIGHTS OF THE FAIR RIDES BURNED BRIGHT in the hot humid air. The Crazy Eight Wheel dipped and whipped sideways, riders held in their seats by centrifugal force, the restraints nothing more than show. David heard a wave of shrill screams, muted by traffic noise and distance, and the faint cadence of music from the carousel.

He had loved going to the homey city carnivals when he was a boy. His father had taken him regularly, unable to resist the blinking lights, the happy screams, the pleading look in David's eyes.

David had been ten when his father left the house to buy doughnuts and never returned. David and his mother had never known for sure what happened, but they had long since mourned him as dead. He was not the kind of man who walked away from responsibility.

There had been no more carnivals, not with his mother slipping into a chronic series of paralytic depressions that landed them on the hard edge of poverty. Carnivals were beside the point while they struggled to stay alive in Little Saigo, the underground underbelly of Saigo City that catered to squatters, gangs; predators and prey.

"Attention, David Silver. Pollution index and allergens are in the danger zone. Temperature and humidity levels are conducive to heat exhaustion."

"Thank you so much," David said.

"You might want to consider closing the windows. The air-conditioning will operate more efficiently that way. You might also wish to know—"

"Shut up," David said.

The car's voice stayed pleasant. "Certainly, David Silver. However—"

"Quiet."

Bad enough that one's children argued over everything. Did he have to take this stuff from the car?

He was missing his little girls. He'd seen them a lot, while recuperating at home from the bullet in his lung. David had had plenty of time to question the doctor's decision to go with repair (cheaper) rather than regeneration. Repair took a lot more out of you than regeneration did. It meant scars, rather than renewal. It meant weeks and months of recuperation, rather than days.

Once he made it back to work, he had lost the drive to put in the hours, unhappy with the old routine of catch-as-catch-can with the kids.

He hadn't been happy at home, either.

He and Rose had lost their ease, and it seemed less and less possible to get it back. He was not sure he wanted it back. He had that separate feeling again, the sense that a wall of glass stood between him and everyone else. It was an uncomfortable feeling, but one he did not want to lose— it gave him awareness; it gave him distance.

He pulled into the parking garage and got out, letting the car find its way.

"I should be back in—" He caught himself, feeling stupid, telling the car his plans.

David heard the screech of tires and stepped out of the way just as String's van tore into the garage. He ducked behind a concrete support. No point enduring the snide remarks about claustrophobia. No law required him to take the elevator.

It was hot in the stairwell. His cough started up again, and his chest ached. He leaned against the wall, trying to catch his breath. Sweat coated his back, drenching his shirt. He looked down, saw streaks of soot on the cuff of his rolled up sleeve, smears of green from the garden, and blue fire-eating gel. His shower was a mere two hours old, but he wanted another one.

He took the stairs slowly, still coughing, and pushed the heavy metal door to the sixth floor. The hallway was brightly lit and so cool David felt chilled as the sweat began to dry on his back. He saw no sign of String and Mel. Likely they had stopped to argue. He heard voices and the faint hum of printers. The air had that static tang of too many computers running hard.

He pushed through the wide swing doors into the morgue. The smell of sweet soap and death was familiar. Every table was occupied. Staff was working double shifts, all hands on deck.

There were a lot of bodies to process.

A man arched his back and stepped away from the table. He nodded as a technician stuffed what was left of a blackened body into a clear plastic zip bag.

"Another piece of toast, please."

David heard a woman call his name, turned, and saw Miriam Kellog in blue scrubs, her long, red-brown hair hanging over one shoulder.

"Miriam," he said, coughing again. "What you got?"

"Where are the other two musketeers, David? I don't like doing repeats."

"Should be in the elevator by now."

She put a gloved hand on one hip and yawned. "How the kiddies doing?"

"Good."

"And Rose?" Her look was sharp, and David frowned. Funny how word got around.

"Rose is wonderful," he said. He heard voices and looked over his shoulder. Mel was walking fast, as if trying to get away, and String was rolling behind him at an impressive clip.

"But, Detective Mel, the paint was *not* chipped before the Warden—"

"Jesus, String, give it a rest." Mel caught sight of Miriam and scooted close, kissing her cheek. "Been missing me, sweetheart?"

David looked from one to the other. Were they dating? If they were dating, Mel would have told him.

He felt lonely, standing in the harsh light of the morgue. He shivered, realized he was still sweating. He was aware of the murmur of voices, the gurgle of water, the feathery sound String made as he skittered sideways across the floor. The Elaki's inner pinkness was draining away, leaving him with ivory splotches. String was never much use in the morgue.

Miriam had moved to the table, and Mel was watching her, smile slow and lazy. She pushed hair out of her eyes with her arm, avoiding touching herself with the soiled gloves. She looked at Mel, seemed to lose her train of thought, glanced back at the table.

It wasn't a complete autopsy. The facial mask had not been peeled away from the skull, and the skin was a livid purple-red, blistered and bubbled and raw. She'd been slit for autopsy, Y-shaped incision reaching from the sternum to the pubic bone, ribs pruned apart, blackened skin peeled away.

No need to open her up, unless there was evidence to collect. David scratched his chin, impatient for Miriam to quit looking at Mel and focus on the job at hand.

"Jane Doe, found on the floor of the house that burned, outside the baby's room, next to the dog." Miriam probed inside the throat with a gentle gloved finger. "Hyoid bone is broken."

Mel looked at David. String came close to the table, then skittered away, eye stalk twitching.

"The significance is what?"

David looked at Miriam. "She was strangled?"

Miriam nodded. "Dead *after* the fire started—there's carbon monoxide in the hemoglobin." She glanced at the computer screen. "But the levels aren't high, so she didn't take in much. Nowhere close to lethal levels."

"Someone strangle this female during fire? This is not right of the ring."

"Yeah, it sounds funny," Mel said.

David looked at the wadded purple lung tissue. "You say she was found in the hall, next to the dog?"

"What dog?" Mel asked.

"There was a dog in the house, near her body."

Mel looked at David, shook his head, then looked back to Miriam. "Any clue who she is? No DNA match? Family claim?"

Miriam shook her head. "No DNA records on the residents. She's too old to be either of the women listed as members of the household, so we think she may have been the visitor. Unless her DNA is somewhere in a listing, we may never figure it out, until somebody misses her. I'm still running it though, and we could get lucky. Won't know for sure before tomorrow. Computer time is at a premium and we got our budget gutted last year, sorry."

"Female," David muttered. "How old?"

"Between forty-five and sixty-five. Every sign of good medical and dental care, cradle to birth."

"Wealthy then," Mel said.

Miriam shrugged. "Not necessarily. She could be in a protected profession."

"Cradle to birth, you said?" David asked.

"Yeah, because of the teeth. She's had good dental care from day one. I see your point. The best money is she's wealthy, or her parents were in protected professions. You know, a cop like you guys, or maybe a teacher."

Mel scratched his chin. "Except lookit where she was found. What's she doing in a housing project downtown? The supper club, okay, plenty of rich people go slumming. But why the house?"

The air-conditioning cranked up, sending a rumble through the duct work. A waft of cool air ruffled the dry strands of hair left on the woman's blistered scalp. David thought of Arthur Jenks, clutching his mother's favorite old sweater when he thought no one was looking.

He had an impulse, and checked his watch. Late, but why not? He would call Rose and tell her to bring the kids in, and they would have a family night at the little carnival down the street. They hadn't had a family night in ages. He thought of his girls, hair streaming in the wind. He thought with sudden hunger of caramel apples, and how happy his daughters would be with a swirl of pink and blue cotton candy on a plastic cone.

"David? You still with us here?"

David looked at Mel, stuck his hands in his pockets. "Miriam, do me a favor. Run a DNA match on a missing person, file origin Chicago PD."

"Who?" she asked.

"Theresa Jenks."

NINE

THEY WERE GONE—THE FLASHING LIGHTS, ANIMAL-SHAPED controls, leering pirates. Unadorned by the holograms, the Crazy Eight Wheel was a twisted utilitarian mass of metal, worn padded seats, questionable restraints. The fair had shut down for the night.

David looked at his watch, thinking that it was late anyway, that the girls were long tucked into bed. He took a deep breath, promised himself that there would be other times.

The fairground smelled just like he remembered, the sour greasy sweet smell that used to fill his stomach with butterflies of anticipation. The metal skeletons of the silent rides had an unmasked look. David jammed his hands in his pockets, thinking of the seats full of people who saw and savored what was not there. He thought of the Crazy Eight Wheel running without holograms, metal rising against the night sky, joints groaning. In his mind's eye, the people rode silently, faces tense.

He heard footsteps. Mel waved a hand; String followed. The Elaki had a plastic roller clotted with dried cotton candy snarled in his bottom fringe.

Mel shook his head. "Well, partner, who would have ever known it?"

"Theresa Jenks?" David said.

"One and the same. Some copper's hunch, David." Mel glanced at String, then looked back again. "Behold, the Elaki equivalent of toilet paper stuck to the shoe."

David tried not to smile.

"Shoe is human fringe cover? I see no toilet paper streams, Detective Mel."

Mel grinned at David, but the smile faded. "Tough on the kid. You want we should tell them, or put it off on Chicago? 'Cause I vote Chicago."

David frowned. "It's too wrapped up in our fire. We'll tell them."

"Want to see Jenks's face?" Mel asked.

David nodded.

String moved sideways. "What will the face tell you that the mouth will not?"

"Sometimes the mouth lies," David said.

"And the face does not?"

Mel waved a hand. "Naw, I know plenty of faces that would lie to you, lots of 'em female."

"Then why would this be the—"

"String, come on, it's a human thing."

"Humans have many things, Detective Mel. I wish to learn."

"Okay, lookit, let's make this as simple as we can. It's like your magic tricks. You got to coordinate."

"Is hard for the human to coordinate face and mouth lies together?"

"Depending on the human, yeah, pretty much. I know it seems complicated."

"No. It is straight, this, I can see it." String balanced on the edge of his fringe. "Humans capable of much in the strangenesses. It brings to my mind something that happened with pouch-sib who would be called the eccentric, even for—"

Mel yawned. "Can we go? Wait, ho, David. Look at your shirt, will you? You don't look clean enough to be calling on bereaved families."

"That's not where we're going."

"Where are we going?"

"The psychic."

"Her? How come?"

"Because she predicted this."

"I didn't hear her. String, you hear her?"

"No, I do not recall this."

"I *did*," David said.

Mel scratched the left side of his rib cage. "I thought you didn't believe in that stuff anymore."

David gave him a hard look. "I don't."

"So then—"

"So then I'm wondering how it is she knew what she knew."

* * *

String rolled back and forth on the oil-stained pavement while they stood in the garage waiting for David's car. David gave the Elaki a second look. Yellow-brown popcorn kernels clotted the fringe around the dried cone of cotton candy.

"Mel, get that stuff off him, will you?"

"Tone down that parent instinct, David, this is a grown Elaki here."

String rolled into earshot. "It will be okay?"

"What will be okay, Gumby?"

"The van, Detective Mel. The dents to be sure. They will have the van in the possession for some of the days is the word to be. It will heal?"

"For God's sake, we're talking fender bender here."

"This Warden is not the good driving force."

Mel grimaced. "Neither of you are. Shouldn't give licenses to Elaki, you ask me."

David heard the crackle of tires on concrete, saw his car rounding the corner.

"The van is what I wish for," String said.

Mel opened the back door of the car. "The van is out of commission. In you go, Gumby."

"I do not like seat of the back, is most uncomfortable."

"Get *in*, will you?"

David gave the Elaki a kind look. "They'll fix the dent, String. Wash it and clean it up, recoat the nicks and stuff. It's going to look great."

String leaned sideways, scooting into the backseat on his side. Mel tucked his fringe in after him, then got in front.

"I am most uncomfortable and do not wish to be the conversationalist."

"Break my heart," Mel muttered.

"Find out where she is," David said.

"Where who is? Miriam?"

"The *psychic*, Mel. I can't program the navigator if I don't know where I'm headed, right?"

"David Silver, please enter location code."

"What's the command for drive aimlessly?"

"Meander drive," String said.

Mel glanced into the backseat. "I thought you weren't talking."

David raced the engine, steered the car out of the garage and onto the congested streets. He wished people would go home at night, go to bed and quit clogging the road.

The car took a curve, veering sharply. String made a soft hissy noise.

"The Jenkses are in a suite at the Rialto," Mel said.

David nodded. He couldn't afford a drink in the lobby. He thought about Teddy Blake. "Nice work if you can get it."

"Not her," Mel said. "Blake's at the Continental."

David looked at Mel, who shrugged and smiled with one side of his mouth. "The Continental? You sure?"

"Yeah, I double-checked."

David glanced in the rearview mirror. There was a smudge of soot on his left temple. "Okay, Mel. I'm not dressed for the Rialto anyway. Drop me off at the Continental, and you and String do the bereavement thing, then come and pick me up."

"That's smooth, David. And if you're going to the Continental, wear your gun outside your shirt. That way you'll blend in."

A weary voice drifted up from the backseat. "Greet the officers from vice for me, Detective David."

Mel grinned. "The Elaki makes a joke."

TEN

THE DISTRICT ATTORNEY HAD ONCE TOLD DAVID THAT HALF the crimes he prosecuted originated at the Continental Inn. Where were you staying, sir? The Continental Inn. Ma'am, can you tell me where the meeting took place? The Continental Inn. Where did you first hear of the incident? The Continental Inn.

Interesting place for Teddy Blake.

Sweat had dried, salty on his back, and David felt grimy.

The sensor that should have registered his presence was out of commission. If this place burned, they'd never get an accurate body count.

The lobby had a musty, sour smell and a thin, blue-patterned carpet that looked like a fine layer of sponge on the floor. In the corner, a fig tree dropped a spray of waxy green leaves in a last-ditch bid for attention.

David felt a thrum of vibration under his armpit and touched his gun, stroking the alarm chip. The hotel had a field going. Weapons would not work here.

Not a bad policy, for a hotel like the Continental.

The desk clerk was short enough that the counter came up to his chest. He was bald, a faint stubble of hair intimating that he was bald by choice. He had a dimple in his chin, and his left ear had five piercing holes but no earrings.

David showed his ID. "Teddy Blake. What room?"

A curious stillness settled over the desk clerk, and his smile was surface tension only.

"Three fifty-two." He did not check the computer.

David gave him a cop look. "Just like that? Off the top of your head?"

The man touched the stubble on his scalp with a sudden, self-conscious motion. He put his hand back on the counter,

45

voice soft and bland to the point of being offensive. "Three fifty-two. Sir."

David shrugged, bypassed the elevator for the stairs.

It was hot in the stairwell, and David started sweating again. He heard footsteps behind him and moved to one side. A familiar-looking man in blue jeans and a polo shirt took the steps two at a time. The guy had the buffed-up physique and expensive tennis shoes that said vice cop, and he carried a grease-spotted pizza box. David sniffed. Onions and sausage.

"String says hello," David said softly, after the man was out of earshot.

The hallway was dimly lit, and cooler than the stairwell, but not by much. Clean enough, David decided, if one did not mind water-spotted ceilings and a grey film of grunge in the corners. Same carpet pattern as in the lobby, this one red.

David turned a corner, frowned, tried to understand a numbering system that stopped dead at one end, then started fresh at random in the middle. He heard the roar of a crowd and an excited male mumble—sportscaster. Someone's television was way too loud. David looked at the number over the door. Three fifty-two.

He ran a hand through black curly hair, thinking maybe he'd gotten it cut too short last time. He knocked hard, wondering if Teddy Blake would hear him over the ball game.

She was psychic, she ought to know he was there.

David waited. Heard screams from the crowd, the announcer going wild. An unladylike shout—"Go, go, go!" David knocked again.

"I'm coming, Detective, have some patience, okay?"

The volume muted. David heard a woman sobbing softly in the next room. He looked over his shoulder, unpleasantly reminded of the kind of motels where the department put him up when he traveled. The only hotel rooms that did not depress him were the unaffordable kind.

The door swung open. He almost didn't recognize her.

Her hair was pulled loosely back, and she wore a thin tank top that was bright orange and said TENNESSEE VOLS. Her cutoff jeans were rolled to an indecent level at the tops of her thighs, making David wonder if the room air-conditioning was on the blink.

She was tan, her arms firm and muscular; the tan was too imperfect to be chemical. David decided she had to be the only person on Earth who hadn't had a fear of skin cancer drummed into her head since birth.

"Come on in, if you're coming." She turned her back on him and dashed back into the room.

He followed her in, closing the door softly. She was watching basketball, no surprise, on an old-fashioned television whose thin screen covered the entire side of the wall. A radio was playing—twangy music with guitars and a sax, and simple, mournful lyrics. A paperback novel was open on the bed.

David checked the book cover. *My Sweet Savage*, etched in gold and pink over a bare-chested man and a bosomy woman who chastely held hands and stared into each other's eyes.

"Good book?" David asked. He smelled pizza.

Teddy turned away from the television with the same look of irritation he gave his kids when they interrupted. She looked confused, followed his gaze to the book on the bed, and blushed.

Her shoulders straightened. "What's it to you?"

She was direct, that much he would give her.

"Kind of late to be dropping by, isn't it, Detective? Back home, we call first, if we think it might be inconvenient."

"In the city, people always find it inconvenient for the cops to drop by. How'd you know it was me at the door?"

"I didn't."

"You said Detective."

"Well. I *am* psychic."

David tilted his head to one side. "The desk clerk called you."

She shook her head at him. "A nonbeliever."

The tank top was oversized, and the armholes dipped all the way to her waist. She wore a white lacy half shirt underneath. David did not think she had on a bra. Maybe the lacy thing was supposed to be instead of a bra.

Her toenails were painted livid red. David looked away from her long slender legs, glancing at the television.

"Who you for?"

She glanced back at the screen. "Volunteers, of course. That's my team."

"You from Tennessee?"

"Yeah."

"What player you hooked into?"

She grinned at him. "This hotel's not what you'd call equipped, Silver. You have to watch it the old-fashioned way."

David glanced around the room. She was reading, watching TV, and listening to the radio, all at the same time.

She turned the music down. Over her shoulders, a coach signaled time out.

"Hang on," she said.

She opened the white pizza box on the bed, put a piece on a Styrofoam slab, then handed it to him. "Hope you like sausage."

She went to a tiny refrigerator that was stashed next to the dresser and a dirty coffeepot, and got out a beer. Retro Beer, the cheapest brand on the market. David hadn't had one since he was a broke kid in Little Saigo. He wondered if it was as bad as he remembered.

"I'm not hungry," David said.

"Pretend. I feel funny if I eat and you don't, and this pizza just got delivered. *Carpe diem*."

David took a bite. The crust was crisp and chewy and the cheese was hot. There was a lot of sausage, oozing orange fat over the cheese and the onions. It tasted wonderful.

"I didn't think these places delivered anymore."

"Not in this neighborhood, that's for sure. Friend of mine picked it up."

David remembered the vice cop running up the stairs. He cocked his head to one side. There seemed to be an interesting microcosm of society in this hotel, and Teddy Blake fit right in. The desk clerk warned her of cops at the door, and the guys in vice brought her pizza.

David opened the beer, watching her eat. She was dainty about it, but fast, like she was starving.

She caught his eye. "Excuse me. Haven't had a bite all day."

"Why not?"

"Forgot."

It seemed like her, forgetting to eat. She opened the pizza box and gave him another slice. Cheese threaded from the bottom of the box, then pulled away. The beer had a bitter, watery taste, but it was cold.

"Jenks and his boy are at the Rialto," David said.

"You think I don't know?"

"He wouldn't put you up there? This isn't the greatest hotel in the world, for a woman on her own. Or a man, for that matter."

"I do okay."

Not good enough for Jenks to put her up in style, David thought.

"Jenks got me a suite there, or tried to. I just told him no. I bill for expenses, and I don't gouge people."

"How much do you charge?" David said.

"That's kind of rude, just to ask."

"Maybe I want a reading."

"I don't do readings. And I don't believe in astrology, so don't tell me your sign. I don't read palms or tea leaves or tarot cards, and I don't charge for what I do. Just expenses, if I go out of town or something, 'cause otherwise I couldn't go. I'm not rich, you know."

David nodded. She did not look rich. But she'd have it socked away, lots of it, good as she was. This was just for show.

She chewed a piece of crust. "Besides, I'm from a small town. Hotels like the Rialto make me uncomfortable. They don't want people like me there."

Her eyes were very large and brown, and David felt an odd pang. She ate all of the crust before she took another piece of pizza. Frugal, David thought. She passed him another beer. It still tasted bad, but he wasn't minding it.

"Pretty bad fire you had. Sorry we intruded in the middle. I tried to get Jenks to wait a day, but he's not the kind of man—"

"He's not the kind of man who waits."

"Nice of you to finish my sentence for me, Detective, but I can do it myself, no trouble."

"Tell me about yourself, Ms. Blake."

She rocked from side to side in her chair. "Like what?"

"History. Born?"

"Flatwoods, Tennessee. I know, you never heard of it."

"Age?"

"Thirty-two."

"You look twenty-two."

"You don't."

He smiled at her. It was cute, her trying to get under his skin. He'd survived worse. "Married?"

"No, thanks."

"Brothers? Sisters? The seventh child of a seventh child?"

"Two. Brother is dead. Sister isn't."

"Sorry."

She rolled her head one way, then another. Grimaced. "Thank you."

"Parents alive?" He saw that there was pizza sauce on her chin. He fought the urge to wipe it off with a napkin.

"My mama."

"Place of residence?"

"Flatwoods, I told you."

"Still there, huh? How did you connect with Jenks?"

She tilted her head to one side. "Guy named Bruer, Chicago Police Department. We've worked together before."

That surprised him. She even had Chicago fooled. Unless she was the genuine article.

Not possible, he thought.

"Where were *you* born, Detective?" A piece of cheese slid off the pizza onto her lap. She picked it up and ate it, then scrubbed at the spot of grease on her jeans with a balled-up napkin.

"Chicago, actually," David said.

"Brothers or sisters?"

"Only child."

"Parents alive?"

David knew his face was red. "I think—"

"Married, I guess." She pointed at the wedding band. "You look like a daddy. *Seven* kids, I'm guessing."

"Three."

"Sexes?"

"All girls."

"You find your lizard?"

He shook his head.

"Sorry I teased you about it. That was mean. I'm like that sometimes."

"Mean?"

She gave him a sideways look and a guarded smile. The brown, sun-warmed skin was oddly erotic.

He settled back in his chair. "Didn't your mother ever tell you that too much sun is bad for you?"

"Every day of my life. I have a garden, I like to be out in it."

"Flowers?"

"Vegetables."

The woman was practical. David thought of his own garden, wild and untended. "You can do garden work at night or in the morning, like regular people."

"I like the heat."

"I don't," David said.

"In Flatwoods, all we got is heat. You learn to like it."

"Do you still think Theresa Jenks is dead? Ms. Blake?"

Her smile faded. She put the half-eaten slice of pizza back in the box and wiped her hands on a grease-spotted napkin, smoothing the wad of paper on her knee.

"If you're feeling friendly, Detective, you can call me Teddy, or even Ted. My friends do. Otherwise call me Ms. Blake, but in a different tone of voice. Be respectful. I don't like it when people say my name like it's an obscenity."

Her gaze was steady.

"Ms. Blake." He said it respectfully, wondering if she was looking for time to collect her thoughts. "Do you still think Theresa Jenks is dead?"

She stood up, turned off the TV. The blank screen was huge, grey, and depressing. It demanded attention, but gave nothing back.

"No, Detective, I don't think Theresa Jenks is dead, I know she is."

"How did she die?"

Teddy Blake put a hand to her throat. "I don't know."

David leaned forward in his chair. "Why did you do that?"

"Do what?"

"Put a hand to your throat when you said you didn't know."

She took a step backward, though he had not moved in the chair. She looked distracted, her eyes focused and inward-looking in a way that made him feel excluded. He stood up, set his beer can on the floor, moving in close enough to touch her.

"You know how she died, don't you, Teddy?"

She seemed small suddenly. She stepped backward and lost her balance, and he grabbed her arms.

He expected her to protest, to pull away. Her arms were strong and firm; he felt the tensile strength of her muscles. He felt ill suddenly, like a bully, and he let her go. His fingers left red marks.

"When I held her sweater, that day in your office."

"What did you see?"

"I saw a dog. A black dog, a cocker spaniel. The dog was barking, it was snarling, it was going to bite. The baby was crying."

"What baby?"

"I don't know. He killed the dog with his fist."

"Who?"

"The clown. I can't see it all. There was smoke, and an alarm." Her eyes were wide and faraway. David wanted to touch her shoulder, but was afraid to.

"What about the clown? What did he do?"

"He put his hands on her throat and he choked her. Her eyes got big and her tongue stuck out. He kept on choking her, even when she was dead."

"What does he look like?"

"I told you, he was a clown."

"How can you be sure it was a man? Was he—"

The knock at the door was loud. They both froze.

"Yo, David? You in there?"

Mel.

"Yeah, I'm here. Come on in."

The expression on Mel's face told him how odd they looked—pizza carton open on the bed, the two of them close together, the air thick with tension.

Mel gave David a sharp look, and David took the cue to back away.

"Sorry, David, they insisted."

David saw the shadowy figure of String, a white-haired man, Jenks, then the boy, running across the room to Teddy Blake. She opened her arms and he ran to her, hiding his head and holding her tight. She held him without hesitation, and David thought sadly that she had an admirable grace with children.

Arthur would not take it well when she went to jail.

Because good as she was, she had not been able to resist playing him along—the con woman had been unable to give up the show. The hand to the throat had given her away, she *knew* what had happened to Theresa Jenks. It was all a nice little scam. The woman, wealthy and vulnerable. Books from the Mind Institute, priming the pump.

Find the link between Blake and the Mind Institute, and the whole nasty thing would unravel.

Teddy's eyes were closed, and she stroked the boy's head. His sobs were loud and painful in the cluttered dingy room.

ELEVEN

OUTSIDE THE CAPTAIN'S OFFICE, THE NOISE LEVEL WAS RIS-
ing. Someone—David wasn't sure who—pressed next to the
glass, scratching the small of his back with short stubby
fingernails.

The man wore suspenders, suit coat draped over one arm. He
was talking to Clements—probably another arson cop. David
did not like this man, standing in the homicide bull pen, talking
too loud and scratching himself.

"David? Are you listening to me?"

David was not listening. He was too angry to listen. Why
should he listen to a long-winded no?

"I'm listening."

Captain Halliday snugged his tie up close to his thin, reddish-
brown neck. He checked his watch.

"Come on, we're late."

David looked at his feet, saw his shoes were dusty.

Halliday paused by the door. "Silver, you coming?"

"How about as a material witness?"

Halliday sighed, opened the office door. "If you folks will
head on out to conference room B, I'll be with you in just a
few minutes."

The knot of cops began to shuffle. One of the Elaki skittered
backward into a desk. David heard Mel shout, "Hey, Yo!" and
wondered if a fight would erupt.

Halliday closed the door and sat on the edge of his desk.
"I'm not getting through to you, am I, Detective?"

"I think the mistake is mine, sir. I'm not getting through
to you."

"You're getting through to me all right, David, loud and
clear. You've got a thing about this woman, this psychic, and
it's affecting your judgment."

"She knows too much, Captain, she's got to be involved. Or do you believe in all that stuff?"

"David, let's think about this, okay? Let's say you're absolutely right. Let's say for some bizarre reason she's involved in the fire and the murder—"

"What's bizarre? She's milking Jenks."

"Say you're right—"

"I'm right and I want a warrant."

"No, you don't. Not if you're right, you don't."

David frowned.

"You're a long way from knowing what the hell's going on, David. The Blake woman is one little thread. Watch her, talk to her, follow other lines of investigation and see where she fits."

David looked back at his feet. Still dusty. He glanced up at Halliday. "You're right, of course."

The captain sighed. "David, you're one of the best homicide investigators I've ever had the pleasure of working with. So what's up here? Because this just isn't like you."

Halliday swung his left leg, sneaked another look at his watch. As always, David knew the proper attitude to take with management.

"Nothing's up."

"Okay then, let's go. Lights out."

The office went grey, dimly illuminated by the light from the bull pen. The computer terminal glowed white on black.

"David? You coming?"

TWELVE

THERE WAS A STIR OF EXCITEMENT IN THE CONFERENCE ROOM.
Detective Clements accepted congratulations and admiration on
behalf of the arson lab techs, who had taken burnt fragments
of several discs stored in sensor units interspersed around the
supper club and restored them well enough that they could be
shown.

Clements should have been excited, but she was solemn.
There was a hitch, as usual, and someone went out for the
inevitable coffee and doughnuts.

David wondered what Teddy Blake was doing today. Pre-
senting Jenks with a final bill, now that his wife's death was
confirmed?

A lot of cops went to psychics. Everybody in the department
knew it; nobody talked about it. Police work was dangerous. A
man could walk into a precinct, ask directions, and open fire
with a weapon that should not work, except for some reason
no one could fathom (or own up to) the field was not on.
An oversight that cost three detectives, and one uniform. An
oversight that meant the walls had to be repaired, the floors
recarpeted.

Police work meant that a woman, newly promoted to sergeant, could get caught in a grid glitch in a neighborhood
that had just been taken apart by holographic troops. That this
sergeant could literally be torn to death by a crowd that ripped
her arms and legs from her body, right outside the tunnels of
Little Saigo where David had roamed as a boy.

Police work meant that a team of detectives could go up
against a psychopath who had killed over twenty children, and
stockpiled every imaginable weapon, and come away without
a drop of blood being shed and the perpetrator weeping on the
way to jail.

All of this could happen and did happen, the point being you could never predict. Some cops had a hard time with that—getting up every day and going to work at a job where you couldn't predict. So some of them went to psychics, trying to exercise a measure of control over something that could not be controlled.

Even him. For different reasons, that were really the same reasons. The inability to live with uncertainty.

It started several months after he'd joined the force. Rose had been expecting their first child, a dark-haired baby with brown eyes, a perfect, pink and white little girl, Kendra. And while Rose stalked the house, heavy-bellied and depressed, David had been ravished by the work. He welcomed it, absorbed it, wondering if his new and formidable skills as an investigator could be used to find out just what had happened that night when he was a boy, when his father had gone out for doughnuts and never returned.

But every tiny thread, any hint of a lead, went nowhere.

He did not think he would ever get over that sense of shame, the humiliation of money spent while bills went unpaid and he and Rose scrimped for baby things. The memory of secrets shared that should not be shared, spilled in his eager need to be fed hope. The shame of having the psychic set limits on how often he could come, when he had grown desperate for news and encouragement.

"Lights down," someone said.

Detective Clements sat on the edge of the table and began the disc. People shifted their weight and moved their chairs so they could see. Someone reached for a doughnut and a napkin. Light flickered on the television and the static cleared.

The images were cloudy, details difficult to make out. There were dark spots like shadows. David leaned forward, wondering if he was mistaken. No. He saw the girl he'd found in the middle of the tracks, her white dress tight, shiny and clean, her hair soft, face young enough to leave no doubt that she was underage. She stood by the bar, talking to a woman in a blue dress, both of them animated and happy, dark hulking shadows of men close beside them. A balloon drifted by, large and purple, a happy note.

The balloon sank behind the bar by the kitchen. Detective Clements froze the image.

"That, right there, is our incendiary device. Our murder weapon, if you will."

David looked up, met her eyes. "The balloon?"

"I think so. We found potassium chlorate and sugar down there, behind the bar."

"Potassium chlorate and sugar, huh?" Mel closed one eye. "I know that's significant, Yo, I just don't know why."

Detective Clements tossed her head sideways, the thick wedge of hair flipping over her shoulder. "Put sulfuric acid in a balloon. Then put that balloon inside another one that's coated with fire fudge—"

String waved a fin. "Fudge chocolate?"

"No, baby, the fudge isn't something you eat. You mix it up with sugar, but instead of chocolate, you add potassium chlorate."

David rubbed his temples, thinking the headache was going to be a bad one. "The acid eats through the balloon?"

Clements nodded. "Yeah, that's the whole point, see. Eats through the first balloon, ignites the fudge in the second one. And you got yourself an A-number-one incendiary device."

David pulled his bottom lip. "How long?"

"How long what, baby?"

"How long does it take the acid to eat through the balloon?"

"Depends on the balloon, and you can layer it. My guess is anywhere between fifteen and forty-five minutes."

"We're still testing it out in the lab."

David looked around to see who'd spoken, saw the man who was scratching himself earlier in the bull pen. David frowned at him, trying to remember his name. Rufus Cobb. Detective Cobb. He had reddish-brown hair and a coarse-looking mustache that needed attention.

Cobb was frowning at Clements, his arms tightly folded next to his chest. "We're still just speculating, Yolanda, you might make that clear."

"I figured you'd do it for me."

He shrugged. "We haven't been able to duplicate this in the lab. We can't make the balloon float like that, the way it did on the disc there, with the fire fudge. Plus, let's face it, folks, this is an exotic."

"Exotic?" David asked. The problem with being a homicide cop in an arson investigation was how often one found oneself playing straight man.

Warden skittered forward, his eye prong twitching. "Is unusual this. Connotes professional behavior."

"Hired torch?" Mel asked.

Clements nodded. "Could be. We're going through our arson signatures, see what we come up with. Get this, Silver." She took a cigarette from her purse and put it in her mouth. The room became silent. Clements rolled her eyes, took the cigarette out of her mouth, and waved it in the air. "I'm not *lighting*, okay, sweethearts? Just tasting the tobacco a little."

David decided that he liked her. She reminded him of Mel.

"We found trace elements of potassium chlorate in that house where you fell through the floor."

David shifted in his seat. He had not been planning on sharing that particular episode.

"Now wait a minute." Mel scratched his chin. "I thought that fire, the one in the house, caught from the supper club. Like an accident."

"It wasn't an accident that we found Theresa Jenks there," David said.

Clements shook her head. "We're still sifting, but there was enough heat and flame to insure hostile fire."

String arched backward on his fringe. "How is this fire hostile? This is emotion?"

"Is human expression," Warden said. "The constant anthropomorphism. Her meaning is the fire seems to be set for the purpose carefully. So it is insured that building will go down to the cinders."

"Ah."

Yolanda Clements sniffed the cigarette. "Listen, while you two translate, I'm a run the rest of the show. It's going to jump around; we've spliced the whole. Got bits from those nasty rooms upstairs."

"Where's vice when we need 'em," someone said.

"Hey, Yo, we get copies of this?"

The image wavered, and bars of grey static fuzzed the clarity. David squinted.

"That an *Elaki?*" someone asked.

"I had no idea they were so . . . agile. What's he doing to that woman?"

"Use your imagination."

"Oh, God. If it wasn't so neat, I'd throw up."

"Beats sheep, I guess."

David heard a chair scrape the floor, looked over his shoulder, saw Della slip away.

The scene switched to the kitchen where an Elaki and a boy, both in soiled undershirts and ball caps, peered into a fryer. The Elaki waved a fin over the grease, and the boy laughed and turned the Elaki's ball cap backward.

David wondered if either of them had survived.

The image blurred, another shift in location. David saw the bar again, people laughing, talking, drinking. Something odd about the scene. He realized that the people and Elaki were mixing freely here, sitting together at tables, moving in and out of mixed groups. The numbers were pretty evenly distributed—human and Elaki one-to-one.

A hallmark of the supper clubs. The only other place David had seen such easy mixing was a restaurant called Pierre's, and even there, Elaki stuck with Elaki, and people stuck with people.

David rubbed his chest, touching the scar. Pierre had saved his life when he'd been shot. Kept him breathing, until the ambulance came. Some days David wished Pierre had not gone to the trouble.

David heard a gasp, an exhalation of breath, someone muttering Holy Mary Mother of God. He looked up at the screen.

A wall of flame rose up from behind the bar. The room was hazy with smoke, and people and Elaki moved in frantic but oddly aimless motion. The Elaki were at a distinct disadvantage—unable to hold their own against the bone and sinew of people who moved in a thickening mass for the door.

Warden turned his back on the screen with a movement so soft, David was the only one who looked up. David glanced at String, wondering if he would feel the need to show respect and consideration for the recorded death throes of the Elaki on disc. String's left eye prong twitched in a staccato pulse, but he was law enforcement through and through. Turning away was not part of the job.

No one moved and no one spoke, and the air was thick with screams that could not be heard.

The image flickered and went dark. Clements lit the cigarette that hung on her lips. David could see the red lipstick stain the filter. The acrid grey smoke curled into the air, but no one looked up, no one objected.

THIRTEEN

DELLA WAS STARING AT THE SCREEN OF HER TERMINAL, A
bright teary hardness in her eyes. A chocolate Twinkie sat on
Mel's desk, untouched. David stood beside her, waiting till
she looked up.

"Yeah, Silver?"

"I need whatever you've rounded up on Teddy Blake."

"Background check is in your reader. Looks clean."

"Della, everything okay with you?"

Her fingers moved over the keyboard, starting slowly, picking up speed. "Everything is fine."

David looked at the display. The words glowed, white on
black.

GO AWAY   GO AWAY   GO AWAY

David went away.

He sat at his desk, reading glasses loose on the end of his
nose. He ran a hand through his hair, thinking it was too short
in the back. Rose used to like it long. He had no idea what
Rose liked these days.

There was a time when such a realization would have been
painful.

He rubbed his eyes. Teddy Blake was thirty-two years old.
That much he already knew. She looked much younger, David
thought, remembering her in the cutoff jeans, yelling at the
basketball players on the big old screen.

She was from Flatwoods, Tennessee, a tiny place in the
mountains with the soaring population of 2006. She had a sister, age thirty, and a brother who would have been twenty-eight
years old last month if he had lived. Her father had worked as a
farm manager for forty years, up until his death five years ago.

Her mother owned a shoe store in Flatwoods and land outside of town. Teddy's home address was a rural route.

She was not wealthy. David studied the accounts and decided that she might be wearing cutoff jeans out of necessity rather than style.

David browsed, studied the compilation. Her travel records were interesting, particularly a three-year segment where she had traveled in and out of Virginia.

David pushed the glasses back on his nose, noting that all the Virginia travel was first-class. He compared the records with the other years. Bus, cheap commuters, all in and out of Nashville.

Who had she worked for in Virginia?

He keyed in a request for more data, and got a green flag that blinked over large red block letters.

CLASSIFIED DATA   CLASSIFIED DATA
DEMONSTRATE NEED TO KNOW

David cleared the screen, aware that his request would be logged by some computer somewhere, and flagged by the people and programs that watched. Likely, nothing would come of it. Those who would watch were drowning in information these days. The data banks were choked; you had to turn inside out to catch anyone's attention. If you knew what the flags were, you could tailor your behavior to avoid the perimeters of the current programs and slip through the system nearly undetectable.

So what had Teddy Blake been up to in Virginia?

David picked up the phone, linking with the Chicago PD. "Detective Bruer, please."

He waited, heard a series of clicks, then a woman's voice. "Chicago Police Department, Calhoon."

David frowned. "This is Detective David Silver, Saigo City PD. Trying to get through to Detective Bruer."

"Bruer's in the john, Detective Silver of Saigo City PD. I'm his partner. Can I help, or you want me to have him call?"

David grinned, thinking that if Mel told people he was in the john he would kill him. "You know, Calhoon, you could say not available."

"Yeah, I could, if my mama had raised me better. Can I help you out here?"

"I'm calling about the Jenks homicide."

There was a pause. "Last I heard, it was a missing person. You guys got a body?"

"DNA match came through last night."

Calhoon sighed. "So all this time, she's dead?"

"Been dead less than forty-eight hours."

"Do I have to play straight man here forever, Silver, or are you going to tell me a story?"

David focused on a spot on the wall. Was everyone in a bad mood today?

"I got more questions than answers, Detective Calhoon. Her body was found in a project house that burned along with a supper club, night before last."

"She died in the fire?"

"Before. Strangled."

"Weird. Any clue what she was doing there?"

"Not yet. Any information you can—"

"Done. We got a lot. Jenks is a big name in this town, so we hustled our butts."

"One other thing. You work at all with a so-called psychic by the name of Teddy Blake?"

"Ted? Yeah, she was in on it. You're sounding a little hostile, Detective. You got a problem with Teddy?"

"No problem. She any help?"

"Yeah, sure, but no onion, my ulcer won't like it."

David frowned. "Pardon?"

"Excuse me, Silver. We were talking about Ted, right? The thing is, I don't know how useful she was. She was sure Theresa Jenks was still alive, but she seemed real worried about her."

"Makes sense," David said. If she wanted to play Jenks, she would keep him wound tight, but hopeful.

"What do you mean, it makes sense?"

"Just thinking out loud."

Calhoon sneezed, said excuse me. "You don't like psychics, do you, Silver?"

"What are you, a detective?"

"The reason I bring it up is, most of the time, I'd agree with you. We got a guy here in the department, goes to a psychic once a week, won't leave the house till he reads his horoscope. He's rude as hell and says it's because of the sign he was born under. But Ted's okay, Silver, you want my opinion. Bruer brought her in when Jenks was agitating for outside help. No stone unturned, you know how it is with families when people disappear."

David winced. He knew.

"I know she worked with homicide in Jackson Hole, Wyoming, and I hear they were happy with her. She was in on that Squire bloodbath."

"Was she? I didn't know they used a psychic on that one."

"They used everything, plus this is Wyoming, the new California, dude. Using a psychic doesn't make the news out there, it's SOP."

"Okay, Calhoon. Thanks."

"You want me to tell Bruer to call?"

"Not till he's through."

FOURTEEN

THE LOBBY FLOOR OF THE RIALTO HOTEL HAD BEEN WAXED to a feathery soft shine. Chrome fixtures glimmered behind a string of double doors. David counted them. Ten doors.

An Elaki-friendly ramp had replaced the stairs, and most of the people David saw were in hotel uniform, hair slicked back on the men and women, no beards, mustaches, or sideburns on the men.

The doorman nodded at String, gave Mel and David a sideways glance. String glided ahead of them across the buffed floors. David's shoes skidded and squeaked, bringing a look of disapproval from the front desk clerk.

David shivered. The lobby was chilled to the temperature he liked his beer on hot summer days. In spite of the occasional well-fed, tanned, and beautifully toothed person crossing the lobby—usually into the bar, which was open already—it was a top-notch hotel, which meant it was nearly Elaki-exclusive.

The desk clerk wore white gloves, and his hair was blond under the heavy gel. Elaki did not like the unruliness of human hair, and a hair in their food was a crisis.

The clerk nodded at String. "May I help you, sir?"

David was aware of the man's sweet powdery scent, the same odor that had emanated from the doorman. Elaki could be picky about human smells. He'd heard of establishments where people had to be perfumed, but he'd never been in one before.

"Detective Silver, homicide." He showed his ID.

The clerk kept his focus on String.

"As in *police*," Mel said. Loudly. An Elaki stopped in mid-glide and turned their way. "We're here to see Bernard Jenks. Can you tell me what room he's in?"

66

"Sir, it is not hotel policy to give out that kind of information."

Mel leaned across the desk. "My partner here showed you his badge, didn't he, Mr., uh, Sam? Sam, huh? Don't use last names in a hotel this nice?"

The clerk lifted his chin. "We are all Sam here, sir."

"Must make it nice if there's a complaint."

The clerk blushed. David noticed that his hands were shaking. He was very young. Likely afraid for his job every day of his life.

David put his ID into his coat pocket. "What's your real name, Sam?"

"Brandon Reynolds, sir."

"It's all right to give us that room number, Mr. Reynolds, believe me. It's even a matter of law. And Mr. Jenks—Dr. Jenks, excuse me—is only human, after all."

Reynolds spoke into his headset, glanced at the computer screen. "Dr. Jenks is in Suite 3017. But it's a secure floor."

"Please to have key for elevator," String said.

"We'll have security take you up, sir."

Mel grinned. "Now, ain't that nice."

David took a deep breath when the elevator door closed. It was roomy inside, even with one Elaki and three humans. The carpet was red and flowered and clean—same pattern but better quality than the one at the Continental. The elevator stopped on the twelfth floor and opened to a knot of Elaki who began a concerted surge forward, then stopped and backed away.

"Room is plenty," String said.

The red-jacketed security woman held the door.

"Thank you, no," said an Elaki. The other three skittered back and forth, then moved away.

All quite polite and civil, David thought.

"At least they're not crowding us," Mel said.

The security woman had the familiar powdery scent. Her name tag said Sam.

Mel looked at her. "You say something?"

Her look was polite, but not engaging. "No, sir."

"How come you slick your hair back like that?"

"I like it this way, sir."

"Can I just ask you one question, while my partner here hyperventilates? He's okay, by the way, he just don't like elevators. Now what I want to know is, you get fired if you don't wear that special perfume?"

"I would if a guest noticed and complained."

Mel scratched his chin. "Okay, one human to another. And I know this isn't delicate, but suppose your stomach is upset. Or you eat burritos for lunch, or—"

"I'm sorry, sir, I don't understand what you mean."

String rolled sideways. "What Detective Mel mean be—"

David cleared his throat. "String? Don't explain."

"Do not?"

"No."

The elevator door opened. Sam held the button for them. "Your floor, sirs."

Mel grinned at her. "Nice meeting you, Sam."

"You too, sir. Sir?"

"Yeah, hon?"

"Ten-day suspension for a first offense. You're out of work on a second." The elevator door shut on her thin, elfin face. David watched, but she did not smile.

Jenks was expecting them. The knot of his tie was tight against the crumpled collar, and his shirttail hung loose and wrinkled. He wore lace-up spensers, but no socks, and his eyes were red-rimmed, his color yellowish.

David went through the ritual of ID, sympathy, and handshaking, and though he mentally cataloged the usual suspicions and questions about angry husbands, wills, and insurance that occurred with the knee-jerk but often accurate prejudice of an experienced homicide cop, he still felt bad for Bernard Jenks, doctor.

"Where is the Arthur pouchling?" String said. He did not sit, of course—Elaki did not sit even when they drove cars— and he towered over them, making everyone uncomfortable.

Jenks inclined his head to the bedroom. David heard the whirs and beeps of a video game. String rolled across the floor and peeped in the doorway.

"The pouchling sleeps."

Jenks took a breath. "Good. He kept me up all night, talking in his sleep and prowling."

David sat forward in his chair, hands loose between his legs, making a conscious effort not to grit his teeth. Jenks was a self-centered bastard. He wondered if the man had found his wife as inconvenient as he obviously did the boy.

Mel settled into a chair. "So, Dr. Jenks, you stand to inherit a lot of money?"

Jenks turned slowly and stared at Mel. "I don't believe I heard you?"

Mel waved a hand. "Yeah, well, it's no surprise, you being short on sleep like you are. I know you're too smart to take offense when I wonder out loud how much you stand to gain by your wife's death. It's just traditional police work."

"Suspect the husband?" Jenks said.

"How's about clear your name, so we can go after the real guy." Mel smiled, showing teeth.

Jenks leaned against the table. David got the impression he wanted to sit, but thought standing gave him an advantage.

"Theresa's money is entailed," Jenks said. "I get a comfortable allowance, but the majority goes to the children."

David looked up. "Children? Arthur's not an only child?"

"Theresa had another child, another son." Jenks sagged and eased himself into a chair. "Martin was only four years old when he drowned. She would never take his name out of the will, though he's been dead for years. That's really where this all started."

David glanced at Mel.

Jenks glared at them. "Didn't that Detective Bruer from Chicago, didn't he bring you up to speed on this?"

"Shsshicago did not mention another pouchling," String said. "This I would be the remembrance of. But I must ask. It is human tradition to leave the money of the life's accumulation to one already dead?"

David tilted his head to one side. "Forgive me, Dr. Jenks, but you said *Theresa* had another child. Neither of the boys were yours?"

"Martin was mine. After Martin I opted for nonbiological parenting." He lifted his chin and gave David a hard stare.

Mel rubbed his forehead. "One of those funny deals."

"I don't consider it—"

"Hey, you mind if I have a drink of water? It's hot outside and the air on our car isn't so good." Mel headed for the polished, black onyx bar.

Jenks waved a hand, including them all. "Please forgive my manners, Detective. Feel free to help yourself to anything you'd like."

Mel opened a small cabinet and bent over, voice mildly strained. "So it's one of those things where the kid's hers, but not yours? Kind of like you're not really married or—"

"It has nothing to do with the marriage. That's the whole point, it separates marriage from the aspect of childbearing. So she could have them, but I didn't have to. The children are her responsibility, legally and—"

"Financially," David said.

Jenks nodded. "Yes."

"So where'd she get the sperm?" Mel peered up over the edge of the bar.

Jenks frowned at him. "I donated it, of course. She *was* my wife."

"Hey, look at this. Popsicles."

Jenks waved a hand, as if swatting a fly. "For the boy."

Mel crooked a finger. "Come 'ere, String. You mind, Dr. Jenks? Come on, Gumby, this you got to try."

David sighed. "Dr. Jenks, let's go back a little here. You said it all started with the child who drowned. Martin. Tell me about that."

Jenks covered his eyes with splayed hands. "I thought she was over it. As over it as any mother heals after the death of a child." He jammed his fists against his thighs. "I thought I'd lost her then. I think if she could have traded me for the boy . . . Of course, she never said as much. It was a bad time, a terrible and very stupid accident. Martin fell out of our boat and drowned. The water was deep, it was dark. We never even recovered the body.

"Theresa blamed herself, of course. And me. He should have been in a life vest; we were both at fault. She's been very careful with Arthur. But it was all history, until about a year ago, when Theresa went to a psychic reading with a girlfriend, just a lark, you know? It was interesting, because the psychic was an Elaki, one of these fellas who read scales." Jenks glanced at String, who held a grape Popsicle on two sticks between both fins. "Is that good, sir?" Jenks's lips were tight, his tone aggressive.

"Is most cold," String said. "What is this scale reading? I have not heard of these. Psychic Elaki do not be the common."

Jenks shook his head. "She wasn't serious about it, I don't think, not right at first. Theresa was incredibly practical. She was physical, she kept busy, she wasn't into that kind of fuzzy navel watching."

String nipped a piece of Popsicle off the end tips. David noticed that a drip of purple juice was inching down the sticks to his fins.

"Go on," David said, thinking he should have left String and Mel in the car.

"Not long after that, she began talking about him, about Martin. Not just the occasional reference, but obsessively."

His tone was tainted with jealousy. David felt chilled.

"She said she was dreaming about him. She started spouting off about reincarnation, for God's sake. Saying what if he'd been reborn, would she recognize him, would she know him? She would cry in her sleep. And when I woke her, she would be *disoriented*, then angry. *Furious*. She even struck at me once, said I had ruined it, ruined the dream." Jenks looked to the window, staring at the heavy gold curtain.

"She started sleeping alone. Sometimes at night, I'd hear her call out. I knew better then, than to go to her. She became obsessed with the idea that Martin was *somewhere*, and that she had to find him."

Mel was quiet, finally, listening. David leaned close to Jenks.

"Was she still seeing this psychic?"

Jenks nodded. "He was feeding her, I know it. It's an organization called the Mind Institute—ridiculous! They gave her reading material, all kinds of outrageous theories and crap."

David thought of the book with the zigzag of lightning across the cover. "What did they get from her?"

Jenks shook his head.

"Sir?"

"I said I do not know. My wife is . . . was a very wealthy woman. I think she gave them money. She was giving it to someone. Large sums, out of her personal account."

"Any chance she was being blackmailed?" David asked.

"Theresa? Not a chance."

"This woman. Teddy Blake."

Jenks smiled fondly. "Oh yes, Ted. Arthur is very attached to her."

"Is she connected to the Institute?"

"No, of course not."

David smiled sadly. "Of course not? Why so?"

"As far as I know, she isn't. Teddy Blake is a straightforward woman. Bruer in Chicago recommended her."

David heard a noise, looked over his shoulder.

Arthur stood in the bedroom doorway, blinking. He wore a sweatshirt, a pair of red cotton pyjamas that were too small, and one gym sock on his left foot. His right foot was bare.

String swooped sideways. "The pouchling awakes. Popsicle, pouchling?"

"No, thank you, I'm not hungry. Careful, Mr. String, you're dripping."

Jenks gave the boy a firm look. "Arthur, I don't believe you're properly dressed."

The boy looked at the floor. "Teddy said I could call her, is that okay?"

Jenks pulled his bottom lip, glancing hard at David. "I'm not so sure that's a good idea."

Arthur's chest heaved. He was breathing hard. "She said she didn't mind."

"No, Arthur."

The boy looked away from Jenks, turned, and went into the bedroom, shutting the door behind him with a careful click. David found the polite control disturbing.

"For his own good," Jenks muttered. "You find any connection between Ms. Blake and the Mind Institute, I'd like to know right away. I'm obligated to protect the child. He is Theresa's boy."

Mel looked at him kindly. "And your own little spermatozoan."

FIFTEEN

DAVID WAS WATCHING DELLA WHEN THE PHONE RANG, watching her scroll through a computer file while a moist chocolate chip cookie sat on the next desk by a can of Coke. Cold beads of condensation bubbled the sides of the can.

He was tempted. A man. Della, a female, had not given it a second look, even though it was chocolate. Her computer beeped at her, but she continued scrolling, shoulders slumped, chin to chest. He wasn't sure what she was supposed to be doing. He hoped it wasn't important.

Mel leaned across David's desk and picked up the phone. "What?"

David reached for the cookie.

"Yo, David. It's Dawn Weiler. You consorting with the Feds?"

David picked up the phone. "Always. Dawn, how've you been?"

"Hi, David. I've been working long hours and eating like a pig at my desk. I bet I've gained five pounds in the last three days."

More like five ounces, David thought. Dawn had always been able to eat anything and stay slender. Much to Della's disgust.

"What is it with women and their weight?" David glanced warily at Della. She paid him no attention. Her computer beeped again, but she kept on scrolling.

"How's Rose and the kids?" Dawn asked.

"Kids are great."

"And Rose?"

She was pushing. David wondered if the word was out.

"Rose is fine."

"Good. Listen, David, you up to your ears in the supper club fire? Anything else going on?"

David frowned. "What's up here?"

"Just something funny."

"Wait for it," David muttered, under his breath. "Should we meet for lunch maybe?"

"No, I don't have time."

"Spit it already."

"You sound like Mel."

"Sticks and stones."

She laughed, and David smiled, picturing her in her office. Her hair would be flipped neatly under, white lace collar buttoned up to the top of her neck, pleated skirt swinging neatly over pale trim knees.

Teddy Blake was tan. Long-legged in cutoff shorts. David put her out of his mind.

"David, your name has come up in an investigation that has no connection to the fire."

"Dawn, are you on your office phone?"

"No, pay phone, and I don't have long."

David rubbed his finger on a coffee ring. "If it's not the fire, then what investigation is it?"

"I don't know."

"Who's sniffing around?"

"Can't say."

"Won't say, you mean."

"Right, David, that's what I mean."

"So why are you calling?"

"Because when our paths cross the paths of local cops, local cops get screwed. And I like you, David, I like you a lot."

Something there he hadn't heard before. There were advantages, sort of, to marriage rumors.

"Tell me what the investigation's about. Just a hint, Dawn."

"No can do. Honest, I don't know. Just a blip I ran across trawling through the system. And somebody stopped by the office, oh so casually, wanting to know what kind of cop you were. Routine hacker or bulldog."

"What'd you tell them?"

"I told them you were in a class by yourself. Tenacious, perceptive, relentless, broad-shouldered, brown-eyed, and obsessive."

"Spare my blushes."

"Take me to lunch one of these days."

"Is that all you're going to tell me?"

"That's all."

She hung up. David looked at the phone, wondering why all the magazines said women put personal relationships before everything else, including work. Evidently the women he knew didn't read these articles.

He wondered why the FBI was interested in him. Something to do with Theresa Jenks?

The phone rang again. He picked it up. It would be Dawn, with more information. The articles were right.

"I knew you couldn't resist me," David said.

"Baby, you been too much in the sun?"

David felt his face get red. "Detective Clements?"

"Um-hmm. Look, you got kids, don't you, Silver? Six or seven or more? Wife always bringing them home?"

"I have three daughters. It's animals my wife brings home."

"Animals, yeah, that was it. She run a pet store?"

"Animal rights activist. Militant."

"Good for her. Anyway, you know kids, right, you got three. So leave your Elaki and your Neanderthal at the office and meet me down by the supper club. Got somebody I want you to meet."

"Is she cute?"

"You married, Silver, or what?"

Or what, he thought. "Married," he said.

"Shame on you."

SIXTEEN

THE NEIGHBORHOOD WAS DESERTED IN THE HEAT OF HIGH noon. A man in oversized shoes and a long black coat mumbled to himself and crossed the street, rather than walk in front of the burned-out supper club.

David thought of the people and Elaki who had perished there in hot narrow rooms. He did not blame the man for crossing over.

He looked around, wondering if Clements was going to be late. The sun was hot, the oil stains on the paved street dark and tarry. Good iguana weather, David thought, wondering if Elliot was still alive. Likely, he was sunning happily somewhere, belly fat, complacent to have escaped the attentions of the girls. He was not an affectionate lizard.

Water dripped from a compressor, and David heard the whine of a ball bearing that would soon go. These were old units, in need of replacing.

The crime rate had dropped dramatically thirty years ago when the Federal government passed a law requiring all housing projects to be air-conditioned. Now they were all going bad, and there was no money for replacement.

A car horn honked; David heard an engine running rough. A battered Subaru pulled up next to the curb in front of the supper club—the curb that had been crushed to jagged chunks by emergency vehicles, angry residents, fire fighters in a hurry.

The Subaru showed traces of two very bad paint jobs—one dull brown, the other tasteless orange. The windows were rolled down. Inside, the beige upholstery was torn in places, showing dull gold padding and a layer of the kind of grime generated by long careless use and children.

Detective Yolanda Free Clements lifted a hand and grinned for one second, then stopped the car and opened the door, bending over the backseat for a canvas briefcase and a bright red plastic bag with a JEEPERS SNEAKERS logo.

David heard the metallic murmur of the car.

"In addition to the oil pan, the engine block continues to accumulate rust, and the leak makes it illegal to allow the cooling system—"

"Just fuck off, baby." Clements put a hand to the small of her back and winced. "Cut off *my* air-conditioning on a day like this? Don't be expecting no oil change any time soon, and you can forget the paint job."

"Yolanda Clements, there is no choice but to obey the law concerning leaks in the—"

Clements slammed the car door.

"You didn't lock it," David said.

"Never do. Keep hoping somebody will take it. Almost happened once, but the damn car talked 'em out of it."

"Might try leaving it here later tonight."

She grinned at him, and he was relieved that her bad humor was only for the car. She glanced at a huge watch with a wide, white leather band. David could see the time over her shoulder. 12:46.

"You by yourself?" she asked.

"Just like you said. What's up?"

She slung the briefcase over one shoulder and headed down the street. "Follow me."

"Where's your Elaki?" David asked.

"Left him back at the office, studying a chi-square analysis of investors in this property." She jerked her head toward the supper club. "Expecting it's changed hands several times the last few years, but evidently it hasn't. We're looking at mortgages and all, see if some familiar names come up in the list of investors."

"Got any?"

"Don't know. My guess is they will. Most of these arson fires are about money, though this one may prove to be the exception."

She stopped walking, leaned against a brick house, checked her watch again.

"I wouldn't lean against that brick there," David said.

"Why the hell not?"

"Side walls in an alley make good bathrooms."

She jerked upright. "Oh."

More suburban than she admitted, David decided. If she'd grown up like he had, she wouldn't need to be told.

"Anyway," she said. "I didn't think it was fair to bring my Elaki when I asked you not to bring yours. And they'd just fight over that van String drives. You ask me, it wasn't even dented. Good Lord save me from obsessive Elaki."

David frowned. "String is very proud of the van. And Detective Warden did dent it."

"I checked, Silver, I didn't see any damage."

"I checked too."

She looked up at him. "At the rate you and I are getting along, we might as well have that Neanderthal here, plus both the Elaki."

"I assume by Neanderthal you mean your buddy, Cobb? The one who scratches?"

"No, I mean your buddy, Burnett, the one who calls me Yo. And *he* scratches too. His *crotch*."

"He was making a point, Clements."

"That's an excuse?"

A silvery tingle of music was palpable in the thick humid air. A pink Sno-Cone jeep crept down the grids.

"Saved by the bell," Clements said. "Look, we're hot and crabby. Let me buy you a Sno-Cone, and let's start over."

She waved a hand. The jeep veered right, just as a stream of children emerged from the side window of a tan brick two-story. The tires made screeching noises and the jeep stopped, rear end jumping the grid.

The side door opened and an Elaki flowed out.

David looked from the Sno-Cone vendor to Clements. "An Elaki?"

"That's right. I warn you, the root beer's not worth getting."

The Elaki held a fin high and swayed sideways, reminding David of a trained dolphin in a water show. His scales were small and close together, no bald patches. He was firm, almost rigid, and his eye stalks were small and close to his head. The happy-face pattern of breathing slits on his belly was elongated, gaping open in the heat.

"Good of the day, sirs, ma'ams."

The voice was high-pitched, but male. David had the feeling the Elaki was very young. He wore a white cotton vest stained with pink and purple juice.

Clements looked over her shoulder. "Now where'd she get off to?"

"Who?" David asked.

"My informant. There she is." Clements raised her voice. "Get on over here, girl, tell me what flavor you want."

The tiny little girl who trudged toward them had her thumb in her mouth. She wore cheap plastic sandals and yellow shorts. Her T-shirt said LAFARGE AND GROAT and showed a fat cat and a dachshund—spin-offs from the old Ren and Stimpy cartoons.

The little girl popped the thumb out of her mouth. "Booberry." Her voice was tiny, but shrill. It carried.

"You mean blueberry?"

The Elaki waved a fin. "No, iss booberry. The flavor that comes in the cartoon."

"Oh," Clements said.

"Oh," David said. They exchanged looks.

The Elaki pushed a button on an oven-shaped lump of brown metal. "One booberry. And ma'ams and sirs?"

"Got grape?" David asked.

"Got grape, yessss. And the ma'ams?"

"Oranges Jubilee."

The Elaki set a dial and pushed a button. "Wait for this beeping, like machine of answering phones. Can pay while the wait goes away."

Clements looked at David. "He's a sociology scholar, on some kind of funded project."

The Elaki slid close. "Joint questions for the sirs and ma'ams. Thissss is to be in the confidence of. No names will be taken. For the anonymousness."

David braced for something personal.

"Please to tell. Any swimming fanatics in family history? Much swimming in early years?"

"That's two questions," Clements said. "You're overcharging."

"Swimming?" David echoed.

"There are three Sno-Cones, ma'ams, it is not to be overcharging." He cocked an eye prong at David. "Do not be of the embarrassed, sirs. Is anonymous this. Please to tell, much swimming?"

David leaned close to the Elaki and lowered his voice. "We swam almost three times a week, during the summers. Sometimes for hours at a time."

The scales on the Elaki's midsection quivered. "Fringe wetting or submerged?"

"Submerged. All afternoon. Just came up for air."

Clements put a hand over her mouth. "I had *no* idea, Silver."

"Keep it to yourself," he said.

"And ma'ams? The swimming?"

"Certainly not. What kind of girl do you think I am?"

"Not even—"

"Hush that talk or I'll smack your fin. And no pestering the kid, her cone's on me."

The machine beeped. The Elaki opened the hinged door and handed out Sno-Cones cupped in thin, edible rice paper. He twitched an eye prong at David, giving him a second look.

Clements bent down and handed a red and blue Sno-Cone to the little girl in yellow shorts. Her hair was a nimbus of tight brown curls. She held the Sno-Cone in both hands, took a test lick, then munched ice sprinkles off the top at a rate that made David's teeth ache just to watch.

"Am I getting old," he said, "or are the informants getting younger?"

SEVENTEEN

THE LITTLE GIRL GRUDGINGLY ADMITTED HER NAME WAS Penny, though she preferred to be called LaFarge after the cartoon cat on her shirt. David, familiar with the cat's habits of personal hygiene from his own daughters' gleeful recitations, was quietly appalled.

Clements sat beside Penny, both of them swinging their legs. Clements wore cutoff army fatigues, a white dress shirt with the sleeves rolled up, and a dark, conservative tie. Penny took a slurp of juice from the side of her Sno-Cone and peered at Clements over the mound of pink and blue ice.

"Most of the polices I know dress nice."

"I ain't most polices," Clements said.

The little girl pointed at David. Pink juice stained the pale white skin of her chin and reddened her lips. "He dress nice, like my daddy."

"Do I remind you of your daddy?" David asked conversationally.

The little girl stopped mid-lick. "No."

Clements laughed quietly, under her breath. She rustled the red plastic bag and took out a small pink pair of chippers.

Penny's eyes got big and she leaned close to David. "Those the shoes that talk."

"What do they say? Tie me? Wash your feet?"

Penny giggled, dribbling pink juice down her shirt. "They tell stories."

"What kind of stories?"

"Spaceships. Little pigs with cones on their heads. Parrots run away to the Big Apple."

David smiled. The parrot story was one of Mattie's favorites. "You know where the Big Apple is, Penny?"

She swung her legs. "Yeah, do you?"

"Omaha?"

"*No*, New York."

"You're pretty smart. Maybe we should get married."

She cocked her head to one side, then glanced at his left hand. "You're already married. Can't be married two at the same, my mama says so."

David looked at Clements. "How old?"

"Four," Penny said.

Clements gobbled ice. "Tell Detective Silver what you told me."

"Which thing?"

"Start with the balloon man."

"He was fat and silly shape, puffy. And he walk funny."

David was intrigued but knew better than to interrupt.

"And he have lots and lots of big purple balloons. I didn't want one." She looked down at her sandals, and David knew her feelings had been hurt. "But Markus got one. He got a whole bunch. I waited to see if he might share or trade me—I got a dead turtle. But he didn't come back out."

"Why didn't Markus come back out?" David glanced at Clements. She looked away.

"Burnt up." Penny's lower lip drooped.

"Where did Markus live?"

Penny twisted sideways and her Sno-Cone dipped. With the immediate reflexes of an experienced father, David grabbed the Sno-Cone and turned it back up before it spilled.

"Hold it straight," he said.

"I know." Penny said. She pointed. "Markus live there."

David looked over his shoulder to the house where he'd found the woman and child in the stairwell . . . where the baby had died of carbon monoxide poisoning . . . where a mother had piled her children on the bed and shielded them as they died . . . where the family dog died outside the baby's room, body next to that of Theresa Jenks, mother of Arthur Jenks.

"That house," David said.

"Markus had talking shoes too. Chippers. And lots of new clothes. And a new scooter *and* a key chain with a whistle. He got lots of new stuff."

"You miss Markus a lot?"

Penny shook her head and a tear slid down her cheek, leaving a trail in the sweat on her heat-flushed face. "He let me ride the scooter and blow the whistle. He let me keep the chain for a while."

David sat down beside Penny, looking at the thin legs, the scabs on her left knee. He pointed to a partially healed scrape.

"How'd you do that?"

"Fell off the scooter. And I stumped my big toe." She pointed to a toe swaddled in a filth-encrusted Band-Aid.

"How come Markus got so much new stuff? He have a birthday?"

"Nope. For his birfday he got a trike with a horn. It was used to belong to his sister, but his mama clean it up and paint it. It had a dent, but it worked good. The scooter was bran' new. It smelled nice."

"You know where he got all the presents?" David asked.

"From the lady. Markus said there was lots more where that came from."

"You know who the lady was?"

"Nope. But she come to the house."

"She did?"

"The day Markus burnt up. She come and then the balloon man come."

"You said he walked funny?"

She tipped the rice paper forward, trailing her tongue in the juice, which ran down her chin and lined the soft folds of skin in her neck.

"Did he limp?" David asked.

She shrugged.

"Just walked funny?"

She dug into the pocket of her shorts, fists bunching them tight against her leg. She opened her palm, showing David a key chain and a whistle. David remembered the woman in the white dress, clutching the ring in her fist.

"I better give this back." Her chin sunk low on her chest.

David closed her fingers around the whistle, pressing gently. "Markus won't mind if you keep it."

EIGHTEEN

PENNY WHO LIKED TO BE CALLED LAFARGE WAS BLOWING the whistle as they walked away. The new shoes were tied neatly on her feet, the old sandals tucked into the red plastic bag.

"You realize her testimony's tainted now, Clements. DA will never get around the Sno-Cone and tennies."

"Like I'm going to put a four-year-old in court."

The whistle shrilled again and David grinned.

"You think this lady Penny talked about was Theresa Jenks?" Clements asked.

"Extremely possible. Interesting that she's giving them money, bringing them gifts. Something very funny going on here, Clements. How'd you find Penny, anyway? Door-to-door?"

"Naw, Silver, my son was with me. He went out to play, and she liked his shoes."

"New police tactic. Take your kids along."

"Kids on the street know more than the hookers."

"Balloon man the torch?"

"We got witnesses saw him deliver a balloon bouquet to the supper club right before the fire. Maybe half hour, forty-five minutes, three weeks. Nobody ever agrees on the time, you noticed that?"

"Excuse me, Clements, but where are we headed?"

She chewed the edge of the rice paper cup that held the remains of her Sno-Cone. "I got two problems. One, this case is going in too many directions, and taken together, they don't make a hell of a lot of sense."

"And two?"

"I'm so hungry I'm going to eat this cup, and I don't care how nutritious they are, they taste like crap. You like Caribbean food?"

"I don't know."

"Come on then, baby. Time you found out."

The Jamaican Café was brown inside—brown upholstery on the booths, brown tile floor, brown doors. The walls were painted in murals by an artist who favored broad strokes, parrots, vibrant shades of green, red, and blue that somehow made David wish for time off and a slower pace.

He noticed two doors in a hallway—one for MONS and one for WOMONS. A ceiling fan swirled and his hair stirred. David looked up, mouth open.

"That's not a hologram?"

Clements grinned at him. "The real thing, right on down to the breeze on the back of your neck."

David watched the wood blades circle lazily.

Clements chose a booth across from the bar. A stuffed parrot sat on a stool next to the kitchen, and he sat alone. Business was slow. The left side of the bar had no stools, though David could see the scars on the linoleum where they'd been ripped from their mooring. The Jamaican Café was Elaki-friendly.

"They put cinnamon in the food here?" David asked Clements.

"They ask first."

He sat down and tapped the menu.

"Silver?"

"Yeah?"

"This is one of those places barely makes it one year to the next. So it's pretty old-fashioned."

"You have a point?"

"You got to *read* the menu. It won't be talking to you."

"Oh."

"The jerk chicken's good. Get the lunch platter, if you're hungry."

David ordered lime water and Clements took iced tea, and they commiserated over their inability to order beer. David leaned back in the booth. It smelled good in here—spicy sweet, mingled with the char of the grill and the afternoon sun. A battered door behind the bar swung open, making the parrot sway. Inside, the kitchen was tiny, overcrowded, hot and steamy. David loosened his tie and rubbed the back of his neck.

The air-conditioning was marginal. Authentic tropical ambience. He wiped sweat off his upper lip with a napkin. Clements drummed her fingers on the tabletop.

"So what's bothering you, Detective Clements?"

"Silver—"

"Call me David."

"Yolanda." She leaned forward and shook his hand, her grip firm and damp. "I got a court order. Went through a storage warehouse that belongs to the owners—a couple of humans . . . Listen to me. Couple dudes, brothers, name of Jimmy and Duncan Bernitski."

"And?"

"And there's a lot of interesting stuff in there, but not what I was looking for."

"Which was?"

"Stuff from the supper club. Stuff they might take out of there, because they know there's going to be a fire. Food packages, like were missing from the kitchen."

"When did you go to the warehouse?"

"This morning."

"They had plenty of time to move it, then."

"Yeah, I'm sure that's it."

Their food arrived—chicken tucked next to a creamy potato salad, black beans and rice with a dollop each of sour cream and salsa, and a piece of corn bread.

Clements sighed. "Heaven."

David took a bite of chicken, tasted lime and the tang of the grill.

"Like it?" Clements asked.

He nodded, tried the potato salad. Different. Wonderful. He made inroads into the black beans and rice.

Clements ate her corn bread with a fork, like it was cake. "The one consistent name we do get is a real estate broker name of Tatewood. You know him?"

David shook his head, picked up the corn bread. It was sweet and thick with bits of things he could not identify. He cut another bite of chicken.

"Mr. Tatewood has two other supper clubs in his portfolio."

David raised an eyebrow, but kept eating. He was getting full, but the food was too good to pass up.

Clements took a bite of chicken and corn bread, a large swallow of tea. "He also handled a refinance for that restaurant that caters to Elaki. Pierre's, you know it?"

David felt the scar throb on his chest. Purely psychological. He set his fork down.

"Yeah, I know it. But it doesn't cater to Elaki, it's half-and-half. Pierre doesn't care who eats, so long as they eat and like it. He's a gourmet. Gives away half his meals to people who are broke but have a palette, charges a fortune for everyone else. He likes Elaki because they'll eat anything. Literally."

"Like what?"

"Beetles in puff pastry. Stuff like that."

She took a bite of potato salad. "Must be five hundred grams of fat in this. Probably why I like it. Not much fat in beetles, I bet."

"Fat's good for you, remember? They've changed their minds again, Clements, keep up."

She shrugged, chewed. "Anyway, I'm a go talk to Tatewood this afternoon. Want to come?"

David scooped a forkful of rice out from under the mushy black beans. "Can I bring my Elaki?"

NINETEEN

A DREARY, HEAT-SOAKED CROWD HAD GATHERED IN FRONT of Tatewood's office building. David got out of the car, saw the attention was centered on a police issue van which had locked bumpers with a jeep from the City Exterminator's office.

He looked at Clements. "I see your Elaki proceeds us."

Clements rolled her eyes, slammed the car door, and ignored the protestations of the driver of the jeep.

"File a claim with our office," she said over her shoulder, herding the three of them inside.

The sign said TATEWOOD REAL ESTATE BROKERAGE, the glow of letters hard to see in the harsh light of afternoon. It was an old building—you could stand in the lobby and judge the success of the occupants. The directory promised a hypnotist, a private investigator, the local headquarters for the Church of Scientology, an insurance counselor, and a schizophrenia rehabilitation clinic. The second floor had an ad agency and a criminal lawyer whose name David recognized.

"Isss most dirt-ridden in thisss hallway." Warden shook his bottom fringe. A web of dust coated the scales.

Clements looked back over her shoulder at David. "This guy Tatewood's been getting threats off and on, last eighteen months."

"Who from?"

"SCAE."

"Iss Skinhead Christians Against Elaki," Warden said.

David grimaced. "Blowhards."

"Don't dismiss 'em entirely. They been blowing up churches down in Florida."

"Everybody blows up churches down in Florida."

"They go after any denomination that—how do they put it—

accepts the Elaki abomination." Clements grinned at Warden.

"They have Nazi affiliation?"

"Not these guys. They just shave their heads and chant the Bible at you. Real perverts." Clements knocked at a thin, pinewood door.

"Coming." The voice was male, a tenor.

Tatewood had the emaciated look and stiff-legged gait of an ex-con who would not thrive in prison, but would be conscientious under house arrest. He had a haunted air that made David think somehow, sometime, something had pushed him so far he could not get back. His cheeks were hollow, there were circles under his eyes, and his hair was black and shiny. The ends curled up in a dip despite the heavy coating of hair oil.

He caught David looking and whipped a comb out of his pocket, smoothing out the flip. He smiled self-consciously, and offered Clements a hand.

"Afternoon, Mr. Tatewood. I'm Detective Clements, we talked on the phone?"

He swallowed hard, Adam's apple prominent. "Pleasure."

He shook David's hand, holding the grip a shade too long, making serious eye contact. David was surprised by the direct, intelligent gaze. Tatewood ducked his head shyly and waved them into the small, dusty office.

There was a desk in the room, an ancient computer, a phone, and a stack of boxes. The window was hidden by grimy white plastic blinds. David had the urge to trace his name in the dust. None of the chairs looked comfortable.

"Got those letters for you, Detective Clements." Tatewood came up with a large battered mailer that had gone through the U.S. postal system one time too many. He waved it uncertainly.

Clements held out a hand. "Come to Mama."

Tatewood went dusky red. "Can I get you anything? Coffee? Coke?"

David saw no sign of a coffeepot or Coke machine.

"Coffee with much of the cream?" Warden said.

Tatewood had been on the verge of sitting. "Of course. Just let me dash across the street for one minute."

Clements folded her arms. "Actually, Wart here is trying to

cut down on his caffeine. Aren't you, Wart?"

"Aren't I?"

"Yes, you are."

Tatewood was red again.

"These threats come through the mail, Mr. Tatewood?" David asked.

"Through the mail, over the phone, tacked to the door. Sometimes they access my E-mail." He tapped the computer.

"They have sssingle you out, these ones?"

Tatewood nodded. "I handle the kind of properties that make good targets. Places where Elaki and people mix together. That's what really gets these people going. The mixing."

"Any direct confrontation?" David asked.

"The windows got broken pretty regularly, before I put the sufplex in. That's mostly it."

Clements waved the sheaf of papers, and David saw that one was actually done in pink and yellow crayon. Some had the letters cut out, some had pictures of burning buildings.

"Let me see," he said.

It was a newspaper photo of a supper club in First Town, Georgia, host to the first Elaki landing. Someone had taken a red marker and put YOU NEXT across the flames.

"How long has this been going on?" David asked.

"Year and a half. Two."

"How long you been handling Elaki/human properties?"

"Since I opened my first office, maybe seven years ago. I specialize. Get established in one city, find someone to manage the place, then move on."

Clements crossed her legs, rubbed the back of her neck. "I guess the supper club was insured to the hilt."

Tatewood's shoulders went slack. "Actually, no."

Clements frowned.

"The Bernitski brothers were having cash flow problems. I warned them, of course." He scratched his chin. "They got hit hard, after the fire, with lawsuits and everything. I'm selling the property for them now, but it'll go cheap. Burned-out building, with liens, mortgaged. We may not be able to give the place away."

"Either way, you still get paid," Clements said.

Tatewood's smile was shy. "Just like you."

TWENTY

STRING SKITTERED SIDEWAYS INTO THE TRUNK OF THERESA Jenks's abandoned car.

"Comes out, comes out, where some ever you are." He cocked an eye prong at David. "This isss what the pouchling says?"

"Gumby, quit horsing around and get out of there." Mel took his left shoe off and peeled back the sock. "Look at this blister. You see this?"

David looked, wished he hadn't. He glanced back up at the hologram Bruer had sent and waved String out of the way.

Theresa Jenks drove a Jaguar, hunter-green. The trunk was a mess—books, many of them from the Mind Institute, a life jacket, a ski boot, and a melted candy bar.

String reached for the chocolate.

"Come on. Quit playing in the hologram."

String's bottom fringe quivered. "Am looking up close, Detective Mel."

"Am driving me crazy, Detective Gumby."

"Move to interior," David said.

The car's nav program light was blinking red. There were, in fact, red lights all across the control panel. The car was upset.

Mel poked his blister. "Bruer tells me Theresa Jenks programmed the car to leave the airport. Said it was chugging along under its own speed before it freaked out there, by the side of the road."

"Isss not possible the car to drive alone. Against regulation laws." String shed a scale and it glimmered in the hologram, seeming to hang off the rearview mirror.

"Sometimes, they'll do it," David said.

"But isss illegal."

Mel peeled back a hunk of skin. "Rich people's cars do

things other people's don't. Besides, it's better than letting Elaki drive."

"Please, Detective Mel. This picking apart of the bubble skin injury is not good of the way. May cause infection and stomach indigestion."

Mel snorted. "A blister's going to upset my stomach?"

"No, mine." David wiped sweat off his upper lip. Even with the air-conditioning going, the humidity was heavy, making the air soft and sticky. The whole building was starting to smell like mildew. Something somewhere was breaking down.

The conference room door opened. Della stuck her head in.

"David? You got a call from that Blake woman. Wants you to stop by her hotel this afternoon, if at all possible."

"Whoa," Mel said. "Can I come?"

"And, David, Captain wants you too, as soon as he's done with lunch."

"How long will that be?" David asked.

"He was halfway through his sandwich, last I saw."

"Thanks, Della."

She was already gone.

"You know, David, this don't make sense." Mel held a flap of skin between two fingers like a pointer. "Jenks uses her own name and credits to buy the airline ticket. Takes money out of her account. I mean, it's not going to be a problem to track her down. Doesn't look like she was trying to disappear, not to start out with."

"She was never trying to disappear," David said. "Move to the Jenks's household."

The hologram jittered like a home movie. A shadow wavered and showed the image of Bernard Jenks. He nodded his head stiffly, pointing.

The master bedroom was a thing of beauty, and David wondered if he and Rose would get along better in such surroundings. The bed was large, high off the ground, making David think of *The Princess and the Pea*. There was a black marble fireplace on one side of the room, hearth cold, a pile of paperback books on the mantel next to gold-framed baby pictures.

"Hold." David got up and crossed the room. The baby pictures were of Martin and Arthur, looking enough alike that they could easily be mistaken for the same child. The difference was in Theresa Jenks. The woman who held Arthur was older and thinner, with a look about her that David had seen before in women who'd lost a child.

The hologram panned Theresa Jenks's closet. The floor was neat, hosting a jumble of low-heeled dress shoes and a stunning array of athletic shoes—two red pair, one black pair, all the rest white. All looked worn, and worn hard. On the right-hand side of the closet, a blouse dangled from a hanger, sleeve caught over the bend of metal, and a jacket was crumpled on the floor over a lingerie bag.

David got up, looked at the books on the bedside table—*The Fearful Parent/The Fearful Child, Scuba in the Bahamas, The Book of Dreams, Reincarnation of the Innocents, Befriending the Dead, Psychic Reincarnation.*

He passed a hand through the hologram, wishing he could thumb through the books, see whether or not the pages were dog-eared, the spines broken. He wondered if Theresa Jenks had found her answers.

David sat back down and flipped through Bruer's file. Theresa Jenks had gone to the Mind Institute with a friend, just as a lark. She didn't believe in psychics, but the friend had talked her into a reading. She had told Bernard about it at dinner, then dismissed the whole thing. No, he did not think she had taken it seriously. Not then.

Then the dreams had started. Bad dreams, about their son, Martin, who had drowned at age four.

David looked up at the picture of the plump-cheeked four-year-old, dressed in well-pressed shorts and a white shirt, tennis shoes unscuffed, hair combed neatly to one side. A happy-looking child—relaxed, compared to the picture of Arthur at the same age. Arthur and Martin had been nearly identical babies, but that changed as they got old enough to walk. Arthur was thinner, he had a habit of ducking his head close in to his shoulders when someone took his picture, and his smile was tentative and fleeting. He had a perpetually anxious look.

David told the hologram to continue.

Double glass doors led into a small room off the master suite. It was oddly shabby inside. The couch was old and well-padded, an ugly shade of green, and inexpensive enough to have graced David's own living room. There were pillows at one end, mashed down as if they had been slept on, and a ratty-looking afghan balled up in the middle. A maroon recliner had an actual tear down the seat of the upholstery, and a table beside it held an open pack of saltine crackers and a juice glass with dregs of milk in the bottom. David saw a Game Boy on top of the television. A pair of undershorts had been thrown over the bookcase, a tie draped over a lamp. Fire hazard, David thought.

"It is the canine death that I find of concern," String said.

"You been hanging out with my sister?" Mel asked. He pulled the sock back over his foot.

"What canine?" David said.

String called up the hologram of the house where David had fallen through the stairwell. "Upstairs pathway."

"*Hall*way," Mel said.

The image wavered and String pointed. "See outline canine there? And body of this Jenks, Theresa, here found."

Mel tied his shoe. "I know there's got to be a point to this."

"Who kills this Jenks, Theresa? Say not the family member. Say is to be the stranger."

Mel leaned back in his chair. "Sensor said only one stranger in the house. Which has got to be Jenks herself."

"Murderer is left," String said. "Has bypassed sensor, this is not to be the difficult."

David was nodding.

"Is thisss a watchdog animal? Is he there at the killing? What does this canine do? Watch? Protect?"

"Lick his—" Mel looked at String. "Never mind. I guess if the dog caused a problem, the perp would—"

"Kill it," David said.

"Might have gotten bitten for his trouble. Which means the killer's hands could be marked."

"Be interesting to know if the dog died in the fire, or before."

Mel was nodding. "We got three detectives in the room, ought to be able to track the remains of one dead canine. Let's flip for it. What you take, String? Heads, tails, or rim?"

"Rim?"

"No, don't take that, it's no fair."

"I take rim."

Mel sighed and pulled out a quarter.

TWENTY-ONE

THE CAPTAIN WAS BOUNCING A PEN ON A BARE SPOT IN THE center of his desk. The surface was covered in computer printouts; the bare spot looked as if it had been cleared specifically for bouncing pens.

The man had his priorities, David decided.

Halliday gave David a small, tense smile and motioned him to a chair. He cleared his throat.

"How are your girls, David?"

"Fine."

"Rose okay?"

I wouldn't know, David thought. "Fine," he said.

The captain leaned back in his chair. "Give me a rundown, will you, on how things are going?"

David frowned, shifted sideways, and told the captain what he already knew. "Fire was deliberately set by incendiary devices housed in balloons. We think the balloons were delivered in a bouquet by a man dressed as a clown, fifteen to forty-five minutes before the bomb threat and subsequent fire alarm were called in. The club had been getting threats from SCAE—"

"Doesn't sound like their kind of thing, David, what I know."

David shrugged. "I hear they've turned nasty down in Florida."

Halliday put his arms behind his head. David saw he was sweating. "Everybody's nasty down in Florida. It's the heat."

"Detective Clements saw some indication that things were removed from the kitchen before the fire, which means—"

"The owners burning it out."

David nodded. "Except that the insurance is screwed up. The Bernitski brothers tried to raise the limits on the policy just before the fire—on the advice of their manager, Tatewood, by the way—but it didn't go into effect, and the other policy had lapsed."

"So they got zip?" Halliday's face creased with delight.

"Clements also says there were some supper club fires in Chicago a couple years ago. She's doing a computer search for arson signatures. The Bernitski brothers have alibis, good ones. If they did it, they hired a torch. But it's a pro job, so we already know that."

Halliday nodded, glanced up at the ceiling. "What's going on with this Jenks thing?"

"There were balloon devices in the house where she was murdered."

"So it didn't just catch from the club?"

"Arson says not."

"Was it the other way around? Club torched to cover her murder? Got any connection between the Bernitskis and Theresa Jenks?"

David shook his head. "Not yet, but Della and Pete are on it. I did run across one thing interesting."

"Which is?"

"The family in the house where Jenks was killed came into money right before the fire. And seemed to think they were headed for more."

Halliday took a deep breath and let it out slowly. His voice deepened an octave, and his eyes looked tired. "I have good news for you, David."

"You don't look happy about it."

"Chief Ogden told me it was good news, so it's got to be good news, right? He said not to be unduly influenced, about the Jenks thing. Just because they're wealthy, doesn't mean we should give them—how'd he put it? An overemphasis. Especially since we got this supper club thing. A lot of bad feeling on how that worked out, with the bomb threat tying up the grid. Ogden doesn't want it to look like we're ignoring the deaths of 248 *poor* Saigo City citizens, to track the killer of one rich heiress from Chicago."

David raised an eyebrow. "What are you telling me, Captain?"

"I'm not telling you anything, David. I want you to tell me."

David sighed and leaned back in his chair. Just a few days ago this would have seemed too good to be true.

And it would have been.

"Captain, the Jenks murder has got to be connected to the supper club fire. At the moment, nothing makes sense, but you can't possibly tell me this is some kind of obscure coincidence."

Halliday closed his eyes. "Of course I can tell you that. The thing is, you wouldn't believe me. Would you, David?"

"No, sir, I wouldn't."

Halliday kept his eyes closed. "Don't blame you. I wouldn't believe me either."

David looked through the blinds at Della, sitting in front of her tube, shoulders slumped. He did not think she had combed her hair in a while.

He wondered if Halliday had fallen asleep. "Captain? What is it you want me to do?"

Halliday didn't even twitch. "You do your job."

TWENTY-TWO

THE DESK CLERK HAD GIVEN HIM A BLANK LOOK, A PROFESsional glaze that made it clear he was purposely not noticing or wondering why David was back again so soon. That bothered David, in a way that the hostility had not. Hostility was the norm for a police detective. Acceptance made him feel the man thought he was up to something.

He knocked outside Teddy Blake's door and waited. Knocked again.

"You'll never get in that way."

She walked too quietly, David decided, noting that she was barefooted, and thinking she ought not be. Her toenails were painted brick red. She wore tight, worn jeans, and an oversized white cotton shirt. The left knee of the jeans was worn through, loose strands of material covering the tan brown flesh. She held three cans of Coke and an armful of candy bars, and her fingernails were clipped short and unpolished, not pretty but clean. Her hair was braided back, pulling loose on the sides, giving her the air of a woman who's had a long day.

David wondered why she didn't wear it down.

"Gets in my eyes," she said absently. She knocked on the door, two staccato taps and one big boom. She gave David a look over her shoulder. She wore large gold hoops in her ears.

"You got to know the secret knock. Come *on*, Arthur, it's me, hon. *Look through the peephole first.*"

"Arthur's here?" David did not like the sound of this.

"I know, I hated to leave him alone in this dump, but I was only down the hall for a second. Poor thing is starving. You know what boys are at this age."

The door swung open. Arthur saw David and took a step backward.

98

Teddy grinned and tossed a candy bar. He caught it, but it bounced out of his hand and hit the floor. David could see the boy's face turn red as he bent over to pick it up. He decided that people who felt nostalgic for childhood were mentally ill.

Blake slammed the door shut with her rear end. "Locks," she said absently and held up the candy bars. "Nestlé Crunch, Almond Joy, or Butterfingers?"

"Almond Joy," David said.

He caught the candy bar in midair, knowing Arthur admired him for this very small thing. Teddy handed David a Coke, gave one to Arthur, and leaned against the door.

David popped the lid on the can. Brown foam shot out of the small keyhole opening and sluiced his arm and the cuff of his shirt, then dribbled down to the worn maroon carpet.

It was an old trick, but that did not stop Teddy and Arthur from being amused, almost to the point of hysteria. Teddy was a young thirty-two, he decided.

He went to the bathroom to clean up. She had just the kind of bathroom that made him crazy. The sink was full of water and suds, and the counters were burdened by tubes of lipstick, a makeup bottle without a cap, a toothpaste tube trailing green paste, and a red toothbrush with bristles so tightly balled together it had probably earned retirement years ago. A woman's razor hung by a cord from the wall, red nail polish was turned on its side. David tightened the cap, then set the bottle upright. The cutoff jeans hung damply over the shower bar, along with a pair of socks.

David let the water out of the sink, found lace thong panties clogging the drain. He shrugged. He was an old married man. He rinsed the panties and rung them out gently, thinking they were awfully small. If she was annoyed about the intimacy, it served her right for leaving them out.

David ran water over the cuff of his shirt, noticing a smear of toothpaste across the bathroom mirror. Had she spit, missed the sink, then not cleaned it up?

He was startled by the way he looked—serious, angry, tired. His face seemed to have settled into permanent lines of fatigue and unhappiness. No wonder people were avoiding him.

Arthur and Teddy were sitting side by side on the bed when he came out, and they had an air of contrition that did not fool him. His Coke can had been cleaned of all stickiness and set on a table next to his Almond Joy. They had even provided him with a chair.

He sat down and took a drink. The can was still three quarters full and he was thirsty. He liked it that Teddy was drinking Coke instead of beer, with Arthur in the room. He picked up the Almond Joy and began unwrapping it.

"You guys didn't do anything to my candy bar, did you?"

This made them laugh again, and David decided that at the moment the two of them seemed very much like brother and sister, and that he felt about a hundred years old.

He took a bite of the candy, thinking how much he loved coconut, and how rarely he ate it. Teddy was eating the Nestlé Crunch, which he considered a woman's candy bar, and Arthur had moved in on the Butterfingers. The boy seemed different today—goofy and relaxed. Was this how he was without his father? Mother's husband, David corrected himself. No wonder the child was tense.

"Arthur has something to tell you," Teddy said.

Something in her voice warned him to go easy. Arthur stopped chewing, swallowed a mouthful of candy, and looked up at David. The boy's shirt was straining at the buttons, and the shoulders were tight. He was growing fast, and no one was noticing.

"I talked to my mom. On the phone, the night before."

David's heartbeat picked up but he nodded calmly. "The night before she died?"

"Yeah."

David kept his voice gentle. "Tell me."

The half-eaten candy bar melted in Arthur's hand. He had been alone in the hotel room eating pizza and playing video games. Jenks had gone to the pool to swim. Arthur was not a good swimmer.

What had she said? Hard to remember, exactly.

She missed him, she loved him, she was very, very sorry. He asked her why. She said because she had a beautiful son she had left behind, to search for something that could not be. That Bernard had been right, for all that he was wrong. She had laughed and said the scales had fallen from her eyes.

Arthur shrugged here.

Yes, she was coming to their hotel. But it was going to be a surprise. He was not to tell anybody about it.

Arthur picked at a hole in the bedspread. "I asked her to please come now, that night. She said could I hang on another day or two, and I said okay."

"Anything else?" David asked.

Arthur shook his head.

"You've talked to her before, haven't you?"

"No, sir. Not since she went away."

"You sure? Nobody's going to be mad at you."

"No, sir. Just that night. I should have told her to come home."

"Do you know where she was? Where she was staying?"

Arthur shook his head.

"Any background noises?"

"She said she was near a place that had great pancakes and hash browns. But then she laughed, so maybe she was kidding."

"Do you think she was kidding?"

"No, sir. She really does like pancakes. Did, I mean."

David put a hand on the boy's shoulder. He glanced at Teddy Blake. "Jenks. He know where Arthur is?"

"Yeah, but he ain't happy about it." She punched Arthur in the shoulder. "Come on, kiddo. The worst is over, and Detective Silver didn't tear your head off." She looked at David. "Thanks a whole lot for stopping by. Arthur was scared to come to your office."

"I *was* not." Arthur's voice cracked, ever changing.

"No trouble," David said, though it was.

Teddy wiped chocolate from her hands on the bedspread. "Come on, Arthur, we'll miss our bus."

David frowned. "This isn't the part of town to be taking buses."

"We'll be okay."

"I'll drop you."

Arthur gave Teddy the anxious look of a boy who was often denied. She winked at him and shook her head at David.

"No, thanks."

Something was up, between them.

"I insist."

Teddy's smile faded. "What good's that do you? I appreciate your trouble, Detective, but Arthur and I have plans."

"What plans?"

"It's no big deal. Arthur saw one of those carnival things and thought we might ride some rides, eat popcorn and greasy pork sandwiches. Maybe get our fortunes told." She winked at David.

He thought suddenly what a kind woman she was, then remembered he did not like her. He wondered if she wore thong panties under the jeans.

"Want to come with us?" she asked, like a woman who knew better.

David looked at her. "Why not?"

TWENTY-THREE

DAVID SHOVED HIS HANDS IN HIS POCKETS, SURPRISED TO find himself whistling. Surprised to be standing in the middle of a carnival ground at the end of a working day playing hooky when the caseload was staggering. Surprised to be happy.

Arthur was eyeing the roller coaster, and David well knew who would be drafted to ride along if the boy headed that way. Teddy swore she got sick on the twisty rides.

"Another hot dog, Arthur?" David asked.

"No, sir."

Teddy rolled her eyes. "Lord knows where he would put it. Would you *look* at that Ferris wheel?"

It glowed neon-blue in the dusky twilight, and the seats looked like silver-coated leather. All illusion, David thought, thinking of the ripped upholstery and stark grey metal under the hologram.

"Quit that," Teddy said.

He looked at her, frowning. "I will if you will."

Arthur looked from one to the other, only mildly curious, as if encoded adult conversation was an everyday part of his life.

"I'll try," Teddy said. "But in return you have to ride the Ferris wheel with us."

Arthur looked at him anxiously.

"It's a deal."

They got stuck at the top, much to Arthur's delight, just as the brown haze of twilight drained away and the night turned black amid glowing carnival lights.

"Look, Arthur, there's that man with the dachshund, see him?"

David did not understand why Teddy and Arthur were so taken with the dachshund man, though it seemed to have

103

something to do with an episode of "LaFarge and Groat." He did not feel left out. He felt as if he had been asleep forever, and was wide awake for the first time in way too long.

It was breezy this high up, almost cool, and David liked the warm press of Teddy Blake's skin against his. He looked out at the people walking the hard-packed dirt and tufty grass between the rides and booths.

Arthur said something that made Teddy chuckle, and David realized that this woman laughed a lot. She clutched the safety bar, and he wondered if heights made her nervous. He took her hand and turned the palm up.

Her face was still soft, the way it got when she thought something was funny. "What?"

"Want me to tell your fortune?"

"You got the wrong hand."

"No commentary, I'm doing this." He studied her pink palm, frowned, pursed his lips, said "ummm" three times.

"Well?"

"You're afraid of heights."

"Nope. I'm afraid of two things—escalators and North Carolina. Nothing else scares me."

"Not even cynical cops?"

"Nah, cynical cops are some of my favorite people. Tell me something I don't know."

"Patience. I see . . . I see a man in your future. A dark-haired man, a man with brown eyes."

She looked at his brown eyes and black hair. She did not pull her hand away. David thought that if Arthur had not been there, he would have kissed her.

But Arthur was there. The boy swung his legs, making the seat sway back and forth. Teddy squeezed David's hand before she pulled hers away, and then she clutched her stomach.

"Arthur, cut it out!"

Arthur laughed and stopped, and the seat rocked gently. The wind blew Teddy's hair into David's face, and he looked down at the Ferris wheel, seeing neon-blue and silver, thinking he had never seen a ride so beautiful.

The temptation to ignore his radio when it went off was almost more than he could bear. Teddy's face took on a closed and wary look, and Arthur ducked his head sideways, hunching his shoulders.

The dispatcher was tense. Bomb threat and arson, Cajun Supper Club, 1202 Ellington and Walford. Mel and String were on the way; he was to get there ASAP. Grids would be held open for emergency vehicles.

"What is it?" Teddy asked.

He saw it in their eyes, the same look of disappointment, of pleasures interrupted, that he saw in the faces of his children when yet another family excursion was derailed by work.

"Fire. Another supper club."

Teddy clutched his arm. "You go on, we'll get home all right."

Arthur grabbed his other arm. "Let us come."

David shook his head.

"No, please, sir. I saw all those pictures before—there were all kinds of people helping. I promise not to get in the way, but I might be able to do something. Some little thing."

"No dashing into burning buildings, Arthur. It's not like that."

"I don't mean that, honest. I'm fourteen, for God's sake. I'm almost grown-up."

David looked into the face of a boy who was always left behind for his own good, and found he could not say no.

"The most likely thing is you'll wind up waiting in the car. You understand that?"

"*Yes*, sir."

David looked at Teddy, who nodded. They dropped their roller coaster tickets and went for the car. As they went, David heard the wail of concerted sirens. The all-city call had gone out.

TWENTY-FOUR

THE FIRE WAS A THING OF BEAUTY, ARCING THROUGH THE roof, backlighting the CAJUN SUPPER CLUB sign with hot orange flares and columns of oily smoke. Flames shone bright and deadly behind windows that were ready to explode.

Teddy opened her door, and the safety kicked in, bringing the car to a halt in the grid.

She pointed. "See the window on the side? No, David, over there. There's a woman right by it. She can't find her way out because of the smoke, and she can hardly breathe."

"How do you—"

"I *hear* her, David. In my head. Arthur, come on, I'm going to need you."

The grids were giving trouble somewhere. David heard sirens, but counted only three fire vans, and a handful of uniformed officers. He clipped his ID to his belt. The scene was completely out of control, and all willing hands would be welcome. Ted was disappearing, Arthur at her heels. David ran after them.

Thick black smoke billowed from the main doorway. As far back as he was, David could feel the intensity of the heat. Teddy shouted and veered left, and David followed, chest aching. So much for Arthur staying in the car.

Why should he? David thought. Because his parents were rich?

A window blew out just as they rounded the corner, and a tornado of glass showered them with shards and slivers. David took a quick look at Arthur. The boy had a smear of blood across his shoulder and was white-faced, eyes dark and excited.

Teddy put her head through the window and shouted. David knocked the rest of the glass from the sill with the flat of his hand, got hold of an arm, and pulled. Whoever he had wasn't budging. He crowded Teddy sideways, his eyes tearing, blinded by smoke and heat.

At first glance, he thought the woman was enormously fat. He focused on the mound of belly and realized she was pregnant and unconscious. He called for Arthur, caught the woman under the arms, and pulled.

The deadweight was impossible. He was aware of sirens, fire fighters, and police officers. His world narrowed to the smoke, the heat, and the weight of the woman.

And then she budged. Teddy had one leg, and Arthur had one arm, and it took all three of them to pull her out.

David checked, saw the woman was breathing. She was young, dark-haired, soot-stained—too young for the sleazy supper club, a child bearing a child. Her face was pretty and pale. David saw that she wore a stained apron. Worked there, then. Hell of a place for a young mother.

He put a hand on the firm belly, hoping to feel the movement of the child within. Her muscles tightened beneath his palm; one hellacious contraction.

He crooked a finger at Arthur. "Grab a medic, quick, she's in hard labor."

Arthur's eyes widened. He jumped to his feet and ran directly into the path of a police car, stopping just in time. David winced, and the boy was gone.

He turned, saw that Teddy was half in and half out of the window, tugging an Elaki out. It rolled into David's lap, surprisingly heavy, and David nudged it into the soft grass.

Teddy put a hand on the woman's belly. "Don't be scared. Help's coming." She looked up at David. "Baby's in distress."

"How would you—"

"Who do you think I've been listening to?"

David looked at her black-streaked face, at the line of blood running down her temple and thought, my God, this woman's for real.

"Hold my shirttail, David, there's eight people in there, every one of them close, but they can't see to get out."

There was no time for careful rescue. They cycled people through like fishermen with incredible luck, piling one almost on top of the last. People and Elaki rolled or crawled sideways away from the smoke.

David held Teddy's shirt, then the back of her jeans as she tipped forward. Behind him, the sirens were louder. On some level he knew when the paramedics arrived and carted the pregnant woman away. He knew Arthur left, manning the stretcher.

Teddy went slack, suddenly, and slumped down by the window.

"Any more?" David asked.

"Not here."

"You hear anybody else?"

He looked at her face, saw the tear tracks moving through sweat, blood, and soot.

"I hear everybody."

TWENTY-FIVE

THIS TIME THE FIRE DEPARTMENT IGNORED THE BOMB THREAT. There had been over two hundred people in the Cajun Supper Club, and the death toll stood at eight—six civilians dead of smoke inhalation, one cop dead of heat exhaustion, and a fire fighter who drowned when he stumbled into an uncovered sump in the darkness.

David heard the drip of water, the beat of media choppers, hoarse shouts from people in charge who knew the worst was over but still had a lot to do before they could call it a day.

He put a hand on his chest where the scar throbbed, noticed a gluey blue stickiness on the cuffs of his pants—likely it would be thick on the bottom of his shoes. Fire gel was harder to get out of clothes than the smell of smoke.

Teddy sat quietly beside Arthur. Her braid had come completely loose, and her sweat-damp hair clung to her neck and back. A dried trail of blood snaked down her cheek.

"*There* he is, I thought that was the car."

David looked up, saw Clements and Warden. A man in a crumpled business suit was wedged between them. He had a forlorn look. He was red-faced, hair blond and wispy, and he moved languidly, as if in shock.

"Ah, Detective Sssilver is not to be hurt so badly?" Warden skittered close and peered at David's hand.

"Very minor," David said.

The Elaki had lost a patch of scales, and his eye stalks were caked with soot. Blue gel gummed the bottom of his fringe.

Clements waved a hand. "Detective Silver, I want you to meet Mr. Cromwell. Give him your sympathy, David. Mr. Cromwell owns this place."

Cromwell hung his head. His eyes were blue and red-rimmed, teary. David assumed the tears were from the smoke.

Clements put a hand on her hip. "David, Mr. Cromwell has a storage unit over on Abner—could you drive us over? Van's blocked in by a fire jeep and an arson chief, or I'd do it myself. That way, Mr. Cromwell can get some idea of what's actually in storage, and not in the club. Help him file his claim."

David wondered what Clements was up to.

Cromwell took a step backward. "Really, this isn't necessary."

"No, no, no, Mr. Cromwell. Unless you object? I mean, if you got some *reason*—"

"I don't want to put you out."

Clements looked at David. "Okay by you, David? We can borrow your car, or you can drive us."

David turned to Teddy.

"We'll get home."

It was Arthur who said it. Teddy met David's eyes; he wished she would say something. He remembered the feel of her, beside him on the Ferris wheel. He remembered reading her palm.

He wanted to take her home, but there was Clements, giving him that look.

"Okay," David said.

They ran the air-conditioning and rolled down the windows, but the car was thick with the odor of smoke, fire gel, and human sweat. Cromwell and Warden were in the backseat, crammed miserably close.

Clements put her elbow over the headrest and gave Cromwell a sympathetic look. "Got insurance, I assume? And I hope you didn't go and do like my brother-in-law, because one, he didn't get replacement value, and two, he was underinsured."

"No, no," Cromwell said. "We just increased the coverage."

Yolanda Clements smiled. David began to understand.

"Isss not like the last we did in place near the Little Saigo." The wind coming in from the windows made Warden's scales ripple violently. He shaded his eye prongs. "Thiss unfortunate human had just put in the order for numerous foodstuffs, and then all goes to ash in the flames."

Cromwell shifted in his seat. "We had a lot of liquor in stock."

"Tell you what, Mr. Cromwell, I'm going to make a list here, on the recorder, while it's still fresh in your mind. Worst thing about fires is people got no update on their list of inventory, and they don't remember half the things they ought to put on their claim."

"No, no, I have a recent listing in the office computer."

"*Do* you now?"

David watched in the rearview mirror again, noting Cromwell's proud apple-to-the-teacher smile. It was a pleasure to watch Clements work this guy over.

"That's good, Mr. Cromwell, real good. But now, you did tell me some of that was in storage. Or am I misremembering? I got no memory, do I, Detective Warden?"

"Not the smallest."

Cromwell pursed his lips. "There may have been one or two things, but most of it was in the club."

"How long you had that storage rental?"

"A long time. Years."

"How long since you put something in there?"

"Couple months anyway."

Clements nodded, smiled like a cat.

The storage bunkers were on the outskirts of the downtown area, well past the comingled overlap of residence and commerce. Marginal residential pockets were interspersed with cheap warehouses of corrugated metal and oddly shaped lots hidden behind barbed wire and makeshift plywood.

David drove past a floral shop that did not sell flowers, and pulled into a parking lot next to a sign advertising STOR-BUNK. It was dark here, though a pale blue stream of light flickered from the sign.

David saw movement across the street, in front of an empty shack that said PIZZA-N-B'CUE.

"Alert," he told the car softly.

The door to the bunkers required a code to get in, or would have if it had not been wedged open with a block of wood. Inside, it was dark. Cromwell called up the lights. A dull yellow haze rose in the darkness, bringing the pitch-blackness up to a nightmarish gloom. David followed Cromwell down the sloping concrete walkway, finding the bunker built oddly like a pyramid. He wrapped his hand firmly on the butt of his gun, waiting for the chip to register his fingerprints. Having the weapon at the ready made him feel better.

Warden skittered ahead, walking close to Clements. David brought up the rear, noticing old scales in the corner. Elaki had been through here, some time ago.

It was hot inside, and humid. The lower they went the cooler it felt. David saw beads of condensation cling together and fall in droplets down the coarse concrete walls. He smelled mildew. His shirt stuck to his back, and the odor of smoke clung to his skin and clothes.

He wondered if Arthur and Teddy were safely home.

Cromwell stopped, squinting. "I think we went too far."

Warden made a fluting noise that sounded amiable, but that David knew to be derisive. Cromwell backtracked and they followed him, uphill now, the slope rising gently.

"Here, this is it."

He went to the sliding metal door and punched in a code. The door jerked, emitted a metallic hum that developed into a full-throated rumble, and began sliding up into the wall.

David saw the hint of a complacent smile flicker across Clements's face and a frown settle on Cromwell's.

Just inside the door were cases of liquor, and plastic tubs of smokes that looked like the pencil boxes David had carried to school as a child. He saw framed family pictures, stacked on top of the liquor, and large bundles of food packages.

Behind was a hodgepodge jumble David could not imagine anyone wanting to keep. A broken wooden chair, cardboard boxes layered in dust, plastic bags, neatly tied. Clements ran a finger across the top of one of the liquor boxes.

"No dust," she said cheerfully.

"I don't get this." Cromwell scratched his head, frowned, took a step inside.

Clements crooked a finger at Warden. "You got the camera, baby?"

TWENTY-SIX

IT WAS EARLY WHEN DAVID WALKED INTO THE LOBBY OF THE Rialto Hotel. A different desk clerk—Sam again—gave him a key to the security floor. His back ached. He had strained something, pulling those people out of the fire. He'd taken Tylenol Twelve caplets before leaving the house, and they were only just now beginning to take effect.

Early as it was, Jenks and Arthur were wide-awake, their raised voices coming through the thick hotel room door.

David's knock was greeted by silence. He waited, knocked again. Someone activated the peephole.

"Please state your business," came the metallic voice from the door.

David held up his ID for scanning. "Detective Silver, homicide, Saigo City PD."

He waited. The door opened.

Jenks wore a shabby plaid bathrobe that was likely older than Arthur. His feet were bare, toenails thick and yellowish, in need of a trim. He looked gaunt, and David wondered if he had been eating.

"Detective Silver?" Jenks was hesitating. "I'm sorry—"

"We need to talk," David said.

Jenks stepped away from the door.

Arthur was dressed, freshly showered, hair wet but neatly combed. He seemed different, more confident.

David winked. "You think you could go downstairs for a while and get some breakfast?"

Arthur nodded. "Sure."

Jenks rocked forward on the balls of his feet. "I've already ordered room service, Arthur."

"I'm eating downstairs."

The door shut softly. Well-trained, David thought. He'd have expected a slam.

"I'm not happy about Arthur's little adventure last night," Jenks said.

"That's not what I came to discuss. Sit down, Dr. Jenks."

Jenks hesitated, did not seem to know what to do with his face or hands. He settled on the edge of the small yellow love seat and his robe split open, revealing blue silk boxer shorts. David looked away, considered telling Jenks to take a moment to get dressed, then decided he wanted the man vulnerable.

David sat in a gold brocade armchair—a grandmother chair, his daughters would call it.

"You and your wife were having serious difficulties when she left." David looked Jenks in the eye, stayed quiet.

Jenks sounded almost bored. "I know it's normal to suspect the husband when a woman is murdered, but I didn't kill my wife."

David said nothing.

Jenks crossed his legs. "Call Bruer in Chicago. He knows how concerned I was when Theresa disappeared. I loved Theresa. I did, you know."

David nodded.

"Just what is it you want, Detective?"

"You admit you were having problems. I need to know how much of it was between the two of you, and how much of it was . . . other things. I need to understand why she left, and never so much as called. If she loved Arthur as much as you say, it's hard to understand. I need to know what was going on in her mind, in her life, those last weeks before she disappeared."

Jenks slid forward on the couch. "Did you quiz Arthur on this last night?"

"Dr. Jenks." Something in David's tone made him sit straighter. "I've seen your little room, off the master bedroom. I've seen the couch you've been sleeping on and the easy chair where you sit up at night and read. The two of you were sleeping apart; your wife was having nightmares. I've seen her books on reincarnation. I know she withdrew large sums of money from her personal bank account.

"You implied, when we talked before, that the problems

started up after she went to the Mind Institute, after she had a reading. I'm trying to understand how that one experience could be the catalyst for so much . . . harm."

Jenks shook his head back and forth. "You don't understand, Detective."

"Then explain it to me, Dr. Jenks."

Jenks looked at David, then studied the backs of his hands. "When Martin drowned, he was four years old, and the brightest, sunniest child. We were so very devastated. Guilt-ridden. There is no comfort in this world, when you've lost a child." Jenks's voice went gravelly. "You have children?"

"Three."

Jenks nodded. "We did not handle it well. We never *talked* about it all that much. It's only dawned on me in the last year or two, how really strange that is. Theresa was raised in the South, and when unpleasant things came up, she didn't deal with them. And really, I was no better. We both fell apart. I finally got to the point where all I wanted was to return to some kind of normal life. I put together a routine, and I followed that routine to the letter every day. It saved me. I didn't have to think, you see.

"Theresa wasn't like that. She was intelligent, impulsive. Passionate." He raised a heavy eyebrow. "Our relationship was the classic case of opposites attracting. And my wife was a very controlling person, Detective Silver, as am I. So much of what went on between us, even the way we dealt with our grief, was a matter of one of us struggling to control the other. No matter what we *thought* we were fighting about, it all boiled down to control."

David thought of Rose, so very strong-willed; himself, a perfectionist. He was getting a glimmer of this marriage, between Bernard and Theresa Jenks.

Jenks clasped his large hands and let them hang between his legs.

"Theresa became unbelievably, painfully depressed. Then she got restless. Anxious. It's hard to explain. Three years after Martin died—" Jenks's voice broke. After all these years, he could not say the child's name casually. "Theresa decided she wanted to have another child, she *had* to have one. I could not bear the thought, the worry—my God, I would never sleep another night. The thing is, Detective, you go through life, and against all evidence to the contrary, you never really believe that bad things can happen to you. You go on every day feeling immune, for no logical reason. And then your son drowns, just by accident, and your innocence goes, you're marked now. You don't believe bad things *won't* happen. I knew if I had another child, I would be afraid for the rest of my life."

David looked at Jenks and began to understand. "So you didn't. And she did."

Jenks nodded. "I don't begin to care or understand why other people make these arrangements. I suppose for the woman it means never fighting for child custody. And for the man, it's complete freedom from child support."

David knew of other reasons. Darker reasons. Child molesters who grew their own victims, but did not want to risk the new death penalty for incest.

"At the time, I thought we both won. She got her child, and I was able to keep my distance. Arthur was *hers*, legally. I donated the sperm, but Theresa was artificially inseminated. Legally, it's not required to do it that way, but she insisted, and I wanted the same. It was not our baby, it was hers.

"Theresa and Arthur started having problems when Arthur turned twelve. She wanted me to intervene, to be a father, and I wouldn't do it. There you have the source of trouble, Detective. Just that simple."

And that complicated, David thought. "So what happened?"

There was a knock at the door, and the sensor said room service.

"Come in," Jenks said.

The locks unbolted. David tensed. Jenks was far too careless. Sensors could be tripped up, even in expensive hotels—especially in expensive hotels.

The door opened wide and a cart rolled in. "Please enjoy the breakfast you ordered, Mr. Jenks of Room 3017. If you require anything further, please dial extension twenty-three on your telephone, and we will be pleased to serve you."

"Join me, Detective?" Jenks dragged the cart closer, setting the voice chip off again.

"Please enjoy the breakfast you ordered, Mr.—"

"Damn it," Jenks said. "Coffee, sir?"

"Please."

Jenks's hands were shaking. David took the pot and poured. Jenks took his small china cup and sat back on the couch. David poured himself a cup, added cream. He took the cover off the food.

Hash browns, a basket of croissants, bacon, and a saucer of caramel candy. David shook his head. Elaki were very partial to caramels. They probably came with every meal.

He looked at Jenks. "You should eat."

"I order meals three times a day, then I can't eat them. Arthur eats for both of us. I think he's grown four inches since we got here."

David took the basket of croissants to the table near the couch, helped himself, and sat down. Jenks took a pastry and set it on his knee. The croissants were small and shedding flakes like Elaki lost scales. They tasted of buttered dough and cinnamon. Not surprising; Elaki liked cinnamon in everything.

"Taste like cinnamon?" Jenks snapped.

David nodded.

"I hate this hotel. No cinnamon in the coffee, you will notice. I raised holy hell the first morning they brought that Elaki pap for my breakfast. They're going to run real people off, if they're not careful."

David kept quiet, thinking that Elaki coffee was superior to the typical brew, and that if Jenks didn't realize that running humans off was the business of this hotel, he was a fool.

"Arthur is a good boy," David said.

Jenks set his coffee cup down. "I told her—Theresa, I mean—I told her that when she started this business up about Martin."

David nodded patiently.

"You know, even though it was a lark, just a chance thing with a friend . . . the reason she went to the psychic was to ask about me. Would I become a father to Arthur?"

This pleased the man's vanity, David thought. He took another croissant. "And?"

"The psychic was an Elaki. It read *scales*, Detective, what a load of crap."

"You hired Teddy Blake."

"She's different. Bruer recommended Teddy, and I think you're wrong about her. I can't get her to take any money, other than expenses. But this guy Theresa went to, he was manipulative. He had her do all kinds of strange things. Meditate three times a day, keep her own personal scale with her at all times. It was ridiculous."

David thought of Candy Andy, his own set of odd instructions, how often he had gone along.

"Before she left, she was really going off the deep end. Nightmares, like I told you. Talked about reincarnation till I thought I would wring her neck." Jenks looked up sharply. "I didn't mean that, you know."

David gave Jenks a reassuring smile.

"Then she stopped talking about it. To me. But I saw her books, and I knew she was still seeing the psychic. She seemed to have some sort of epiphany, she came to a decision. At first I thought, thank God, she is over this. Then I realized she had just gone underground. I caught her in Arthur's room when he was at school. She had his Eight Ball—you've seen those things the kids have, like a black bowling ball? Ask it a question and the answer comes up?"

David nodded. He'd had one himself, when he was growing up. How many times had he asked it if his father would come home?

YES . . . NO . . . IT SEEMS SO . . . ASK AGAIN LATER . . .
ANSWER HAZY AT THIS TIME

Jenks grimaced. "Those things, they're just kid toys. They're a joke. And there she was, with this Eight Ball in her hands, tears running down her cheeks. It was *important* to her. It *mattered*."

"Then what?"

"It shook me. I started watching her. And I realized how completely she had shut me out of her life."

"Did you argue?"

"I wish we had, but we couldn't even do that. She was polite, she just slid away. I let it go awhile, but she even shut Arthur out. Her own son, she had no right to do that. Someone had to focus on the boy, and he was hers after all."

"Did you tell her that?"

"Hell, yes, till I was blue in the goddamn face. And you know what she said?"

David waited.

"Said he wasn't mine, by legal contract, and I could mind my own business."

Jenks picked up his coffee cup, then set it down. David saw that he had shredded the croissant into a pile of brown flakes.

"Then what?" David said.

"Then she disappeared."

TWENTY-SEVEN

DAVID SLOUCHED NEXT TO THE PAY PHONE IN THE LOBBY OF his precinct and dialed Teddy's number. He decided not to think about why he didn't go up to his office and call from his desk. He let the phone ring, wondering if she was in the shower, counted three more rings. He hung up, disappointed, but relieved. The camera disc recorded his presence, and he ducked into the stairwell.

There were three messages in his reader. Two from Detective Warden, one from Clements. Mel was sitting on the edge of Della's desk, being ignored.

"Hey, David, you had breakfast yet?"

"Twice."

"Once with your mistress, and once with your wife?"

"Talked to Jenks this morning, Mel. No surprise, but he and his wife were having Serious Marital Strain."

"Business as usual," Mel said.

String rolled in, carrying a white bag that reeked of cinnamon, garlic, and chili powder. The bag said HOMEBOYS on the side.

"Good of the morning, I have brought breakfast."

Mel shook his head. "You have brought *tacos*. How many times I got to tell you that ain't breakfast?"

"Goes in one hearing orifice and proceeds out the other. This is the proper expression?" String opened the bag. "Who will care for the taco?"

"They got cinnamon in them?" Mel asked.

"All are Elaki-style."

"Give it here. Take mine, Della. You like stolen food better anyways."

David shifted his weight. The Tylenol was wearing off and his back ached. "Della, did you do that background for me on the Mind Institute? There hasn't been anything in my reader."

Della's voice went low and apologetic. "I got it started, Silver, just haven't quite finished it up. System's slow."

Mel gave David a knowing look.

Della pushed her chair back from her desk. "Look, I'm serious here. I know my work's not up to par, okay? But this wasn't me. I got most of the stuff together, including a client listing, did some cross-referencing, and somehow in the middle of all this I lost data. Haven't been able to retrieve it."

String took a bite of taco, tearing the shell loose and showering filling on the desk. David fished a napkin out of the bag and slid it across the table.

"Of what nature be the data?"

Della shrugged. "Names. Mainly people that were on the list the first time through, and now they aren't. And I can't figure out where I dropped the entries. I transferred everything to a shell document, and put it through a keystroke program, but it's a simple routine and—"

"Wait a minute," David said. "You're saying you have names that were in the data bank, and now they're not?"

Della nodded.

Mel scooped up meat that had spilled from String's taco. "But what's the significance? Who are the people on the list?"

"Clients of that Mind Institute," Della said.

"How many names are missing?"

Della slapped the desktop. "How am I going to know what's missing if it's not there?"

Silence settled, broken only by the crunch as String ate another taco.

"I do have two of the missing names. Shut up, Mel, let me finish. It's only because I ran a test subset. That's how I knew data was gone in the first place."

David frowned. "Della, you think there's any chance anybody got into your drive crystal?"

"No, Silver, I was right there the whole time, working late. I ran the subset, got a call from the central operator. Said they were running a data compile, and the system would be down. I got up, took a break, came back."

"So if somebody messed with it—"

"They'd have to get to the actual data file, Silver. Who's going to do that? The Feds?"

"Give the girl a taco."

String fished in the bag.

"It's an *expression*, String, okay? He's kidding." Della chewed a thumbnail. "You don't really—"

David held up a finger. "Here's the funny thing. Captain Halliday told me that if I wanted to back off on this Jenks murder, work just the supper club—"

"Nah, come on, she's a rich bitch, that don't sound right." Mel cocked his head sideways. "And even if they did tell you that, it's bureaucratic bullshit. Management isn't smart enough to actually hatch a plot, they're just blowing in the wind."

"Please, most distressing mental image."

"Sorry, Gumby. What else makes you say Feds, David?"

"Dawn Weiler called me, said my name came up over there. Why would that be?"

"Senior detective on this supper club fire."

"What's got the FBI interested?"

"If it's a hate crime, David, it's up their alley. Especially since this business agent, real estate broker . . . what's his name?"

"Tatewood."

"You said he'd been getting letters from that group. SCAE. And you know those supper clubs always catch the hate groups, right? Mixing Elaki and people?"

Della dropped the taco she had picked up.

"I don't know, Mel. Clements is pretty sure these fires were set by the owners."

"Two in the same month?" Mel said.

"Ah, it will be the feline faker."

Della looked at String. "The what?"

"Feline faker. It brings to my mind an incident of happening when I was but young in law enforcement."

Mel put his feet on the table and closed his eyes. "Excuse me for interrupting another ever fascinating story, but are you trying to say copycat, String?"

"Yes, that is it."

Mel looked at David. "For the life of me, I can't figure how Theresa Jenks fits into any of this."

"Wrong place at the wrong time?" Della said.

David shook his head. "Not if she's murdered. We have the same incendiary devices used in the house and the supper club. Making sure it burned and burned good."

"Same somebody that killed Jenks did the fires," Mel said.

String chewed taco shell. "Is most surprise the dog does not protect."

Mel scratched his left armpit. "Much as I hate to admit it, he's got a point. You get anywhere on finding Bowser's remains?"

"The Bowser cannot be finded in the morgue."

"Should be in evidence," Mel said.

"But yes, Detective Mel, and much is the altercation, which does not change the one true way."

"The one true way?" David asked.

"That this animal of remains has been tossed for the cookies."

Della frowned. "Thrown up?"

"Thrown away, I bet." Mel put his feet back on the floor. "That's what you mean, ain't it, Gumby?"

String twitched an eye stalk. "Have speaked with a one who believes Bowser remains given the heave-ho at site of origin. The fire. So this will be perhaps found in the Euclid dump?"

Mel looked at David. "You think it's worth going through days of garbage?"

"I want to know what the dog died of. If somebody killed it, or it died in the fire."

"A murdered dog, David? You don't have enough crime to solve? Or maybe he bit the killer, and still has their hand in his mouth, or their class ring in his belly."

David waved a hand. "If the dog died of smoke inhalation, then it didn't interfere in the struggle in the hallway. Which means maybe it knew the killer. And, Della, I want anything you have on this Mind Institute in my reader today. Plus, take the two names you have that disappeared from the data set and give me what background you can, quick and dirty."

"Okay, but David?"

He sighed. His back hurt. "Yeah?"

She leaned close, turned her back on Mel and String. "Can we talk a minute?"

"Okay."

Della slipped into the interrogation room and closed the blinds. "I want to ask you about something."

"Okay."

"I want your opinion."

"Okay."

"This really isn't a joke, David."

"Okay."

"Stop saying that."

"Oh . . . sorry. What is it, Della?"

"I'm afraid to tell you. You'll think it's disgusting."

"No, no I won't. What is it?"

"I think I'm in love," Della said.

David smiled wanly. "What's wrong with love, Della?"

"It's not what you call a natural love."

"Another woman? There's nothing so bad about that."

She shook her head, looked him in the eye. "An Elaki."

David swallowed hard. No, she didn't look like she was joking.

"Pretty weird, huh? You think it's sick?"

"I don't think it's sick, Della. It's just, it seems strange, that's all. Not String?"

"Good Lord, no. No, he's . . . don't laugh, but he's handsome, Elaki-style. You know, like he's eight feet tall, and black as coal on the outer loop, dark red in the middle. Really, he's very striking. And he is so kind. So wise and childlike, and so focused on me. He cares about me. He's considerate." She closed her eyes and groaned. "Oh, God. I know how this sounds."

Bizarre, David thought.

"So schoolgirlish. He wants . . ." Della looked at her hands. "You sure you want to hear this?"

David did not know if it was fair to judge this Elaki by the standards of men, but he had a good idea what the Elaki wanted.

"Yes?"

"*You* know."

"Ah. Is it . . . possible?"

"I don't know. I thought maybe you would?"

David swallowed. "What does *he* say?"

"He says he wants to understand and experience human intimacy."

"Did he say how?"

"Maybe he's just going to read me poetry or something, I don't know. Did you . . . you saw that supper club tape?"

David cleared his throat. "Yes, Dell. Yes, I did."

"Everybody was laughing. They made it all seem . . . it seemed so dirty. God, Silver, I don't know what to do. Do you think I'm evil? Unnatural?"

David put a hand on her shoulder, thinking how fragile her bones felt. "I think anything between two consenting adults is their own business. And, let's face it, women are always saying they'd like an alternative to men. Think of yourself as a pioneer."

He expected her to smile, but she didn't. She looked at him quite seriously.

"So what exactly should I do? Should I—"

"You should do whatever you want to do, Della, whatever feels good . . . uh, *right* to you, and not worry about other people. Or Elaki. Or whatever."

She nodded, sighed, smiled. "Thanks, David. And David?"

"Yes?"

"You should do what you want, too."

"What I—"

She patted his shoulder and left him sitting alone with his mouth open.

TWENTY-EIGHT

THE RETRIEVER WHO WORKED THE EUCLID TRASH DUMP HAD a storefront office. David saw the telltale lines of sensors—better than iron bars, unless the system was down. He glanced over his shoulder. In this neighborhood, he'd opt for the bars.

The thick green plastic of the front door reflected cars going by on the grid. The plastic was warped, which made the cars look like they were going over a hill. A hand-lettered sign was taped over a buzzer.

Mel squinted.

"What's it say?" David asked.

"It says ring the bell."

A dog barked, somewhere inside, and shadows moved behind the plastic.

"This is the Bowser I am hearing?" String asked.

Mel shrugged. "Unless it's an ostrich."

"Detective Mel, you joke me. This reminds me of a pouchmate—"

The door was opened by a woman who gave them a wary look. She was short and thick, and wore a pink T-shirt, stretched too tight over broad shoulders and enormous breasts, and a pair of white shorts that had gone dingy. Her black hair was cut short, soft and feathery. She had dark eyebrows and big brown eyes.

"Thank God for you," Mel said.

The woman raised her eyebrows. David had the feeling she was not used to people being glad to see her.

"You looking for somebody?" The dog barked, and the woman looked down. "Hush, Barclay."

The dog barked louder. He was a yellow, shorthaired something or other—one ear was missing a chunk, and the other

126

tipped at the end, giving him the look of a dog you would trust with your children.

"We're looking for a retriever," David said.

"That's me. Come in."

It was cool inside, and dark. Displays showed an unpredictable array of very used items—wire hair rods, a package oven, a bent and rusty pizza slicer, an encyclopedia of *Birds in the Southwest*. The shop smelled like mildew and dust. There was nothing on the tables that David would not have been happy to throw away.

Mel stopped suddenly, and String rolled into him. "Lookit here. I haven't seen one of these in ages."

String twitched an eye prong. "Is it gone for the bad, or are these holes intentional?"

Mel poked his finger through the center of the black metal. "Intentional. This is a pie composer. You just put the ingredients in the side here, see? Then the nano machines cut loose and it makes a home-baked pie. All you got to do is put it in the oven. My aunt used to have one of these."

"But why would the human not purchase a pie?"

" 'Cause then it wouldn't be homemade."

"This is pertinent?"

Mel put the composer back on the table, looked at the woman. "So you're the retriever, huh?"

"Yeah. Do the Euclid dump, right next door." She inclined her head toward the back of the shop.

"We're homicide detectives, Ms.—"

"Clay. Ellis Clay. Homicide, huh? I usually don't get anybody but the vice guys. And even them not too often."

"You should do garbage in a better part of town," Mel said.

"I've put in bids. I don't have the pull for it, no matter how much money I come up with. You want me to put this on the department's account?"

David nodded.

"If it's more than a year back, forget it."

"Just a few days. The night of the supper club fire."

"That was some roast, wasn't it, Barclay?" The dog jumped up and licked her on the nose. "Is that cute? He's smart, too. What you looking for, anyway?"

Mel scratched his nose. "A dog, actually. A dead one."

*   *   *

"The dungeon's down here." She led them down steps thinly covered by mildewed carpet, looked over her shoulder at String. "Sorry about the stairs."

"Is not to be a problem," String said.

The small dog trotted close to String, sniffing at the Elaki's fringe.

"Barclay, no," Clay said. Without conviction. She shook her head. "He's got a mind of his own."

"People always say that when they don't train their dogs," Mel muttered.

String waved a fin. "Why does this animal wear a scarf for the neck? The Bowser hair coverment does not suffice?"

Ellis Clay shrugged. "I think it's cute. He looks in the mirror when I put it on him. Some people think dogs don't look in mirrors, but Barclay does. He watches vids too. 'LaFarge and Groat' is his favorite show. He liked that one with the dachshund man, you catch that one?" Her breathing got deeper and faster—the stairs were causing problems. "That was a classic. You know what, if I throw a piece of popcorn in the air, Barclay can jump up and catch it in his mouth."

"Truly the amazing animal."

David looked at String, wondering if the Elaki had learned sarcasm.

"Lights," Ellis Clay said, moving ahead of them.

The basement was cavernous, the single fluorescent light defeated by dank, murky corners. The computer sat on a scarred metal desk in the center of the room, placed just under the fixture. David touched a concrete wall, found it beaded with sweat. He smelled something awful too close by.

Ellis Clay scooped Barclay up under her arm and settled him on her lap. "Computer up." She scratched the dog's neck. "Now tell me about this dog."

David gave her the times and particulars of death and location and she keyed it manually into the computer.

David looked over her shoulder as the grid came up on the screen. At the bottom, the signal flashed: SEARCHING.

"Just threw him away, poor little thing." She clutched Barclay.

String rippled his bottom fringe. "Is animal that is deceased from life. Should there be special deathwatch for the Bowser?"

Mel waved a hand. "You do 'em up like Vikings, Gumby. Put 'em in a little boat with all their favorite bones, launch it in their water bowl, then set it on fire."

Ellis Clay clamped her hands over the ears of her dog. "Don't listen to them, Barclay. Don't listen."

The computer beeped.

"List matches." Clay squinted at the screen. Her feathery black hair fell forward, too short to get in her eyes. She kept a hand on the dog's head, scratching absently.

"We have about six hot spots here, guys. Let me do some eliminating. Dog will likely be dumped with some of the debris from the fire, you think?"

David nodded.

She keyed in a command. "Kill that one and that one. That leaves . . . four possibilities. Let me activate the keystroke grid, here." She drummed her fingers on the dog's collar. He licked her wrist and it glistened, sticky under the light.

The computer screen went neon-blue, a white waffle of lines descending. Four red-orange dots glowed. Numbers appeared, across the dots.

"We can do it one of two ways. I can go for a single target search, which means I get the garbage from one spot together, you look through it, if what you want isn't there, then we try again. Or I can dump all four at once, then go through. Your first way is cheaper, if we hit on the first look. After that the price goes up and you're losing time and money."

"And you recommend?" David said.

"If you feel real lucky, and you have all the time in the world, do it one at a time. Otherwise, I say dump the whole thing."

"The whole thing," David said.

"Go get lunch, then come back. You just want the dog, or you want a look through?"

"Just the dog."

She raised both eyebrows. "Most cops want a look through."

David got the feeling he'd failed a test.

TWENTY-NINE

ELLIS CLAY LED THEM THROUGH THE BASEMENT ROOM INTO a tunnel, where strong odors permeated the darkness like an echo. David was sorry he'd had lunch.

Mel gave him a look.

"I'm fine," David said. He took a breath. He was fine.

Barclay the dog tripped along happily, pink tongue hanging thickly from the left corner of his mouth, showing healthy black gums and white needle teeth. He padded close to String, running in and out of the ripple of the Elaki's fringe. A shred of napkin had adhered to one of String's scales, bonded by barbecue sauce from lunch.

Mel was grimacing. String's inner pink belly was showing ivory, the way it did in the morgue. Ellis Clay did not seem to notice.

Garbage was her business, David thought.

"See, it's a great system. Trapdoors all over, big iron ones, but if they get kludgey you got a problem. That's the major drawback to this whole setup. A door gets sticky, then you have to go in, work in the mess, or clean the whole thing out. Use scuba gear when you go in."

"Scuba gear?" David said it politely, proud he was able to talk.

"Yeah, makes perfect sense if you think about it."

David nodded. The pork sandwich he'd eaten was becoming a problem.

"So, anyway, all three dumps went clear, except the last one, wouldn't you know. Man, that thing was stuck like nobody's business."

"But you got it loose?" Mel said.

"Yeah, you wouldn't believe how. Trade secret, but think Vaseline."

130

"Rather not," Mel muttered.

"This way." Clay unlocked a metal hasp, freeing two iron doors.

David looked at the locks, knowing that outside on Euclid there were hookers who left their children alone all night while they worked. This woman guarded her garbage.

"I sorted it for you," Ellis Clay said, and opened the door.

The smell rolled out in a wave. David and Mel stepped backward and String skittered sideways.

The room was the size of an airplane hangar. Garbage had been dumped in the middle of the floor, a mountain of it, bits and pieces still clinging to the seam in the ceiling like loose teeth hanging by the root. Inside, the lights were bright but hazy, and flies were noisy and thick. David waved a cloud of them away.

"What's that pile?" David pointed to a slag heap, out of the way in a dim corner.

Clay scratched her head. "That's mine. Just stuff I found, thought I might sell."

"You find the dog?" David asked.

"*Something* in there died," Mel said.

Clay grinned and chuckled. "You guys are great, you know it? Bunco cops, some of them get sick when I open that door, but homicide doesn't flinch. Where'd the Elaki go?"

"He had some business back down the hall."

"The big load here's what I went through. And that over there is fire debris. Here's your dog."

The dog was limp and wet, a black cocker spaniel with oozing fly-specked eye sockets. The fur was singed. David smelled smoke and grit, sweet putrescence, and the sour sick smell that coated every garbage dump in town. He'd smelled death before, death and garbage, but usually not on top of a pork sandwich.

"That the one?" Clay asked.

How many could there be? Mel roamed the room, moving toward the pile Clay had set aside.

"So, would you like me to wrap it in plastic?"

"Blood doesn't do well in plastic," David said. "Leave it here, and I'll have a CSU van pick it up later."

Mel moved toward the center pile. "What the hell . . . this looks like a foot."

Clay looked over his shoulder. "That's what I thought."

"You didn't bring it up?"

"I find all kinds of things, Detective."

"Definitely a foot," Mel said. "Not too fresh."

"Male or female?"

"Hard to tell, David, it ain't got genitalia attached."

David wandered around the edge of the pile. "Is that a goat?"

"Yes, it's a goat." Clay was sounding irritable. "Take a poke through the whole thing if you want."

David waved a swarm of flies on their way and went to the small pile of garbage gathered in the corner—Ellis Clay's private stash. A doll, headless, unless . . . no, thank God, just a doll. Tins of food, rotting packages, a bow and arrow in surprisingly good shape.

David frowned and took another look at the delivery address on the tin. He squatted and used his handkerchief to clean something wet and yellow that he did not wish to speculate about off the top of the can.

Fourteen Reidy Street. David looked over his shoulder at his partner. "Mel?"

"Yeah? David, this foot looks like somebody hacked it off with a fillet knife."

"That's nice, Mel. What's the address of the supper club that burned? The first one?"

"Something Reidy Street. Why? What you got?"

Clay gave David a hard look. "It won't hurt if I sell this stuff. It's not illegal if I identify it as being retrieved. It was silly to throw it away, just 'cause it'd been through a fire. There's no smoke damage through those seals."

David's back ached and he was queasy, but that was background noise. He looked at Mel.

"They threw it out before the fire, not after."

Mel scratched his head. "Another point in this case which makes absolutely no sense."

"It might," David said. "If you wanted to frame the owner."

THIRTY

DAVID CRADLED THE PHONE BETWEEN HIS CHIN AND SHOULDER. "We need to talk."

Clements sounded depressed. "Serendipity, baby, I'm headed your way."

"Here?"

"I'm not dropping in at your house, Silver. Don't you people talk over there? You and me are scheduled to do a joint interrogation of this Cromwell guy, owns the Cajun Supper Club. Your territory, of course. Homicide always takes precedence."

"You want me to come over there?"

"No, but don't go stomping through this with both feet, okay? Arson's different. It takes time, it takes patience, it takes computers. There's ways to ask questions on these things, and ways not to."

David wondered why he was getting so much flak from Mel about moodiness. Now Clements, *she* was moody.

"I'll follow your lead," David said.

"Where have I heard that before?"

David caught his finger in his center desk drawer and winced. "I don't know, Detective, and I don't much care about your love life. But while I've got your attention, consider this an official request to leave your Elaki at the office, since he makes so much trouble with String."

David set the phone down firmly, but did not slam it.

Della gave him a knowing look.

"You got that list of names?" he asked her.

"If you call two a list." She ripped a piece off a printout, folded it into a paper airplane, and launched it toward his desk. "Names, addresses, and phone numbers. And don't you *start* with me."

The plane took a nosedive and landed on David's foot.

133

*   *   *

David detected a decidedly wary note in the voice on the other line.

"Yes, this is Alice Caspian. Who did you say you were?" The woman sounded intelligent, and busy, and very, very old.

"Ms. Caspian, I'm Alwin Lemm, comptroller for the Mind Institute."

"Is everything okay with Janet?"

"With who?"

"Is everything all right? Look, I'd like to see her again. I know you said it would be best if I didn't, and I understand that. But I just . . ."

The woman trailed off. David thought she might be crying.

"I'm calling about another matter," he said. "I handle the financial end and—"

"She needs more money?"

"We've had an error, Ms. Caspian, in our financial matrices. We think there may have been some overcharges, and in your case they would amount to something. I thought if we could go over the services you've already—"

"Please. Put any credits in the account we set up for Janet. Could I please . . . I just want to see her. Again, just once?"

David said, "May I call you back?"

"Of course."

He hung up. The address was in Arizona. He wanted a face-to-face, he wanted to go see this woman and talk to her. He did not like the edge of desperation in her voice. He dialed the other number.

"Ford residence." The metallic voice gave it away. Phone butler.

"Jefferson Ford, please."

"Who is calling, please?"

"Alwin Lemm, Mind Institute."

"Please wait."

David waited, his mind on Alice Caspian.

"This is Leah Ford. Who's calling?" This woman was younger than the last and her voice trembled, but she spoke in hard tones as if her teeth were clenched.

"Alwin Lemm, Mind Institute."

"Alwin Lemm? I don't believe I know you, Mr. Lemm. I believe my lawyer instructed you people not to call. I believe we made it clear that we do not intend to pay the settlement from my husband's estate. You are more than welcome to contest the decision, and if you do, we will fight you in court. I have two young children to support, sir. And we can prove my husband was *not* in his right mind at the time of his . . . of his death."

"Ma'am—"

"So you can by God hire every lawyer you want and I'll see you—"

"Ma'am. My apologies. Please excuse the call."

"What?"

"I'm sorry," David said. He was.

THIRTY-ONE

DAVID HEARD STRING'S VOICE IN THE HALLWAY, LOUDER than usual. Was that a hiss? He looked out the door, saw Warden and String, facing off.

"This van obsession for object that is inanimate and not a personal possession is perhaps a sign that all does not go well in the chemaki," Warden said.

David winced. String did not have a chemaki. It had seemed at one time that he might put something together with an Elaki emergency room doctor, but that had yet to materialize.

"Eat the corncob," String said. David grinned. His partner was fighting like a human.

Warden skittered backward and waved a fin. "Clearly you have had too much human consortation."

David looked at Della, hoping she hadn't heard. She was staring at the door, chest heaving. She stood up and headed for the hallway.

"Della?"

She did not hear. David moved out of her way, wondering if she would have walked through him if he hadn't.

"Excuse me." Her voice was loud enough to be heard on the next street. "Are you saying that there is something wrong with an Elaki and human friendship? Because I have had just about all the bigoted, racist, narrow-minded—"

David rubbed the back of his neck. What had Rose been telling him? To stay out of things that were not his business, and to quit trying to handle everybody's problems and give them a chance to do it themselves. Being right, she said, was often beside the point.

Now seemed a good time to turn over a new leaf. David took the back door out of the bull pen. Likely Clements was here, if Warden was. Which meant she'd be headed for the interrogation room, if she wasn't already there. That's where he'd go, but he'd get there the back way.

He smelled fresh coffee as he went and considered going back to his desk for his favorite mug. Probably not safe yet.

"There you are."

David turned, saw Detective Clements standing outside the interview room, left hand on her hip. Her hair was sweat-damp at the temples and hairline, and hung thick and hot over her shoulders. She lifted it with one hand and wiped the back of her neck.

"Good Lord, Silver, what happened to you?"

He had cleaned up when they'd come back from the retriever's, but there was only so much he could do. "The usual garbage."

"I was rude on the phone, David, and I apologize. Now what have you done with my Elaki?"

"Want coffee, Yolanda?"

"Baby, it's ninety-eight degrees outside and my air-conditioning doesn't work. Correction, won't work. I want a cold beer, two of them, one for each hand, but I can't while I'm working and these days I'm always working."

David found a clean blue mug by the coffeepot and decided not to worry about who it belonged to. "I didn't ask what you wanted, I offered you coffee. Yes or no."

"No. I see *you* need a cup. Drink it down fast, dude, and let's see if it improves your disposition."

He added cream. "Warden is in the hallway with String, and they're arguing over the van."

"Good thing we're above that sort of nonsense." She rested her back against the wall. Her smile faded. "David, these supper club fires are the biggest mess I've seen in my life. Nothing is typing. The patterns don't fit."

David nodded. A sign of Elaki involvement.

"We're busting our butts—used more CPU time than we got budgeted for the rest of the whole year, and we're still going under. I tell you, baby, I'm tearing out my hair."

David leaned close and tugged a swatch of her hair. "You got plenty left to go."

She rubbed her temples.

"Want something for the headache?" he asked.

"What you got?"

"Tylenol Twelve."

"Shit, *that* ought to do it."

David stood in the vid room, watching the interrogation on camera while Clements swallowed Tylenol caplets. The Elaki questioning Cromwell was moving in too tight. The district attorney in Saigo City insisted no Elaki get closer than three feet—there would be no intimidation pleas in her jurisdiction. Juries didn't much like Elaki law enforcement, and an Elaki towering over a seated suspect was a mental image the DA liked to avoid.

"That Warden?" David asked. He looked closer, knew better. This Elaki was narrow in width, with the usual thickness, which gave—David checked the side pouches—*her* more of a pencil shape than was average. The cameras took the images in black and white, so he couldn't read her coloring.

"Who's this Elaki?" he asked.

"Smokar."

"Smokar?"

"You know how they make jokes with the names. God knows what her Elaki name is. She's with Alcohol, Tobacco, and Firearms."

"She's a cowboy? I didn't know they used Elaki."

"Baby, everybody that's anybody uses Elaki these days. They're the latest status symbol in law enforcement. You're considered a pioneer."

"What's ATF want with Cromwell?"

"That little balloon trick—sulfuric acid and fire fudge. That tripped their computer wire. They've seen it before, and they think they got an arson ring by the tail."

David raised an eyebrow. "What do you think?"

"Don't make me talk about this before the Tylenol kicks in."

David sat on the edge of a desk, gave her his patient look. Waited.

She looked back at the video image. Closed her eyes, then opened them. "I tell you what it is, it's screwy, that's what it is. Let's say somebody's hired a torch, okay? You accept that?"

"Makes sense. Bomb scare, sophisticated incendiary device, multiple points of origin."

"Right. So first thing we look at is who holds the mortgage. We look to see if it's changed hands several times. Sniff around for creative financing, you know, selling it back and forth, higher price each time, inflate the property values."

David nodded. "And?"

"No go. First one hasn't changed hands in six years. Second one in three. So we put the owners through the CLUE program. Looking for priors, arson priors—claims and losses. Nothing. We got two fires, same exact MO, got to be the same guy, right? So we look for links."

"Tatewood?" David said.

"Give the Elaki a taco. Of course, it makes sense. Not just anybody is going to deal in properties where humans and Elaki mix—too many bigots in real estate. Now Tatewood, he holds the mortgages. Not his own money, but he puts the investors together, handles the loan, manages the property."

"Tatewood's got to be our guy, Yolanda. Tell me he's increased the insurance coverage sometime in the last two months."

"That's where you're wrong. Tatewood handles the escrow, and he's got cash flow trouble. Both policies had lapsed. According to Tatewood, that's because both the Bernitski brothers and Cromwell are behind in payments, and the books bear it out. So do both of the owners, but they also say they didn't know that the insurance policies had lapsed. *Insurance* companies show notarized E-mail notification for all of them, Tatewood and the owners."

David ran a hand over his chin, thinking he needed a shave already. He shook his head. "I hate to admit it, but I think you're losing me."

She stuck a strand of hair in her mouth and chewed. "Join the club, baby. The upshot is, nobody's making any money off the deal."

"This insurance thing can't possibly be coincidence, Yolanda. We just have to figure the angle."

"Only one I can think of."

"Which is?"

"They don't want the insurance companies on their back. I

mean, face it, David. Having insurance investigators in your face—might as well screw with the Organization. Those people never let up." She glanced up at the vid. "Uh-oh, Smokar's coming in too close, this girl don't know the local rule. We better get in there."

David followed her down the hall and into the room. Cromwell did not look good. He was white around the mouth and there were circles under his eyes—circles of illness, not fatigue.

David settled into the corner. This one he'd watch. "How are you, Mr. Cromwell?"

Cromwell nodded. "Detective Silver. I guess my fire's classed as a homicide, all those people inside. It's murder by my book too. It's a wonder most of them got out. A miracle."

The word murder made Clements look up. She dropped the don't-mess-with-me attitude, smiled, and shook Cromwell's hand.

"You know, we really appreciate you coming down here like this. You okay, Mr. Cromwell? You don't look too well."

"I have stomach problems, my esophagus. Well. You don't want details on that, I'm sure."

"We'll give you a break, you want to take your meds," Clements said.

"My medication was in my desk drawer at the club, so now it's soaked in fire gel. I'm on the waiting list for more."

Clements made sympathetic noises.

Smokar swept close to Cromwell. "Any tally yet on personal damages?"

Clements froze, then turned her head slowly, facing the ATF Elaki. Smokar was brown—black on the outside, like the hard outer shell of a roach, and orangy-red in the midsection. Her eye prongs were tight, small, close to the head. Her side pouches sagged loose.

A Mother-One, David realized. A Mother-One who was about to get blindsided by an arson detective.

But Clements smiled sweetly. "I meant to tell you, Smokar, that you have an urgent message from your office. If you'd check with my associate, Detective Warden, he'll pass it along."

"I will see to thisss at the later moment."

"I said urgent, does the Elaki understand that?"

Smokar skittered backward. Left the room.

David tried not to smile, and Cromwell shoved a paper toward Clements.

"We had a contents tally in the computer," he said. "But, as usual, it wasn't up to date."

She studied the list, then handed it to David. "Are you sure this is all there was?"

Cromwell frowned, shrugged. "It's hard to remember everything."

Clements smiled. "No food in the kitchen?"

David thought about the cans and packages he'd found in the Euclid garbage hoard. He'd forgotten to mention it to Clements.

"Oh, yeah," Cromwell said. "I didn't think about that."

David decided on a change of tactics. Cromwell had a past. "Mr. Cromwell, have you ever been arrested on a felony charge?"

"Why, uh . . . no, I've never been convicted of anything."

David glanced at Clements, wondering why cons, who grew up with computers, thought they could use weasel words to get out of admitting they'd been up for something on the felony level. They had to know their records would come through on the instant.

Just didn't like to admit it face-to-face, David decided.

Clements took the list back. "There's things on here that we found in the storage unit, Mr. Cromwell."

He folded his arms, mouth turning down. "I don't know how that stuff got there. I've told you that, I've told that other Elaki guy, that Detective Warden. How many times you want to hear the words come out of my mouth?"

"You want to change your mind about the paralegal?" David asked.

"No. I got nothing to hide."

David looked at him. Everyone had something to hide. "How about enemies?"

Cromwell smiled, showing teeth. "Not me. Haven't got an enemy in the world."

"Everybody likes you," Clements said.

People were always embarrassed to admit someone out there didn't like them, David thought. As if life was still run by the standards of junior high school.

He kept his voice low and kind. Good eye contact. "Mr. Cromwell, you run a supper club that caters to Elaki and human clientele. You know, I know, everybody in the building knows, the world is full of bigots."

Cromwell rubbed his stomach. "I get threats, I told you that. That group, SCAE. Those guys, they're just jacking off. They paint graffiti, call and hang up, that kind of thing. Then they go buy some beers or packages of Jackie and feel big and mean. I've seen them, I've dealt with them, they're nothing. Little pissant jerkoffs."

David liked the sound of that. Little pissant jerkoffs. "You say you had phone calls? Hang ups?"

"Yeah."

"Trace back?"

"Didn't bother. Blocked it."

"Anything else unusual?"

"That wasn't unusual, it was the norm, been going on since I opened the place."

Clements waved a hand. "Mr. Cromwell, we've had two supper clubs burn in the last four weeks. Now, you didn't burn your own club down, did you?"

"No."

"No what?"

"No, I did not burn my club, or kill those people inside, or take that stuff out of there and squirrel it away in that stupid storage bin."

Clements nodded sympathetically. "Okay, Mr. Cromwell, then tell me who. Who did burn down the club? Kill the people? Cause a pregnant woman to die in childbirth?"

David flinched. The woman had not made it. He wondered if Teddy and Arthur knew. Why wasn't Teddy answering her phone?

Clements leaned back in her chair. "How long you known Tatewood?"

"Three years or so. We do business."

"What you know about him?"

"Not a lot. We don't socialize much. He's got a sick mother, spends most of his spare time with her. He's good at what he does, or so I used to think."

"Meaning?" David asked.

Cromwell sagged in the chair. "We're screwed on the insurance and I'm ruined. One lousy late payment, and they cancel us. I think we should take them to court, but Tatewood, he's working something out with the investors, so we'll see."

Clements tapped her chin. "Guys who hold the mortgage. Do they—"

"You'd have thought they'd have seen it coming," Cromwell said.

David tilted his head sideways. "What's that?"

"I said they should've seen it coming. They're psychics, aren't they? Bunch of fakes."

David kept his voice matter-of-fact. "Your investors are psychics?"

Cromwell shrugged. "Not very good ones, obviously. Tatewood made some kind of comment, day I got the loan. My credit, see, well hell, you probably know more about it than I do. I had a bad credit history, needed to refinance or go under. Tatewood helped me out. So, I ask him, how come *he* can find people to lend me money when nobody else will? I mean, it bugged me, kind of like too good to be true."

"And what did he say?"

"Just that it was some kind of psychic institute. Something like that."

"Mind Institute?"

"Yeah, that's right. Said they knew I was okay. Can't be too good, can they? Didn't see this fire coming. I took their money, but I always figured Tatewood was kidding."

"No," David said. "I don't think he was."

Cromwell shrugged. "It's all a racket anyway."

THIRTY-TWO

DAVID DID NOT KNOW WHAT HAD HAPPENED IN THE HALL-
way between String, Warden, and Della, though someone told
him later that the presence of the ATF Elaki, Smokar, had
somehow banded them all together. By the time he and Clements made it back to his office, the three of them were clustered
around Della's terminal—Della at the keyboard, the aliens at
her back.

Mel pointed a finger. "Harmony of the races." He offered
a bag to Clements.

"Doughnuts? I'm hungry, Burnett, I didn't get any lunch.
Don't you guys ever send out for sandwiches?"

"This is homicide, Yo. In homicide we eat tacos in the
morning, and doughnuts in the afternoon."

"Tough guys, huh? What you eat for dinner?"

"Arson detectives."

Clements sat on the edge of Mel's desk and leaned close.
"Typical cop, I bet. All talk, and no follow-through."

David had the unique pleasure of seeing Mel blush. He
sorted through the doughnuts—all caramel, chocolate, and
white powder. No plain ones. He looked at Clements.

"You think Cromwell torched his club?"

She licked caramel icing off her fingers. "Hard as hell to
prove. His alibi holds."

Warden flicked an eye prong at Clements. "But of course
this human be the responsible party, Yo Free. This storage
bunker holds many of the choice goods, hidden to be the
squirrel."

Della looked at David. *The squirrel?* she mouthed.

"Squirreled away," David said.

Clements crossed her legs. "And no dust on anything, so it
was all put there a day or two before we found it. But two
things bother me, Wart."

Mel scooted his chair away from the desk. "Come on, Yo, this guy led you right to the storage bin where all the stuff was stashed? You think he's that stupid?"

"He could be related to you, Burnett."

Warden swiveled toward Mel. "But this happens the most frequent. In the arson, the perpetrators not always the criminal profession. Many the mistakes are to be made."

Mel nodded. "So what you're saying, is even your low IQ cops got a chance working arson."

Clements rose to the challenge, but David didn't listen. He thought about Teddy, wondered why she did not answer the phone. Was it a psychic thing? Did she know it was him on the other line? Did she know he was going to kiss her on the Ferris wheel? Did she know all his thoughts?

He was being paranoid. Besides, Rose always said it didn't take a psychic to know what was on a man's mind.

"I say *David*."

He looked up. Blinked. "What, Della?"

"I got no other real similarities between the two names, but—"

"What two names?" David asked.

Della studied him a moment, and when she spoke her voice was kind. "The two names on the list my computer ate. Alice Caspian and Jefferson Ford. Both of them have money. Caspian's mom won a lottery and hung on to enough of it to leave Alice money to invest—which she did, and I may say shrewdly. And Ford's a pretty big gun at Nano-Dirt."

"Those guys who do garden soil?" David said. He bought from them all the time.

"Fat salary, stock options, stuff like that."

David looked at Clements, who was rummaging through the doughnuts. She found one with chocolate sprinkles. "This looks like your speed, Wart, want it? Last one."

David wondered why Elaki were invariably attracted to any food that was messy, sticky, or runny. Like two-year-olds, he thought.

"Yolanda?" David said.

"Yeah?"

"Don't you mean yeah, baby?"

She grinned at him. "You homicide guys do stand-up on your days off?"

"We don't get days off," Mel muttered.

David waggled a finger. "I want to know what you think of Cromwell. I want to know what two things bothered you."

Yolanda folded her arms. "Okay, one. His little caddy, where he keeps all his bills and stuff? Everybody has something like that. Most of the time, somebody torches the place, or hires it done, they take it out. It's so damn inconvenient to lose all that stuff, you know? Account password numbers, all those things. And his is sitting in the office, smeared with fire gel."

"Probably all on a disc at his home computer anyway," Mel said.

"Maybe. But what about the man's medication? You know how hard it is to get what you need these days, much less *replace* the stuff? Worse than trying to put an unregistered car through the DMV, which is damn near impossible. People *always* take their meds out."

"Then please to explain items in storage," Warden said. A rainbow of sprinkles shone on his chest scales.

Clements opened both arms. "That's what I'm saying. This case doesn't hold up no matter what direction you run it. I mean, you should have heard the guy in interrogation, Wart. He says, '*I did not burn my club.*' Said it twice, didn't he, David?"

"Words to that effect."

She frowned at him. "They told me you were obsessive."

Obsessive? David thought. Did he have that reputation?

"Anyway, most guys I talk to? They use weasel words, if they're guilty. Never come out and say the touchy stuff. Caused this accident . . . incident, problem. This guy wasn't any kind of mealy mouth. Said the deaths were murder." She frowned. "It could just be his personality. Could be a real cool guy."

David shook his head. "No, because when I asked him if he'd been arrested for a felony, look how he answered."

"*That's* right. Said he hadn't been *convicted*. And he's got to know we got the information in the computer."

"So if he's worried, he weasels, that what you're saying?"

Mel stuck a finger in his ear, wiggled it around.

Clements looked at him. "You got serious allergies or something? You're always scratching."

Mel wiped his finger on a handkerchief. "You know how I know you're a good arson cop, there, Detective Yo?"

"How's that, baby?"

"See, my old sergeant, he always said arson was a tough job. Hard to convict. Said it took a cop with two things to do the job."

"I know I'm a be sorry I asked, Burnett, but what two things?"

"One's a tape recorder, the other's a big mouth."

David decided to change the subject. "We found the dog."

Clements looked at him. "The dog? What dog?"

"One killed in the first fire. The house where we found Theresa Jenks."

"The one with the people in the closet? Where you fell—"

"Yeah, yeah," David said.

"Where'd you find him?"

"Garbage. We also found food packages from that first supper club, the one the Bernitski brothers own. You remember when we went in the kitchen, and you said they'd probably been taken out by—"

"The owners, yeah. And you found them in the garbage? A lot of them? Not just one or two?"

David nodded.

"That tears it," Clements said. "These guys are being framed."

Mel frowned. "By who? What's the point?"

"Somebody does desire this property?" Warden asked.

"They want the property, be easier to buy it than open yourself up to three hundred counts of homicide."

Clements shrugged. "You'd be surprised, Burnett, I promise you. That Smokar from ATF—" Both String and Warden hissed. Clements looked at David and rolled her eyes. "Anyway, like I was saying, you-know-who may be right. She thinks we have a serial arsonist. You remember two years ago? Guy that was going after all the dental clinics?"

David was nodding. "You think we got somebody after supper clubs? Or places where people and Elaki hang together?"

Della's hands froze on the keyboard. "Hate crimes."

Warden waved a fin. "The Federal Bureaus will be looking into this then. We can ask them to consult for knowledge."

"No. They will be like the sslugbartoners and not share."

Mel frowned. "Like the what, String? Run that by again."

David looked at Clements. "You talked to any Feds yet?"

"Yeah, about that hate mail Tatewood showed us."

"You go to them or they come to you?"

"Actually, you know, they came to me."

"They ask about me?" David asked.

She looked at him. "As Wart would say, the ego is a very big thing."

"How about Jenks? They want to know about her? They ask about the Mind Institute?"

"Shoot, Silver, I don't remember. We talked about a lot of stuff. I even told them they should talk to you some. I see they didn't."

"Theresa Jenks is the key to this whole thing," Mel said. "Her murder ties the arson and the Mind Institute—which by the way may hold the mortgage on at least one of the supper clubs."

"I'll check the other one," Clements said. "And try to confirm the first."

"We figure Jenks out, we'll have it," Mel said.

Warden turned to String. "Please explain to me one thing."

"And this is?"

"What does this mean, eat the corncob?"

THIRTY-THREE

THE DESK CLERK GREETED HIM LIKE AN OLD FRIEND. DAVID lifted a hand, said hello. He wasn't noticing the smell of mildew anymore, or the stain on the carpet. He took the stairs slowly, tucking the loose ends of Mel's best shirt down into his pants. Mel often went out after work; usually kept a clean shirt in his desk. David had kept Mel talking while Della raided the drawer.

The shirt was big in the middle, sleeve length a hair too short, but made of fine quality cotton.

The hallway was quiet. David checked his watch—seven P.M. He ought to call Rose and tell her not to expect him. He ought to go home and have dinner with his kids.

Another tense night on the home front.

He knocked. Waited. Knocked again.

The door opened.

Teddy was barefooted, wearing the cutoff jeans and an oversized white shirt that hung down past the shorts. Her face was freshly scrubbed, and she wore no makeup. Her hair hung long and straight, past her shoulders, making her look very young. There were deep circles beneath her eyes, and the animation had gone from her face.

"Teddy, are you ill?"

She gave him a half smile. "I'm fine. Want to come in?"

He felt awkward. Wondered if she was unhappy to see him. If she'd notice the scent he wore. If she'd figure it out and hate him for it.

She pointed to a chair. The television wall was dark and quiet. Radio off. No book in sight.

"You sure you're all right?"

"Of course." She sat down on the bed, put a pillow in her lap. Raised an eyebrow. "Get you a Coke or something, David?

149

I didn't know you were coming. If I had of, I'd have put on some makeup and brushed my hair. But I didn't know." She pulled a thread on the pillowcase, unraveling the hem.

"What is it?" There was no reason for her to confide in him, no reason for her not to shut him out. "Tell me," he said again. Willing her to talk.

She was quiet a moment. Years of interrogation had given David a good sense of when to shut up.

She tilted her head sideways. "It's a funny thing about you, David. I knew when I met you that you were important to me." She had the thread again. Unraveled three more inches of hem. "Knowing things, like I do—see, to me it's just a natural part of every day. It's there, David, that's all. It's in the air, it's all around you, you just tease it out. Or you can ignore it.

"Everybody has their way. Like other psychics? You always find each other—takes one to know one, believe me, it's true."

David settled back in his chair, enjoying the sound of her voice, letting it wash over him.

"My brother's dead, happened a long time ago. And at the time, I knew it was coming, but I was a kid, and nobody believed me."

He moved toward her, but she scooted backward on the bed. This was an area not to touch. Like his father.

She was circling, something big she hadn't said.

"See, David, the mind takes in so much, then stops. That's why psychics only get bits and pieces." She leaned toward him. "But what I think is, it's *all* out there. Every single bit. You just have to stop being scared to go and get it. So many psychics, they're content, you know, with tiny little insights. They think that's all, they won't run with it. Because it's like taking a running jump off a cliff, and thinking, yeah, okay, you'll know how to fly once you get out there. But there's this voice in your head that says, come on, get real. People can't *fly*, what are you, nuts? I mean, David, *I* have doubts. I'm no different from any other neurotic human being. I have doubts, even when I *know*. There's always little nasty voices in your head, they say . . . they say, God, girl, you're such a faker. You're three bricks shy of a load. My mom used to say that to me all the time—three bricks shy of a load."

David moved from the chair and settled on the edge of the bed. "What happened when your brother died?"

She was close to him, so close he could smell the hotel soap on her smooth, tan skin. Camay. It smelled sweet.

"He just died, David. A dumb accident, at my grandparents'. I told my mom, I told my dad, don't let him go. Nobody listened. I didn't trust my instincts then. Knowing what I know now . . . I wouldn't *let* him go. Still, I was just a kid, it wasn't my fault. If anybody's to blame, it's my mom and dad, for not listening. At the time I was so sure, everything was really clear. Then after it happened, I shut down."

"What do you mean, shut down?"

She put her hand on his arm and he moved closer on the bed. "Shut down, David. The psychic stuff. It all went away."

"How long?"

"Two years, and then some." She squeezed his arm. "You know, this sounds stupid, but sometimes I think I meet people for a reason, because they need me in their life. I thought you needed me, David."

Maybe I do, he thought. "What is it, Teddy? The fire?"

She was trying not to cry.

"Have you shut down, Teddy?"

"It's gone. Everything's quiet, everything's dead. There were so many people, David, and I heard them, clearly, like I was at some peak. And then that pregnant woman, in the ambulance. She died, and everything went dead. It's like I'm lost, David. I'm a long way from home and I can't find my way back."

"You feel separate? Like everybody is behind glass and you can't get to them?"

"Don't want to," she whispered.

"Welcome to the club." He leaned close and kissed her.

It was a risk, of course, and when he thought about it afterward, he wondered how he'd found the nerve. He had never kissed another woman this way, not since he married Rose.

She could have been angry, she could have pointed out, quite accurately, that he was taking advantage of a vulnerable moment.

But she didn't. She kissed him as if she'd been waiting on him for a very long time.

He touched her throat, brushed his knuckles across the soft sweet skin. He kissed the tears that wet her cheeks, and pressed his body gently into hers, easing her backward on the bed.

"You sure?" he asked.

"I'm sure."

He felt an acute elation, surprise that was not surprise. He put a hand beneath her shirt; it was loose and slipped easily over her head. She wasn't wearing a bra, and her breasts were small and firm and cool. He put his mouth on one breast and squeezed the other in his hand. She made a low noise in the back of her throat and arched her back gently, saying his name three times fast.

He put his hand into the loose leg of the cutoff shorts, wondering about thong panties, and found she wore no panties at all.

"Bad girl," he said softly, biting the edge of her ear.

She unfastened the buckle of his pants. "I'll show you bad."

David cradled Teddy in his arm, her head in the crook of his shoulder. She ran a finger up and down his chest, and her touch made him sensitive, ticklish.

"I came to ask you about the Mind Institute," he said.

She went tense beside him, and he was sorry he had brought it up.

"You got a funny way of asking."

"We'll talk about it later." He turned sideways and kissed her, sucked her tongue into his mouth. He sighed. "I have to go home."

She nodded. Watched him while he got dressed. He went to the bathroom, looked out the tiny, frosted window. Still dark out, that much he could see.

The bathroom was still cluttered, worse than ever. David smiled and borrowed her toothbrush.

When he came out, she was sitting on the side of the bed clutching a pillow, breasts welling up over the top. He bent close and kissed her shoulder.

"David?"

"Hmmm?"

"You should know I'm not entirely what you think."

"I know what you are, Teddy Blake. I've seen quite a lot of you."

She grinned, rolled her eyes at him. "Seriously, David. There's things about me you don't know. I'm talking about the case, the murder of Theresa Jenks. I'm talking about the Mind Institute. There's more to this than you have any idea."

"You want to tell me about it?"

"Not now, I can't."

He thought about it. She watched him carefully, expectantly. She bit her bottom lip and blood welled over the soft red flesh.

"Whatever it is can wait till tomorrow, Teddy. What I know about you, I *know*. I like. You understand me?"

She nodded. Kissed him. He licked the blood off her bottom lip.

"Call you tomorrow," he said, and walked out the door.

THIRTY-FOUR

DAVID HAD THE CAR WINDOWS DOWN ON HIS WAY HOME FOR what was left of the night. The wind was soft and humid, and he could smell fresh cut grass. The radio was turned low, the DJ's voice was pleasant and peaceful, and he smiled in the darkness as the woman promised the thirty-eighth remake of that Stone Age classic . . . "Unforgettable."

He could only just hear the music over the noise of traffic, the rush of wind. He squinted into the rearview mirror, thinking how tired he looked, knowing that tonight he would not sleep.

David turned into the long gravel drive of his house, stopped halfway down and got out. He shut the door carefully, told the car to kill the engine and the lights, and stood in the darkness.

Wife and kids inside. One cat, one dog, one errant iguana. Two bunnies in the barn and a yearling cow that liked candy. A list of overdue bills in the computer.

He walked to the house, unhurried, gravel crunching beneath his feet. In the back of his mind, he planned. He would take Teddy to dinner tomorrow, he would take her to Pierre's. He checked his watch, saw it was after three-thirty. Tonight, then, since it was already tomorrow. He would wear the blue shirt, it was his favorite.

There was a light in the living room—the reading lamp, turned to the lowest setting. The petunias by the porch had crumpled and turned brown from lack of water, something he should have seen to.

The porch swing creaked as he went by. David told the front door to open locks. He went in quietly. The living room was medium neat—ice cream wrappers on the floor, licked clean by the dog, school discs on the chair, right by a backpack and one pink tennis shoe.

Rose, asleep on the couch.

He was able to look at her with an objectivity that surprised him. She was something of a beauty, his wife. Small and fine-boned, dangerous. Thick curly black hair, blue-violet eyes, the lashes dark against her cheeks. She wore nothing but a linen shirt and panties, and had wrapped herself in a blue wool blanket, like a moth inside a cocoon.

Asleep, she looked very sweet. He had seen her kill with her bare hands; she had a past in the DEA branch of the military that haunted her still; she was a hired mercenary in the fight for animal rights.

He was shocked not to feel any guilt. He had never once strayed, all the years of their marriage, but he knew what he should be feeling now, and he did not. Could they be so very alienated, that infidelity was beside the point?

Perhaps it always was.

He heard footsteps in the hall—one of his daughters. Lisa stumbled toward him, arms out, her voice small and heavy with sleep.

"Had a bad dream, Daddy."

He pulled her close, smoothing hair out of a face so like his own, thinking how glad he was that he was home when she had a bad dream and needed him.

THIRTY-FIVE

DAVID WAS DOZING WHEN THE PHONE RANG, AND HE PICKED it up on the second ring, thinking it would be her.

"Yo, David, wake you up?"

"What?"

"It's Mel. You remember me, we work together?"

"It's still dark out, Mel."

"Yeah, well, it's almost five A.M, so it would be. Figured I better remind you, we're doing an early bird on Tatewood."

"Tatewood?"

"Yeah, David, Tatewood, guy you wanted to talk to? Supper club fire, business manager, mortgages, Mind Institute."

"I got it, Mel, I'm awake now."

"You get anywhere with Teddy Blake last night?"

"*What?*"

"You know, the psychic. Said you were going to see what she knew about this Mind Institute. Thought you said you were awake?"

"Mel, let me get a shower. I'll meet you in front of Tatewood's place, we can talk then."

David looked for the battered green Buick, saw it was parked four houses down from Tatewood's duplex. Mel had the seat on recline, his head turned to one side, eyes closed. His tie was loose, collar open, sport coat wadded in the backseat.

David shook his head. Early as it was, this was not a place to fall asleep with the windows open and the doors unlocked. Even in a car this old.

"What you looking at?" Mel's eyes stayed closed.

"Lipstick on the front of your shirt. Midsection, Mel, that's interesting. You sleep in your clothes?"

Mel opened one eye, then the other. "Not exactly. Somebody took my clean shirt, and to tell you the truth, I didn't sleep."

"You should save this stuff for the weekend."

"It is the weekend, David."

"Miriam?"

Mel smiled.

"We have good relations with the coroner's office, Mel."

"Relations are just getting better, David. This could work for us."

"And it could backfire."

"Get in, will you? I brought coffee."

David opened the door to the passenger's seat and a red light flashed on the console.

"Security breach."

"Guard off," Mel said.

David paused, hand on the door. "You got this rigged?"

"I called it off. Go on, get in, it's safe."

David sat down carefully, but nothing happened, and he let his breath out in a rush. He sniffed, smelling cinnamon.

"Elaki coffee?"

"Cinnamon rolls and human coffee. Bakery near Miriam's place."

"She wouldn't give you breakfast, huh?"

"She doesn't like getting up this early."

David opened the brown paper bag. "Me either."

"The one on top is black, that's mine. The one with cream is on the bottom."

It was a big cup, double order. David opened the top spout and wet steam escaped, coating his upper lip. He reached into the bag of cinnamon rolls, and Mel held out a hand. David gave him a napkin.

"Did I ask for a napkin?"

David handed him a cinnamon roll. "Where's String?"

"Gumby's meditating in a bog somewhere. He won't be in until later."

"He's still mad about the van."

"C'mon, David, he can't just not come to work because he misses his van. Can he?"

David took a bite of cinnamon roll. It was warm and soft,

and the icing was crisp like he liked it. "These are great, Mel."

"Yeah, they smelled good. So when you want to go in here?"

David looked at his watch. "When does he get to his office?"

"Not till around nine, I think."

David looked at the duplex. The windows were dark, soulless. "He's not even up yet."

"The nice thing to do, David. We should let him wake up, go to the bathroom, have his morning cup of coffee."

David chewed a bite of cinnamon roll. "What do you want to do?"

"First we finish our coffee, *then* we wake him up. Be good police work that way, get him off guard. Speaking of which, tell Rose I'm sorry if I got her up this morning when I called."

"No, she slept right through it."

"She on the couch again?"

David swallowed coffee the wrong way and coughed. "What do you know about this guy, Mel?" He took another bite of cinnamon roll. Looked at Tatewood's house. Still dark.

"No priors. Keeps himself to himself. Minimal education. Only child . . . or did he have a brother? I think he may have a brother."

David licked icing off his fingers, checked his watch. The left-hand side of the duplex showed a light.

"Come on, let's go."

"Yeah," Mel said. "Guy should be about midstream, time we get to the door."

Tatewood greeted them in a flannel plaid robe, belted high up over his hips. Wrinkled yellow pyjama legs could be seen beneath the bottom and long-sleeved yellow cuffs peeked from the sleeves, though it was high summer and hot. Tatewood wore tatty brown slippers on his small feet.

Vinyl, David decided, thinking they would rub blisters and make Tatewood's feet sweaty.

Tatewood's hair stuck up in the back, an oily-looking muss, and the left hem of the robe had ripped loose and trailed blue thread. David felt a surge of pity. Something about this man's earnest awkwardness stirred his sympathy.

"Mr. Tatewood? Detective Silver. This is my partner, Detective Burnett, homicide. We spoke the other afternoon?" David showed his ID.

Tatewood blinked and ran a hand over his face. There was a dried smear of toothpaste on the man's sleeve.

"Did you want to come in? I'm not really—"

Mel smiled broadly. "Don't give it a second thought, Mr. Tatewood. Homicide cops are like doctors, see people in their pyjamas all the time." Mel chuckled. "Some of them still breathing."

Tatewood smiled hesitantly, trying to please. He unlatched the storm door and pointed to the wall. "Mother's still asleep next door, so we'll have to keep our voices down."

"You live with your mother?" Mel said. He gave David a look.

"She lives next door in the other duplex. It's convenient that way."

"Convenient for what?" Mel asked.

Tatewood frowned at him. "She's not in good health."

He led them into a living room that was paneled in dark wood and carpeted in gold sculptured wall-to-wall. At first, David thought there were no windows, then realized that they had been paneled over. He felt creepy. Glad he carried a gun.

Tatewood sat on a brown vinyl couch—matches the slippers, David thought—and shoved a stack of newspapers to one side. A stuffed parrot sat on a perch in the corner, glass eyes glittering. Tatewood got up, turned on another lamp. David settled into a bentwood rocker, Mel into a dark green recliner.

David smiled kindly. "Sorry to get you up, Mr. Tatewood. We saw the light and thought you might be awake. You'll be glad to know we're working night and day on these supper club fires."

Mel crossed his legs. "Yeah. Me and David, I think we forget what normal hours are."

Tatewood blinked at them. "You saw the light? Were you watching the house?"

Mel smiled, showing teeth. "Why would we be watching the house, Mr. Tatewood?"

Tatewood looked from one to the other, licked his lips, frowned. He searched the right-hand pocket of the bathrobe and came up with a Chapstick. He pulled off the white cap, unrolled the fleshy-looking wax, and coated his lips.

How do people get this way? David wondered.

Mel crossed his legs. "Mr. Tatewood, we want to know if you'd had any more E-mail threats, phone calls, that sort of thing?"

Tatewood shook his head. "I told the woman. Clements?"

"Detective Clements, yes."

"I said I'd tell her if I got anything else."

"That's funny," Mel said. "I would have expected it." Tatewood shrugged, and Mel made a sympathetic noise. "Real shame about the insurance money."

"Yes, I really fell down on that one." Tatewood gave them a sideways glance.

David frowned. He could have sworn the man was smirking. Surely he was mistaken?

Mel picked at the bottom of his shoe. "They must be mad, huh? They going to fire you? You got some kind of malpractice insurance as a business manager?"

"They were upset, but we've come to an agreement. I've found buyers for the property."

"Did you now?"

David glanced over his shoulder at the parrot. Tatewood saw the look.

"It's not real, Detective Silver. Mother doesn't like pets. She's allergic, you see."

"Shame," Mel said. "My partner here, now he's got all kinds of pets."

Tatewood gave David a tentative smile. "Really?"

Mel held up fingers. "He's got a cat—big fat cat, looks like a possum."

Tatewood covered his mouth with his hand and laughed.

"And he's got a dog. Couple rabbits. And—you still got the cow?"

David nodded.

"Yearling," Mel said. "He used to have an ostrich, till it . . . left. And he had an iguana that just ran away from home."

Tatewood's eyes widened. "A lizard? How big?"

David held his hands up.

"Not counting the tail? That's sizable."

Mel gave Tatewood a sympathetic look. "Mom doesn't like lizards either?"

Tatewood shook his head.

David shifted in his chair. "Mr. Tatewood, did you know a woman named Theresa Jenks?"

"No, sir."

"Ever hear the name before?"

"No, sir."

"How about the place next to the club, the people who lived in the house that burned. Hart, that's what the name was. Did you know them?"

"No, sir."

"They had a five-year-old son, Markus. You ever see him out playing?"

"No, sir." Tatewood looked cooperative, polite. No frustration or anger at the line of questions.

Mel pulled something off his shoe, looked at it, balled it up. "You read your horoscope, Mr. Tatewood?"

David tensed. Gave Mel a look.

"No, sir," Tatewood said.

"Never?"

"No, sir."

"That's unusual. David here was just telling me—read it somewhere, didn't you, David? Eighty-seven percent of the population reads their horoscope. Every day. You read your horoscope today, David? Mine said, let's see, how'd they put it? Watch for prevaricators. You know what a prevaricator is, Mr. Tatewood?"

"Yes, sir."

"You do? It's someone who lies, right?"

"Yes, sir."

"You wouldn't lie to me, would you?"

"No, sir."

" 'Cause I would have figured you knew those people. The Harts."

"No, sir."

"Never said hi on the street?"

"Not that I know of."

"Or been to their house?"

David saw it for sure this time, the man's head tucked to

his chin, the flicker of a smile. But when Tatewood looked up, his eyes were stricken, chin unsteady. He seemed on the verge of tears.

"No, sir. I have never gone in their house."

Mel pulled into a Quik Pak Food Shop, left the engine running. "Got to make a pit stop, too much coffee." He looked at David. "Like to meet his mother, huh? You don't reckon he's one of those guys, mother is dead but he's still got her body?"

David frowned, wondering if he'd imagined the man's hidden smile.

Mel yawned, stretched. "Tell you the truth, I kind of felt sorry for him. I read you right back there, David? I was going to use horoscopes to lead into the thing with the Mind Institute, but you gave me that look."

"I should have warned you. I'm not ready to fish in that pond, rather look into them quietly."

"I thought my recovery was good. Went on the offensive. That lying thing."

"Yeah," David said. "Pat yourself on the back."

He waited till Mel was in the men's room, then showed his ID to the clerk behind the counter and asked for a phone. The woman pointed to a wall extension and David dialed the Continental.

"Room 352." He checked his watch, wondering if they'd ring through this early. But it was the Continental. Likely they'd ring through at any hour.

Teddy didn't answer. David let it ring a while longer, wondering where she was this early in the morning.

Shower, he decided, hanging up.

THIRTY-SIX

DELLA WAS GLIDING LIKE AN ELAKI WHEN SHE CAME INTO the bull pen.

"*Good* morning, David. Like the tie."

David did not remember putting on a tie. He looked at his shirt. No tie.

"Hi, Mel." Della took the white bag off the corner of Mel's desk and fished out the last cinnamon roll, taking a dainty bite. She booted up her terminal, smiled at her reflection in her compact mirror, and applied a coat of deep red lipstick to her lips.

Mel hung up the phone. "Della girl, I hate to see you this depressed."

"I love weekends." She glanced over her shoulder. "Where's String?"

"He and Warden are still trying to run down where Theresa Jenks stayed before she died. They're hitting every pancake house in the city."

David looked at Mel. "You get hold of Miriam?"

Mel put his feet up on his desk. David could see the delineation where the sole of the left shoe had been replaced.

"Looking bad," Mel said.

David rubbed the back of his neck. "Nowhere with the dog, huh?"

"Dog was killed by somebody ramming a fist down its throat."

Della looked up. "Silver, if your wife finds out about this, all hell's gonna break loose."

David ignored her. "Sounds like somebody who knew what they were doing."

Mel nodded. "Got a DNA sample off one of the teeth. Human. Male. Miriam's running it right now, but so far no matches."

"She got DNA off the tooth?" David leaned back in his chair. "Let me play this back, Mel. I said what's up, and you said it didn't look good. Were you hoping the dog ate the killer's ID and had it partially digested with the kibble?"

"Last meal was cereal, bone meal, and beef by-products. Dog food."

"Naturally she looked."

"Miriam's very thorough. The bad news is she's not happy. A, she did not like doing the dog. Said it made her feel bad."

"She never objects to cutting up people," Della said.

Mel rubbed his forehead. "B, she's pissed as hell because I didn't call her this morning after . . . this morning. What time is it, David?"

"After four."

"Good grief, the woman's obsessive."

Della's hands stilled on the keyboard. "Did you *tell* her you'd call this morning?"

Mel shrugged. "Why's it such a big deal? I told her I would call, and I would have eventually."

"Yeah, Burnett, but you *said* this morning. Didn't you?"

"Hell, I don't know. If I did, it was just a euphemism."

"A euphemism for what, not calling?"

"For Chrissake, Della, I got a job here, I got stuff going on. I just didn't think about it."

"Then why bother saying it? She's got stuff going on too. Now how can she concentrate, if you don't call when you say you're going to?"

Mel tossed a pencil in the air, caught it. "Okay, Della let me ask you this. A guy tells you he's going to call soon. When you expect to hear from him?"

Della tilted her head from side to side. "Sometime in the next twenty-four hours. Or at least forty-eight."

"*Hours?* Not days?"

David looked at his watch. He'd tried all day and still couldn't get Teddy on the phone. Maybe it was time to try again.

Della's voice went up an octave. "You think a month is soon, Burnett?"

"What's the big hurry?"

"So she knows whether or not you're really going to call. So she can quit wondering one way or the other."

Mel threw up his arms. "Then why can't she pick up the phone? 'Cause if you do call, it just starts back over again. What's the point, here?"

"The point is that men are—"

"Yeah, yeah, men are pigs. Women say that all the time, it gets old, Della."

David shifted his weight, receiver in his ear. The first floor was a zoo, no surprise. He put a hand over his other ear. The phone rang four times. Pick it up, he thought.

"Hello."

David took a deep breath. "Teddy?"

The chief at the front desk looked up. David turned his back.

"David?"

"Yeah."

"Hi."

She sounded strange.

"You okay?" David asked.

"Fine, sure. You?"

"I'm wonderful. I was thinking about dinner tonight. There's a—"

"David."

Something in her tone made him wary. "Yeah? Is everything . . . I mean, you're not having regrets, are you?" David kept his voice low, hoped no one was listening.

"Are you?" she asked.

"No. You?"

She didn't answer.

David had not realized how happy he'd been till it went away. He cleared his throat. "You are, aren't you?"

"Look, David, I just don't think it's a good idea for me to start something up right now. I'm sorry, I know I'm not explaining this very well. We should talk, but I just can't right now."

When, how, where, why, what, he thought. She had seemed so close last night. How could he have called this one so badly?

"David, are you okay with this?"

Jesus, what a question.

"Sure," he said.

"I'm sorry, David, I've got to go."

"Of course. Good-bye, Teddy."

David hung up, rested his head on the wall, saw the chief looking his way.

THIRTY-SEVEN

DAVID CLOSED ONE EYE, THEN THE OTHER.

Mel opened a bottle of aspirin. "I could send her flowers. If I had money, I could. David—"

"Broke." David rummaged in his desk drawer for the bottle of Tylenol Twelve.

Della stopped humming and looked up. "David, you are *pale*. You sick?"

David's phone rang and he ignored it. Mel reached across the desks, letting the phone cord cut across David's chest.

"Homicide, *what?* Yeah, String. No. No kidding? Where?" Mel made a notation on a pad. "That's great, String. Really? I didn't know Elaki threw up. Nah, go on ahead, we'll meet you. Yeah, I'll bring it, don't worry."

Mel hung up and grinned at David. "String found it. Been to just about every pancake place in town, but he found where Theresa Jenks was hiding out."

David tried to look pleased.

"Quit making faces, will you, and come on. We got to make a stop on the way, pick up some Shredded Wheat and Wrigley's Spearmint gum."

Della waved at them. "Don't come back without chocolate."

Mel waited till they were in the hallway, then glanced back in the bull pen. "I say she definitely got laid last night."

They found String draped over the steering wheel of the van, cushioned by pads that had been installed to give increased traction to Elaki fins. The van looked good—nicks smoothed and painted over, freshly washed.

String hissed.

David peered in through the window. If it hadn't been for the hiss, he would have thought the Elaki was dead. A scale fell off String's soft outer hide and got wedged in the rubber lining of the window sill.

"Pleasse to see I become deceased," String said.

Mel walked to the front of the van, knocked on the hood, waved. He raised a bag. "Yo, Gumby. Got your Shredded Wheat and spearmint. Hey, you okay in there?"

String lifted his head, hissed again, and slumped back over the steering wheel. "Am not okay, Detective Mel."

"What did you do, Gumby, eat your way through every pancake house in town?"

"But yes, it is the necessary. Pleassse, a biscuit of wheat, most quickly."

Mel ripped open the box of cereal. "String, nobody said you had to *eat* there."

"But she, this Jenks, she says the pancakes are most of the delicious, yesss?"

"Yeah, but—"

"So thorough investigation requires to taste."

"Better make sure he never works vice," Mel said.

David shook his head. "You sure about that biscuit of wheat, String? I don't think you should eat anything else."

"Is not to eat."

Mel took a step backward. "I'm not sure I want any details on this."

String straightened up and pressed the wheat to the lowest slit in the happy-face pattern on his inner belly. He made a whistling noise, and his muscles relaxed.

"This like an Elaki antacid?" Mel asked.

"More direct. Please, Detective David, another biscuit."

"Where's this place Theresa Jenks was staying?"

String took the biscuit out of David's hand and plastered it over the one on the slit. "Two places down on the side with streetlights is rental room. Possessions still intact."

The room was clean and small, and not what Theresa Jenks was used to. According to the landlady, Ms. Jenks had walked by, seen the sign, and stopped in on impulse.

Not a bad impulse, David decided. The bed was narrow, tarnished brass, covered by a beige lace spread. There was a padded Victorian rocker, a mahogany dressing table, an electronic center. No one was likely to track her here, not her husband, or the Mind Institute. She had paid in cash, and the landlady had been leery of taking it.

David opened the closet. The clothes were still there—simple, expensive; cotton whites, khakis, a camera. David checked. No film. The pictures were the instant kind, they'd be around somewhere.

"Look at this." Mel held up a child's Eight Ball and tucked it under his chin. "Will we find Theresa Jenks's killer?" Mel turned the Eight Ball over, squinting at the answer.

"What's it say?" David asked.

"*Without a doubt.* Will Miriam forgive me? *Message unclear, try again later.*"

David opened the dresser drawer. Bras. Lipstick. Paperbacks, zigzag lightning on the covers—books from the Mind Institute. He opened another drawer. Interactive CDs. Socks. The third drawer held the treasure.

"Mel, look at this."

Mel put the Eight Ball down. "Pictures? Isn't that—"

"Yeah. The Hart's house before it burned. This must be the little boy that died in the fire. Markus."

David frowned, thinking the boy looked familiar. He flipped through the stack, found the boy posed in front of the supper club, one foot propped up on a brand-new scooter. He wore expensive new shoes and a pricey ball cap. Every picture showed him standing near the project house or the supper club. All except one.

This one was older, and it showed another child, a boy who wore jeans with the knee torn out, a boy who stood next to a large, expensive house, a miniature football tucked under his arm.

David felt Mel's breath on his collar. "It's the same kid?"

David held the picture up, comparing it to one of the others. "No. This is Martin. Theresa's first son."

"The one who drowned? Yeah, right. One with the football's got a dimple in his chin. He's built sturdier too."

"Amazingly alike, though, aren't they?"

Mel nodded.

David studied the older picture, thinking that this chubby-cheeked child would be the apple of any parent's eye. The child looked to be four or five—the picture had likely been taken just before he died. David flipped the photograph over, found an inscription written in neat, upright block letters.

MARTIN ON FOURTH BIRTHDAY, CHECKING OUT THE NEW FOOTBALL.
                    A FUTURE LINEBACKER!!

David flipped the new stack of pictures. Found one inscription.

                         MARTIN?

Same handwriting.

"Here's our scam," David said.

Mel's voice was flat. "They convince her that her little boy's been reincarnated, right? They getting money out of her?"

David picked up the Eight Ball. "She'd been withdrawing large sums of money a while before she died. Probably buying things for the boy, and giving money to the Institute. Look how they can work it, Mel. Find a child that looks like Martin— same age as he was when he died, so she gets that sense of recognition, that emotional jolt. Then they say, hey, the kid's in a bad situation here, needs help."

Mel was nodding. "Pay off the boy's family, pocket the rest."

David tucked the Eight Ball under his chin, thinking of Teddy. Will I see her again? he wondered. He turned it over, looking for comfort.

                      UNDOUBTEDLY SO

"It's a beautiful little scam, David; they can hit her up indefinitely. But here's what I don't get. Didn't Jenks say she was dreaming about the kid? How do they do that?"

"Maybe they don't. But remember, it's Elaki we're dealing with. Maybe when they do the psychic 'scale' reading they hypnotize her, make her open to suggestion, give her some kind of drug."

Mel frowned. "You hear something?"

David listened. Footsteps, women's voices, deep male resonance.

"String?" Mel said.

"Not unless he brought friends."

The footsteps got close, and the hallway darkened.

Teddy Blake walked into the bedroom, and David dropped the Eight Ball on his foot. The black plastic casing cracked open, spilling thick syrupy liquid on the slated wood floor.

Teddy nodded at David, gave him a cold professional smile. "Good to see you, Detective Silver. I hope your foot's okay." She waved a hand at Mel, then turned to the two men who hung back in the hallway. "Looks like they're here ahead of us. I told you they were good."

THIRTY-EIGHT

THE PANCAKE HOUSE WAS NOT CROWDED THIS LATE IN THE afternoon. They'd snagged a large round table, tucked privately into a corner. Everyone had coffee, and there was food on the way.

It had taken all of Mel's wiles to coax String inside, then he had propped the Elaki against the wall, giving him a podium to lean on. It was a family-run restaurant—a sick Elaki brought out the paternal instinct in the owner's husband, and he'd been happy to help String out.

Teddy sat across from David, wedged between two agents of the FBI. One, John Brevitt, was a traditional—six two, short sandy hair, green eyes, and chiseled jaw. The other was the surprising Agent Peterson—tall, overweight, thick black hair, small brown eyes, and a diamond pinky ring in the shape of a horseshoe. His voice hit the lower registers, and when he smiled at David, one of his teeth glittered with small diamond chips.

Not a style David associated with the Feds.

Peterson told them to use his first name, which was Grey. He wrapped a huge hand around a mug of coffee, tasted it, added sugar. He winked.

"Teddy's been wanting to bring you in on this awhile now."

Brevitt nodded and scratched his smooth-shaven chin.

David did not look at Teddy. He knew she was not looking at him.

Peterson shrugged. "We couldn't get the go-ahead from—"

"Aw, cut the crap, Grey. You were the one didn't want to bring them in on it."

Peterson smiled good-naturedly. "Don't you just love our Teddy? She doesn't put up with much, does she?"

David did not like the man's possessive air. He allowed

himself to meet Teddy's eyes and kept his voice matter-of-fact. "You're an FBI agent?"

"I'm what I told you I was. A *psychic*."

There was something there, in the way she said it. Or maybe he was reading too much into everything.

"*David?*" Mel pointed over his shoulder. The waiter was barely hanging on to a platter of hot blueberry pancakes and a bowl of hash brown potatoes. David moved his elbow and coffee cup, and the waiter smiled with relief. A waitress set a pitcher of fresh-squeezed orange juice on the table, made sure they all had a glass.

"Teddy and I go way back." Peterson poured maple syrup over four pancakes.

"You worked together in Virginia," David said.

"Been checking her out, have you?"

"That's my job."

Teddy nodded, but did not look friendly. "And only fair. They were checking you out too."

David took a sip of orange juice, but it did not sit well. He noticed Teddy wasn't eating either.

"What's the connection?" he said. "Between the Mind Institute and the supper club fires? How did Theresa Jenks get in the middle?"

Peterson and Brevitt exchanged looks. Brevitt smiled, and David was instantly wary. Any cop would be, when a Fed smiled that smile.

"I'm sorry, but—"

David gave Brevitt a hard look. "I already know the Mind Institute holds the mortgages on the supper clubs, and I know it's not an insurance scam. Somebody went to a lot of trouble to make sure both properties were *uninsured*, I assume to keep the insurance companies off their backs."

"That's one part of the plan you can admire," Mel said.

Teddy tapped a spoon on her coffee cup. David looked at her, thinking she could not be still. "David, you ever hear of a group called the Kahaners?"

Peterson frowned and hunched forward in Teddy's direction, but she seemed unconcerned.

"I told you, Grey, it's all or nothing with these guys. No mind games here, and no secrets."

String hissed. "Kahaners. Isss Elaki hate group."

"They hate Elaki?" Mel asked. "Like the SCAE?"

"No, isss Elaki group that hate the human."

"It's the racial mixing that tears them up," Peterson said. "We've had targets burned out all over the country. Supper clubs. Restaurants with open seating. Churches with mixed congregations—not too many born-again Elaki, but there are a few, mostly in the South."

David thought of Pierre's. Worried about it.

Mel scratched his ear. "If they're out there, and they got that much presence, how come they aren't taking credit, like all the other terrorist groups? How come Tatewood's getting that mail from the SCAEs?"

"Isss not Elaki way," String said. He was upright now. Interested.

"Feeling better?" Mel asked.

"Be wary of these Kahaners, Detective Mel, isss dangerous grouping. Many Kahaners in Izicho, try to keep the track. Is suspicioned one or two have become to infiltrate. I myself have been warned to take much care."

"You've been threatened?" David asked.

"No, iss the warning, by friendlies. Am known to consort with the human overmuch, so could be target. Not likely, just the maybe."

Peterson poured salt in his palm, licked it. "Their focus seems to be twofold. The fires are set with maximum carnage in mind. That way you get punishment, and what they call 'cleansing.' They buy the property afterward, if they don't already hold the mortgage. Then they leave it sit, burned-out, and it becomes a message, a sort of haunted, holy place."

"And they hire a torch to do the dirty work. Set the property owners up, throw the blame that way, that right?" Mel said.

Brevitt nodded.

"Which means Tatewood," David said.

Peterson leaned back in his chair. "We've been after Mr. Tatewood for longer than I want to count. Same MO every single damn time. Dresses up like a clown, delivers balloons full of sulfuric acid and fire fudge. Calls in a bomb threat to tie up the grids, so the fire fighters can't get there, and the place burns to the ground."

David looked at him. "You could have stepped in a whole lot sooner, Mr. Peterson. Maybe kept the second place from going up."

"Yeah, I got the same line from Ted here, Silver, but *you* know how it works, even if she doesn't."

"Why bring us in now?"

"Hell, you're one step ahead anyhow, and Tatewood is a great big prize."

"And ATF is breathing down his neck," Teddy said. "They been after Tatewood for years. Grey's just decided he's got a better chance of bringing Tatewood down, with you and Burnett at his back."

It made sense, David thought—the acid burn of interdepartmental rivalry, with the local guys caught in the middle, taking the risks but left out of the glory. At least he knew where he stood.

"I don't care what you want with Tatewood, so long as we get him and get him good. He's my killer, isn't he, Peterson? He strangled Theresa Jenks?"

"He's your man, Silver. Don't know why he killed her, but she was obviously some kind of threat. And it's the mistake we've been waiting for. I'm hoping it's the one that'll bring him down."

"We have his DNA from the crime scene. Got it off the tooth of a dog that bit him."

Peterson grinned and shook his head. "No match in your records, right? That's an old one, he's pulled it before. Up in Oakland, and other places. Likes to plant DNA that belongs to some hapless John Q. Tatewood's smart, Silver. He's nasty, and he enjoys his work. Playing mind games with the cops is just part of the fun."

String tilted back on his fringe. "Is very Elaki, these Kahaners. The circle within the circle. Study human at Mind Institute. Read his secrets and take him money, for use to kill the mixers."

Teddy looked at Peterson. "We already made up our minds on this, Grey. Quit dragging it out."

Peterson put a slab of butter in the center of a stack of pancakes, then dribbled syrup down the sides. "Let John tell it, I'm eating."

Brevitt smiled and shredded the corner off a napkin. His manner was low-key; he was the kind of man who stayed calm in a crisis.

"Gentlemen, let me start at the beginning."

The victims all had the usual thing in common—money. Family money, like Theresa Jenks; lottery money; one woman who'd hit it big in Vegas.

Brevitt leaned across the table. "What is it that makes a man walk away from a good job, a happy marriage and two babies, in search of a lost love he supposedly knew from a prior life?"

"Mid-life crisis?" Mel said.

David shook his head. "Not when there's money involved."

Brevitt gave him a smile and a wink, and David felt like a prize pupil. He thought of Theresa Jenks, and the Eight Ball. Of Martin, and of Markus, who had hidden in a closet and died in a fire, thanks to his parents' greed and Theresa Jenks's obsession.

And what of Arthur? What made Theresa Jenks leave a living, needy, and rather delightful boy, to look for the ghost of another child whose death she would not accept? What had made her so desperate and so vulnerable, that she turned to a child's toy for guidance?

In his mind's eye, David saw himself and Mel, asking the Eight Ball questions of the lovelorn.

David remembered the women he'd talked to on the phone, the clients of the Mind Institute. "This man, the one who left the wife and two babies. His name wouldn't be Jefferson Ford?"

Brevitt nodded. "Put a gun in his mouth and blew out the back of his head. Wife found him on the floor of their bedroom closet."

Peterson set his fork down, wiped his mouth. "Bullet went right through the wall, lodged in a quilted bunny rabbit, hanging over his daughter's crib."

"That's one that went wrong," Brevitt said. "You have to understand, this man actually had a pretty good marriage, and all the evidence showed he was a devoted father. Business stress is what sent him to the Mind Institute, as far as we can tell. He'd been getting mailings; his wife confirms it. We think they did something to him—drugs, hypnotism, something."

Mel shook his head. "Hypnotism alone won't do it, Brevitt. Can't make somebody go against the grain."

"Granted, Burnett, we're hazy on the mechanism, but rest assured there is one."

"Elaki very good with the tailor drugs," String said.

Mel wadded a napkin. "He means tailor-made. And he's right. You okay over there, String? Need another wheat biscuit?"

String hung his head, leaning hard on the podium.

"This guy ought to be home in bed," Peterson said.

"Elaki do not have the bed, is human thing. And may as well be miserable getting on with job as soon as molting at home perch."

Mel leaned back in his chair. "Hate to say it, guys, but unless you got evidence of drugs here, you don't have a crime to go after. Nothing that'll hold up, anyways."

String hissed. "Would not need such carefully catfooting about, if could work in Elaki Izicho police methodology."

"Yeah, we could send you and Wart to cho-off all the psychics, guilty or not, which might make David happy—"

Teddy gave David a sharp look.

"But," Mel continued. "Is kind of beside the point."

Peterson rubbed his jaw. "We want to send Teddy in. Set her up as some big lottery winner or something, dangle her out there as bait." He gave her a grin, and she rolled her eyes. "I personally think she'd be good at it, but she says it'll never work."

Teddy pushed hair out of her eyes. She was wearing the khaki pants again, the white blouse. Her hair was coming out of the braid, as usual. It struck David that the objectivity he had gained with Rose was lost with Teddy. He was too close to her now and could not see her as others did.

She sounded tired. "It wouldn't work, Peterson, we've gone over this before."

"But, Ted, you'd be just the one to spot them. You're the expert, aren't you? You're the one who can say if they're real or not. You're the one who can spot the scams."

"Takes one to know one," Mel said.

"That's it exactly, Burnett. And when I spot them, they'll

spot me. Then the whole thing'll be blown, and they'll be warned, and you'll never get that close again."

"She's right," Mel said. "Send somebody else."

"You volunteering, Burnett? You don't think they'd be a little suspicious of a cop?"

Mel pursed his lips, looked at David. Frowned. "Not me. But my partner here would be perfect."

Teddy folded her arms. "Why? He's not a cop?"

"He's a cop with a history. Cops go to psychics, right? And David here—" Mel stopped. "You want me to shut up, David, I'll shut up. But you see what I'm saying?"

"I see."

"I don't." Peterson sounded polite, but his eyebrows were raised and he was jiggling his knee so hard the table shook.

Mel waved a hand. "Thing is, David's already been to psychics. His father . . . you sure this is okay, David? His father disappeared, see, when David was a boy, and David's been kind of looking for him ever since."

"My father is dead," David said.

Mel nodded. "But you *did* look for him, right, David? You did pay that guy, that Candy Andy, and you got took for some serious money before you got your head straight. So what I'm saying is, you guys set it up to look like David comes into some big money. Something that makes headlines. And David takes some time off, now he can afford it, to settle this business of his father once and for all."

Brevitt looked at Peterson. Picked away at his chin. "I like it."

"Works for me," Peterson said.

Teddy bit a fingernail. "It doesn't work for me, it's a terrible idea. For one thing, it's way too obvious. And you don't know for sure what they *do* to people." She looked at David. "Don't you see what you could be getting into here? Just because these people are bad news, it doesn't mean they're not good psychics."

"You can coach me."

Mel looked at him. "You sure about this, partner?"

David thought of little Martin, drowned at four, and Arthur, left behind with a man too cold to admit to fatherhood. Had Theresa Jenks finally come to her senses? Was that why she called Arthur? She had said she was coming home, but it was going to be a day or two. What did she have to do? Was she going to blow the scam?

Of course he'd do it. Nobody knew better than he did, the kind of pain these people could inflict.

He nodded at Peterson. "Put the bill on your expense account, and let's get started."

Teddy frowned and folded her arms. "You know what I'm thinking, Grey? I'm thinking it's a good thing you brought them in on this, or before long, you'd be eating their dust."

That was when David knew for sure that he loved her.

THIRTY-NINE

DAVID HAD NEVER SEEN ROSE SO NERVOUS. SHE BRUSHED Mattie's hair, pulled it up on the sides, and fastened it loosely with a wide yellow bow. She straightened David's tie, though it didn't need it, surprising him. She rarely touched him these days.

"Go get ready, Rose. The girls are perfect."

She looked over her shoulder at her daughters. "They are, aren't they?"

They had not stinted, he and Rose, with their orgy of spending at the expense of the FBI. David looked through the window at Kendra, sitting alone on the porch swing, wearing her first low heels and stockings. His baby. Lisa, wearing a pretty dress instead of the usual jeans, leaned against the kitchen table, elfin face clean, for once. It went against the grain, involving the children. But when it meant new shoes, new dresses, new hair bows and ruffled slips, and, he suspected, new lace panties . . . when it meant not looking at price tags, just this once, and indulging their every whim, it was impossible to resist.

Anyone paying attention would be convinced that the Silvers had come into money.

He did not know who had originally been slated to win this year's Racial Harmony Award given by the Elaki Benevolent Association, but whoever it was had run into bad luck. The EBA, brought around by the promise of a large donation and their own inclination to see a hate killer brought to justice, agreed that if making Detective David Silver a very public cash award would accomplish both of these things, it was an arrangement that made perfect sense. If it also won them friends and future favor with the Federal Bureau of Investigation, so much the better.

Elaki, David thought, favored obscure and manipulative goings-on anyway.

The EBA had been intrigued, of course, as to how that much money deposited to the account of a local homicide cop could have any bearing on a maniac who torched supper clubs, but the Mind Institute had not been mentioned. Agent Peterson had somehow made it clear that details would not only not be revealed, but that any kind of leak could easily be traced.

"I hate having my picture taken," Rose said.

"Why do they want a picture of us while we eat?" Mattie asked.

"It's a celebration," David told her.

"Of the award?"

Lisa touched her brand-new sparkley tights, and David was uncomfortably reminded of Markus with his new scooter. "Mama says you might even be on TV."

"Maybe. Nothing major."

"The Comedy Channel?"

"Funny girl. No, the Elaki Channel."

"Good. None of my friends watch that one, it's boring. So what is this EBA anyway?"

David stuck his hands in his pockets. "An Elaki charitable group. Promoting racial harmony."

"So basically, they pay people who hang out with Elaki and get along?"

"Something like that."

"And they give you money, just like that? How come String doesn't get any? Or Uncle Mel?"

"That's just the way it works. Every year, fifty people get the award. One from every state." David hoped the Kahaners would not be as hard to convince as his children.

Mattie touched her hair bow carefully. "Where are we eating again, Daddy?"

"We're eating at Pierre's."

"That costs lots of money."

"It'll be okay."

" 'Cause we got lots of money, right?"

"For now we do."

"Forever, or for now?"

He looked into his daughter's face, wondering how to be straight, but not compromise the investigation. He picked her up, the frills of her dress bunching at the waist.

"Nothing is forever, Mattie-girl."

The phone rang. He put Mattie down, warned her not to play with the dog. Could it possibly be Teddy calling? She had told him in a whisper that they needed to talk, but the opportunity had never come.

"David? Mel. Just touching base. Miriam and I will meet you at Pierre's. If we get there first, we'll be at the table."

"Made up, huh?"

"Ain't it wonderful?"

"I'm happy for you, Mel."

"David, it's just a dinner date, okay? My nieces all fluffed up and ready to go? Rose ready?"

"She's still getting dressed."

"I'm right here." The voice came from the hallway. David looked over his shoulder. Rose.

"See you, Mel." He hung up, pulled the cuffs down on his shirt. Told Rose she was beautiful and wished that he cared, thinking life would be simpler that way. "Shall we go?"

"David." She touched his arm and spoke softly. "I know things are as bad between us as they ever have been. For the first time since I've known you, I really think we might not make things work, no matter how hard we try."

Where was she going? he wondered. And why now?

"But all that aside, I feel like something's happened. *To* you. Something that doesn't involve us."

"Nothing's happened, everything's fine." He knew he sounded wooden, but didn't know how not to.

"Don't tell me that, when I know better. I can't tell if it's this case you're working on, or if there's something else. And I'm not worried about me or us or the future. Just you, David, because you're so very . . . crushed. I want to help you, but you're so faraway, I don't think I can."

The tears came, streaking Rose's makeup, making the mascara run. He put his arms around her and told her not to worry, but he was the one who pulled away first.

FORTY

THE RESTAURANT LOOKED THE SAME—WORN, RED-CHECKED curtains, bar painted in gold letters on the front window, RESTAURANT PIERRE on the front door. Same scarred mahogany bar, cracked plaster ceiling. There were no bloodstains on the floor where David had fallen, and the broken table had been replaced. The shocked patrons were long gone, and there was nothing left to disturb the diners who ate calmly, happily.

Tonight David was well-dressed and clean, accompanied by his wife and daughters. Then he had been unshaven, in dirty blue jeans and a grimy shirt. Something had happened to him that night in Pierre's, when he'd brought down an Elaki he had considered a hero, and found the venal underbelly of fanaticism gone bad. Maybe it was the aggregate of years of mind-numbing work, but in his mind, that night was the point of no return. He had lost more than blood in this restaurant.

Mattie reached for his hand, and he looked down into the small upturned face, smiled, and led her to the back of the restaurant.

Pierre was waiting, dressed in black as always, distracted by secret thoughts and a melancholy that separated him from the world. David met Pierre's eyes, saw the spark of interest, wondered if the two of them were more alike than he knew, wondered if they had both crossed that boundary that set them apart—not sure he liked the concept.

The back section of the restaurant was six steps up from the rest of the dining room. Pierre had closed the area off with battered, floor-to-ceiling mahogany shutters. David found the dark wood oddly comforting.

He studied the menu, listening to Rose's voice rise and fall softly as she quizzed the children on their orders. Most of the Elaki and his youngest daughter, Mattie, opted for the *pannequets aux laitances*—an aromatic dish of mushrooms, chopped fish sperm, and unsweetened crepes, bound by a fish-based béchamel sauce, and sprinkled with grated Parmesan.

David felt adventurous trying *canapés à la moelle*, figuring that if he could eat Jell-O, he could eat beef marrow marinated in olive oil, lemon juice, and parsley. The canapés came coated in tempura and deep fried, and he shared them with the girls, who had ordered fruit cups.

He drew the line at *anticuchos* (barbecued hearts) and *Hjerneboller* (brain dumplings) as a main course, and settled for a sedate and delicious chicken marsala that he combined, to Pierre's displeasure, with a heavy cabernet.

He watched Mattie eat her crepes, saw that she picked out the mushrooms but devoured the rest. The child had a palate, and he saw Pierre watching and felt a swell of pride.

Atta girl.

It was wrong of him to want Teddy there, but he did, and he wondered what she would have ordered from this, the most interesting of menus. He watched Lisa cock her head and imitate String, saw Kendra eating so self-consciously, so painstaking in her efforts to pass for an adult, that he wanted to hug her and tell her she was fine just like she was.

The children were enjoying themselves—the expensive restaurant, the new clothes, the Elaki all around.

Dessert was Elaki coffee and a simple chocolate cake. Pierre served it himself, on white china plates bordered by delicate blue flowers, and he watched David's girls as he passed the cake around. David caught Pierre's nod of satisfaction at his daughters' delight over the moist and beautiful chocolate, and he guessed that the cake had been made with the children in mind.

Teddy would have loved it.

An Elaki, short and squat by alien standards, but much taller than David, glided to the front of the room, shedding scales as he went. He waited till he had their attention, or as much of their attention as he could get, with chocolate cake on the small round tables, and he began a small speech.

"Each year, in States every one, we of the Elaki Benevolent Association select a human who has done the advancement of human and Elaki relationships the smooth."

Lisa grinned at David and he winked.

"For this year in Saigo City, we have found the human who has worked side by side with the Elaki, before the fashion is to follow."

David noticed that Mattie was swinging her legs. Vigorously.

" . . . so we are to be the pleasure of awarding this year's Racial Harmony Award to the Detective David Silver, of the Saigo City Police Department."

David stood up. Nodded at the applause. Saw the camera following his every move as he went to the front of the room. Someone took his picture and he made a little speech, talking off-the-cuff. Afterward, he had no memory of what he'd said, just that it seemed well received, that people laughed once or twice, that his little girls were smiling and looking interested, that Mel gave him the thumbs-up sign. Teddy, of course, was not there. He did not look at Rose.

Afterward, a newspaper photographer wanted a family picture, and David sat with Rose by his side, Mattie in his lap, Lisa and Kendra on his right. Last family portrait? he wondered.

The reporter asked if he was going to take a vacation. He said he had something of a personal nature to work out, with the help of the money and a little time off.

"My father has been missing since I was a child," he said. "I'm going to find him."

"Find Granddaddy?" Mattie asked.

David looked at his daughter, felt a pang. But that night on the Elaki Channel, he was featured with the caption RACIAL HARMONIST. The film clip was followed by a video on "*Dealing With the Difficult Human.*" And the next morning's paper had his picture with the caption: HOMICIDE COP USES AWARD MONEY TO FIND MISSING FATHER.

Everything was going according to plan.

FORTY-ONE

A VOLCANO HAD ERUPTED, MILES AWAY AND MONTHS AGO, on an island David did not remember studying in school. For that reason and that reason only, as far as the current art and science of meteorology could divine, the day was deliciously cool, the sun hard and bright.

By the end of the week, the miserable weather was due to return, but for now, it was perfect.

It seemed that a weight had lifted from the city along with the heat, that everyone had gotten up that morning in an exceptionally fine mood. David wondered if the ills of society were more tied to the weather than anyone suspected.

He parked blocks away from the Mind Institute and sat in his car. Two boys with chains hanging from their belts, divots of hair in the back, and a top stubble on their heads, gave David what they likely thought was a hard look. Then one of them smiled, sweet and friendly.

Weird day.

He had parked at a distance on purpose, feeling the urge to walk through the Psychic Fair, an area he had avoided for years. It was nothing more or less than a few city blocks offering a labyrinth of storefronts, boutiques, and parlors for those seeking advice, guidance, and diversion from psychic phenomena. Signs showing a black palm glowing on white background were common.

David passed a house with a front door painted like a tarot card—the card of love. A sign in the window said APPOINTMENT ONLY. Beneath the sign was a hand-lettered note that said WALK IN—SPECIAL HALF-OFF READING. The note had yellowed with age.

Candy Andy's place had no such sign. His business was brisk, and all word-of-mouth, and he had the cachet of catering to clients in the know. David stood outside the glass door leading up to Andy's apartment, looking inside at the dusty staircase, sporting those worn brown rubber treads. It was all so familiar. He felt bad for the young police detective he had been, looking over his shoulder as he traipsed up those stairs for another fix of hope.

He had decided years ago that Candy Andy had been nothing but a con, but maybe Teddy was right. A little bit of talent and a lot of panache could go a long way toward manipulating vulnerable people.

David blushed to think of the things Andy had made him do—stand under the shower for fifteen minutes with the water as hot as possible. Cleanse your body, your heart, your mind. The deferential way Andy had accepted his fee, as if financial transactions were embarrassing and beside the point. The limits he had set—you may come no more than every two weeks, but you may call every week.

The man had wanted the money, but he had enjoyed the power.

A curtain twitched in an upstairs window—the kitchen, as David remembered, smelling again the cloying fragrance of the tea laced with whisky that Candy Andy liked to drink.

One of these days, David thought, looking up the dark staircase.

The area picked up as he closed in on the Mind Institute. David passed two hookers heading the other way. One of them shook her head sadly.

"He's a *john*, honey, he's not going to fall in love."

"But it's in my palm, Vanna, she *said*—"

David kept moving.

The Mind Institute did not blend—not possible, it was complete Elaki design, a milky-white dome of thick glass over a snarl of small, narrow rooms. A billboard blinked with moving images—an Elaki behind a table reading scales. Elaki did not trust people to read.

The front door was not a door at all, just an open space, tall and narrow, Elaki-shaped. David went inside.

A feminine voice echoed. "Pleassse wait. Pleassse wait."

It was dark in the foyer. Heavy wood latticework had been layered under the dome, blocking the light. David stood under diamond-shaped patterns of muted sunlight, remembering Teddy's advice. Perfectly okay to be nervous, she'd told him, but watch that hostile edge. Some hostility is normal, but your best bet is to keep your mind on your daddy.

Your daddy. Such a Teddy thing to say.

It was harder to do than he imagined. He had perfected the art of putting his father out of his mind and was rusty now, when it came to calling him up.

David realized that an Elaki was in the room with him.

"Please, do you have the appointment?"

Male, David decided. Old. "My name is Silver. David Silver."

And yes, indeed, he had the appointment. The Institute had accepted his initial call with a cautious nonchalance, but after they'd had time to check his financial records, they had been eager to accept his business.

"You are to be exsssspected, David Silver. Pleassse follow."

The Elaki crept ahead, hunched over to one side, the right fin making rhythmic, jerky motions that looked involuntary. Gravel beds lay in strips on either side of a walkway that was uncomfortably narrow by human standards. The light here was blinding, no latticework beneath the glass, and David blinked, eyes aching. He knew his every move and physical reaction was being monitored by Peterson, Clements, Mel, and String, but he wished his partners were there with him. He missed Mel's crude but effective way of diffusing situations by making vulgar remarks. Mel was like Alice in Wonderland—he had to say three outrageous things before breakfast.

The Elaki stopped, and David skidded to keep from running into him.

"Pleassse to go to the right, onward this way."

David moved through an open doorway and squinted, eyes adjusting to the gloom. The room was covered in some kind of brown fabric—walls, floor, ceiling, like a sensory deprivation chamber.

"You are the David Silver?"

"Yes, I'm Silver."

"You are made welcome. Please, do come all the way forward. I am Jordiki. Be hospitable here. Will you not have this chair?"

David went, nearly blinded by the change in light. The Elaki was hard to see, but David had the impression of unusual bulk, heavy, almost muscular eye stalks, stark white belly encased in a black outer section. David stepped up onto a platform and sat down. The chair and table were simple bleached oak, and the elevation allowed the Elaki to stand while David sat, eyes and eye prongs at a level.

Which meant the clientele was human, David thought. Prey was the word that came into his head.

David looked down at the desk. A collection of Elaki scales fanned across the top.

"When you have given information for this Institute, David Silver, it was not of the personal nature."

No, David thought, it was of the financial nature. Which was really more to the point. You didn't afford the Mind Institute on anything like detective's wages—not if you had a family and the usual load of debt.

"These scales are of my person, and I must ask that you do not touch."

David nodded. The Elaki twitched an eye prong, casting a look over David's shoulder. The old Elaki came in with a mug, steam rising from the top. The smell was familiar. The same brew of tea used by Candy Andy.

The old Elaki set the tea on the table, a good ways from the scales.

What if I spill it? David thought.

"Please to drink. It will relax you, this liquid warmth, and is only tea leaves in water." The Elaki waved a fin. "No drugs of caffeine or any other toxin to pollute the body and mind. Please to forgive me that I do not join. I eat, drink, and smoke abstinence before scale reading, so the focus is complete and full circle."

David picked up the mug and sipped, finding the tea hot and weak. He wondered if there were any extra additives, knew Miriam would be monitoring his blood chemistry.

The things he did to make a living.

"You have questions," the Elaki said. A statement.

"I want to—"

The Elaki waved a fin. "No, please to wait. See this scale in the middle? This one you will pick up, you will handle. Please.

Do not be shy with this. It is fragile, but can be manipulated safely. You may please put it here and when you leave, you will take this scale. You will keep it with you, and the future readings, if you desire such, will improve and intensity grow. Yes? This is understood?" The Elaki folded David's scale in with the others, then fanned them back out again.

His voice became matter-of-fact. "I see two women, one dark, one light. I see one heart, your heart, which goes in two directions."

David thought of being monitored. He could shrug it off, tell everyone it was bull.

"This is a difficult path, but worth the journey."

Does this mean things will work out with Teddy? David wondered. And realized how vulnerable he was.

"The missing pet is in danger," the Elaki said.

"Elliot?"

"I do not know. I see danger."

"But he's alive?"

"For now." Jordiki paused. "Missing. This is a theme for you, David Silver."

David nodded. "My—"

"Please, do not feed. Must not confuse what you will tell with what I will see. I see your makers, your parents. A cloud of dark for the mother. I see her eyes. She is deceased?"

Cruel, David thought. So very cruel.

"And the father is . . . alive."

"Is he?"

"You do not know?"

"He left when I was ten years old. Disappeared. We haven't been able to find him."

"Ah. Please, a moment. Think of this man, this father, as you remember him. In the out loud, for my own benefit."

"A tall man," David said. "Broad-shouldered. Brown eyes, like me, we were . . . alike. He has—he had a large smile. A sense of humor. He liked playing jokes. He was religious. He had a code of morals and ethics which—"

"He held in reverence," the Elaki said.

"Yes."

"I see him."

The statement, so matter-of-fact, so convincing, made the hair stir on the back of David's neck.

"He is alive, David Silver. The father is alive."

"Then where is he? Why didn't he come home?"

"This I do not know." The Elaki gathered the scales together slowly. "Perhaps another time, we can discover the answers that you seek. Good of the day, David Silver."

FORTY-TWO

THAT NIGHT DAVID DREAMED OF HIS FATHER. HE WENT INTO work feeling shaky and ill.

"Nothing in the tea," Miriam told him.

"Nothing?"

"Just tea. Good notion, spilling it and wiping it up on your shirtsleeve. Don't you carry a handkerchief?"

Mel gave him a sympathetic look. "Everybody's a critic."

Rose stood over him, shaking his shoulder. "David? Aren't you working today?"

He opened his eyes. He had been dreaming again, something about his father and a baseball game. "What do you want?"

"David, it's late, you—"

"Don't *ever* wake me up again."

She looked as if she was going to say something, then turned and walked away.

The phone rang and he picked it up. "Yes?"

"David? Mel. Where the hell are you?"

"Home, Mel, obviously."

"Still sick, huh?"

David coughed. "Yes."

"When you going back to the Institute?"

"Next week, probably. He said not to come till then."

"Be sure you get in here first and get the monitors set up."

"Sure, Mel."

"Feds have Tatewood staked out, trying to get some kind of connection there. Peterson's trying to get a warrant to search the Institute, get into their records, get a paper trail going. Nothing so far, so a lot is riding on you. Oh, and Teddy called again. You ever get back to her? She says—"

"Look, Mel, can a man be sick without all this fuss and bother? I'll be in tomorrow, and I'll deal with it then, okay?"

"Yeah, okay, sorry. Get well, David. We're counting on you."

David hung up and got dressed, making sure the scale was safe in his pocket.

FORTY-THREE

DAVID SAT IN THE SMALL BROWN ROOM, FACING THE ELAKI. He dreamed of this room.

"I have found the father for you."

David bowed his head so Jordiki would not see the tears that filled his eyes.

"Is time of much emotional joyousness, do not be the shame, David Silver. You must ease this well of hurt. This father does not know you."

David cleared his throat. "I don't understand."

"He has experienced the permanent memory lapse."

David's head went up. "Amnesia?" Somewhere in the back of his mind, warning bells went off. Amnesia. No memory. Very pat.

But it made sense, did it not? There had never been a body, yet his father had not come home. He would never have abandoned them, never. Every milestone, David had expected to see him. Graduation from high school, then college, then the police academy. His marriage to Rose, the birth of his daughters, the suicide of his mother. Amnesia explained it all away.

He is telling you what you want to hear, came the thought.

"Where is he?" David said.

The Elaki waved a fin. "He is alive, but he does not thrive. His health has not been good, since this blow to the head of amnesia. He is a long way from here with the menial work. And on the list, the long list, for medical care."

David felt a chill like ice. "He's not going to die?"

Jordiki's scales rippled, like a shudder. "Without the treatment of medical he needs, death is a possible outcome."

"Where is he?"

"He is south in a New Orleans satellite town."

194

"Rough places," David said.

"He has been there some time and survived this."

"Which one?"

"The one of the south loop. It is called Meridian. He brings the fish to a place of restaurant."

"Name?"

"Crawdaddy's. I do not know what this is, the crawdaddy. We will contact him for you."

"I want to go myself."

"As you wish it."

"And I want to get him his treatment. Bring him here and—"

"David Silver, this father has been gone many years. He is an abuser of substances. He may not desire the homecoming. He may not desire the help."

"I'm going."

"I wish you well. Perhaps we can help with him—to arrange the treatment, if you cannot bring him home. Pleasse to go, to see. And to come to me if there be troubles. I wish you well, David Silver."

David nodded, picked up his scale, and left.

FORTY-FOUR

NO ONE HERE SPOKE ENGLISH, DAVID THOUGHT, NOT THE way he knew it. And it was hot, really hot, the kind of heat that would make you gasp, if it hadn't sapped your energy first. The day before, David had seen a woman slump against a wall and slide down dead to the ground. Heat.

It was a bad place, Meridian; a place where nobody who had anything ever wound up. As was the way in places like this, places where life dealt you nothing or worse and said take it or die, people took it, and gave it a dirty spin, creating a complex underbelly that had its own set of rules, its own pecking order, its own class of haves and have-nots.

People were the same, really, top to bottom.

David turned the faucet of the sink in his room and the fixture came off in his hand. A thin stream of rusty yellow water dribbled into the mildewed drain.

What had he been going to do? Wash his face?

He looked in the mirror, seeing with some surprise that he had not shaved in a while. Sweat glistened in the heavy growth of beard, giving him a grey look of illness. There were deep swollen circles beneath his eyes, and his hair was long and thick.

His shirt was not clean. The collar was grimy, the underarms yellow with sweat stains.

What would his father think?

Not your father, came a voice in his head. *Not your father.*

It would be so good just to see him, just to say hello. He would show him pictures of the girls, even of Rose. He would explain about Teddy, ask him, man-to-man, what to do.

He would take his father home.

He himself was a long way from home, that he was sure of, and he could not think how to get back. He felt homesick for something, he did not know what. The names of his daughters went through his mind. Lisa. Kendra. Mattie.

First he had to find his father.

He did not know how to turn the water off with a broken faucet. He left it dribbling into the sink.

FORTY-FIVE

IT WAS HIM, NO DOUBT, THOUGH HE LOOKED YOUNGER THAN David expected. Everything was right—the way he moved, intense, focused, *wired*. A trademark self-confidence that was so very attractive. A handsome man, dark and energetic, out of place here in this hot Southern city full of wispy sunburned men who moved languidly, as if they walked through soup and not air.

David decided then and there, no matter what, to help him. Even if things did not work out between them, even if there was no spark. It could only be a good thing for such a man to get another chance at life—such a man as his father.

Hi, Dad! Hey, Pop! That you, Daddy? Hello, you used to be my father. I look familiar to you, sir? How do you do? You don't know me, but . . . Excuse me, I know this is going to sound strange . . . Could I just have one minute of your time?

David realized that the man was speaking.

"Sorry, I know this seems strange. I just got the oddest feeling I know you somehow?"

David felt warmth in his chest, right where the bullet scar throbbed. He knew that if he opened his shirt, the tissue would be red and livid.

"I beg your pardon," the man said.

Then he smiled, and David knew that smile. He'd pay money for that smile, he'd lay his life down for it. If his mother could have seen that smile again, would she still have felt the need to string that rope and die?

The man inclined his head to one of the outdoor tables. "You look kind of shaky there. Sit down for a minute."

The chairs were black spindly wire. David sat on the tiny round seat, hooked his toes on the precarious legs, and rested his elbows, making the table wobble back and forth.

His father steadied it with one hand, and his look was kind.

"Tell me," he said.

The warning voice that had come and gone went away for good. David knew that his hands shook, that he looked ill and dirty. He sighed deeply and tried to smile, not quite sure what to say, but knowing that words didn't matter all that much.

FORTY-SIX

DAVID WAS HARD ASLEEP, VAGUELY AWARE THAT SOMEONE had been knocking, knocking a long time, that the door opened and someone walked in. He felt a presence by the bed.

He sat up in a panic, reached for his gun. The woman flinched, but did not touch him. He felt a twinge of fear, a conviction that she could have taken the gun if she wanted, that she held herself in check. He felt that he knew her.

She was dark-haired, violet-eyed, extraordinarily pretty. He rubbed his eyes, wondered what she was doing here, standing by his bed, unsmiling, wearing cutoff shorts and a white cotton shirt with the sleeves rolled up.

His tongue felt thick and sticky. "I forget to pay?"

She cocked her head to one side, gave him a reluctant smile. The room was hot, quiet, no sound of the air conditioner, which was no longer making a pretense. He ran a hand over his beard.

"You need a shave," she said. "And a bath."

He cleared his throat. "Who are you?"

"Right now? Right now, I'm your worst nightmare. My name is Rose. I'm your wife. Here, take this."

"What is it?"

"It's just a Coke. It's cold."

David took the can—so cold it seemed precious. He held it to his forehead and closed his eyes.

She grimaced. "My God, it's hot in here. You look dehydrated, David. Drink and take some of these. No, no, it's just aspirin, that's all. You look like your head hurts."

It did hurt. He took the aspirin, reached for more. She snatched the foil pack out of reach.

"No, that's all for now, did you want the whole pack? You don't look like you've eaten in days."

"I have . . . no money."

"Considering that you cleaned out every account we have, it's hard to be sympathetic. Come on, get up."

"Why?"

"There's someone I want you to meet."

There was a fat man on the sidewalk, standing beside his father. David smiled at his dad and waved.

His father did not smile or wave back. He was handcuffed, and the fat man had him in a grip that looked painful.

David was amazed at the intense surge of anger. He raised his gun. "Let him go. Let my father go." He liked the way that sounded. My father.

The fat man looked at the woman who called herself Rose. *"You let him keep his gun?"*

She shrugged. "I didn't want him to feel threatened. Besides, I know David. The only person he might shoot would be you, Peterson, which would suit me just fine."

David clenched his teeth. *"Let my father go."*

The safety chip glowed green as it registered David's fingerprints. Ten more seconds, and he'd be able to shoot. He aimed for the center of the fat man's chest.

Peterson looked at Rose. "Now what?"

"I guess you let him go. Otherwise, I think he's going to shoot you."

Peterson let go.

"Cuffs off," David said.

Peterson said something under his breath and keyed in the cuff release.

"It's okay," David told his father. "We'll sort this out."

Rose curled her lip. "Tell him your real name. Tell him who you are."

David's father looked at her, rubbed his wrists.

"Tell him and don't take off. I run faster than you, 'cause I wear Keds."

The man looked at her shoes, then at David. He turned and ran.

"Shit," Rose said. *"Mel!"*

David's father dashed toward the street, Rose right behind him. David saw it before it happened—the police car bearing down, the screech of tires, the thud of the body being thrown. He called out and ran, praying as he went. Not dead. Not now, not after he'd found his father at last.

The police car stopped, frozen in the tracks which had clamped the wheels as soon as the man crossed the grid. David got there just as Rose tackled his father, bringing him down hard.

"Don't hurt him!" David lunged, but someone caught his arm.

"She won't hurt him, I already made her promise."

David turned, thinking he should know this man. Blue eyes, thick brown hair, solid build.

"David? You recognize me?"

David did not know what to say.

"It's Mel, David. Your partner? Your best friend?"

David shook the man's arm off, helped his father to his feet. "You okay?"

The man curled his lip. "I don't know who the hell you think I am, *chère*, but I don't know you. Get him off me, for Christ's sake."

FORTY-SEVEN

DAVID SAT ON THE FRONT PORCH, HIS DAUGHTERS CURLED around his feet. They had barely let him out of their sight since he got home, forty-eight hours ago. He did not have the heart to send them away, though they should not have been up so late, out on the porch, hearing the conversation.

Mattie blinked, head nodding forward, and David tucked her into his lap. She laid her cheek on his shoulder, touched his freshly shaven chin, and closed her eyes. Lisa went into the house and came back with pillows from the beds. She and Kendra curled up next to his chair.

David caught Rose looking from him to the girls.

String came out onto the porch, beers cradled in his fins. The screen door banged behind him.

"For Rose Silver, and Detective Mel, and Detective David."

David shook his head, waving the Elaki aside. For now, he had a horror of anything that might take the edge away. The disorientation of the last few days had been a nightmare.

String settled against the support post by the porch swing—his favorite spot.

"When did Miriam figure out the toxins were coming from the scale?" David asked.

Mel took a long drink of beer. "Miriam got worried the second time you called in sick, so she took another look at that tea sample. Didn't find anything. So she starts studying the tape, that monitor sheet of your blood chemistry when you were there on your first visit. Said she saw some elevated histamine levels—not much to speak of. Looked more like allergies, and was just the barest trace at that. But then she compared them to the monitor sheet on your second visit, and your levels had gone up a lot—and that was before you even set foot in the place. So either you had really bad hay fever—which

203

was possible, because you said you were sick—or you were
being exposed to something outside of the Institute. Which
had to mean the scale, because you kept it with you all the
time. Handled it, right?"

David shivered, and Mattie sighed in her sleep. "Yeah.
I did."

"Miriam said you were unusually sensitive to whatever it is
that's on there—kind of like an allergic reaction." Mel took
another drink of the beer, looked out into the night. "The guy
we arrested in Meridian, his name is Alford Crumbo, David. If
he's your father, he'd have to have married your mother when
he was fourteen."

David knew they were looking at him. He didn't like it. He
stroked Mattie's hair. He was mourning his father all over
again. Whatever he'd settled in his mind all these years, had
come unsettled.

"Did they hypnotize me?"

Mel shook his head. "Not that we could see, unless it
was awfully subtle. Miriam's still working on the drug—
actually, she's handed it off to the Feds. Working theory is
it worked like an allergy, like an irritant, and it made you
very suggestible, very vulnerable. Suppressed some parts of
your brain, stimulated others."

String swayed sideways. "Much testing will be the necessary."

"Anyway," Mel said. "We went in stomping, into the Institute. Got a warrant after you disappeared, on the grounds we
had an officer in peril. So that worked in our favor, otherwise
no judge would ever let us in there."

"You're so welcome," David said dryly.

Mel grinned.

String waved his beer can, spilling droplets on the porch.
"This Jordiki psychic. He is to be back in tomorrow. To talk
and sign. To face off the interrogation onto you, Detective
David, will be most of the interesting."

David shuddered, saw Mel watching.

"David's just going to be observing, String. Me and you
will be talking to him, and keep it in human-speak this time,
hear me? We'll catch him tomorrow, before Peterson gets to
him. You can invite Yo, David, she promises to be good."

"You sure he'll come through?" David asked.

Mel hid a small belch behind his hand. "He's ready to go. Worked everything out with his legal aid already. We broke Alford, got one other worm that turned—woman who played the reincarnated lover to the guy that blew his brains out."

"We still don't have Tatewood," David said.

Mel reached for the beer String had brought David. "We got Jordiki, and he's dealing. We're hoping he'll bring us Tatewood, and one or two of those Kahaners."

David frowned. He wanted Tatewood. Tatewood had strangled Theresa Jenks.

The phone rang. Rose got up from the swing, silent and graceful.

"Pouchlings all sleepset?" String asked.

David looked at his daughters. "Like babies."

"Ah. So glad to have the Father-One."

"Hey," Mel said. "We're all glad to have the Daddy-One home. How come you shaved the beard? I kind of liked it."

Rose opened the door. Looked from David to String to Mel.

"Now that you have our attention," Mel said.

"Clampett called."

"Clampett?" Mel asked.

"What iss thiss Clampett?"

David frowned. "You mean Clements? Arson cop?"

Rose nodded. Her lips went tight. "Bad news. You no longer have your witness."

String arched back on his fringe. "Is thisss the Jordiki? He is to recant?"

"Dead," Rose said. "The Mind Institute burned, right to the ground, no more than an hour ago. I didn't do it."

David stood up.

"No, don't go, David. Clements said there was no reason for you to come out, and you still . . . you're still shaky. The place went up in minutes, nothing left but ashes and remains that they're pretty sure belong to Jordiki."

David sat, settling Mattie back on his lap.

"Isss justice of the rhyme," String said.

Mel crushed a beer can. "Poetic justice, Gumby."

Rose settled back on the swing. "She said to tell you one other thing, David. That somebody saw a clown there, a half hour before the place went up. With a fistful—"

"Of purple balloons?"

Rose nodded.

"That's our Tatewood," Mel said.

FORTY-EIGHT

DAVID WAITED TILL ROSE AND THE GIRLS WERE ASLEEP BEFORE he left the house. He drove two hours in the night heat, windows down, arriving as the sun came up.

The Psychic Fair was quiet. You would never know that the streets had been crawling with fire fighters, psychics, palm readers, and residents just a few short hours ago. David passed his ID through the sensor box and stepped through the crime-scene tape.

The smell of smoke hung heavy. The glass dome had shattered and melted, nothing left but incinerated garbage up to the waist.

He felt almost ill standing there, thinking of himself in that little brown room. He felt as if his father had died all over again. He would be sorry if they lost Tatewood, but he was not sorry Jordiki was dead.

David hoped the Elaki had suffered.

Something moved, back in the rubble. David felt sweat roll down his shoulder blades. He took a breath. Peterson. Just Peterson.

The FBI agent raised a hand.

"Don't have a gun with you this time, do you, Silver?"

Actually, he did, but he shook his head. "You been here all night?"

Peterson nodded. "Watched it burn to the ground. Jordiki was dead by then. Went fast, Tatewood did it up good."

"Hurts, losing him."

Peterson hitched his pants up, stuck his thumbs in his belt. "If you only knew, Silver. I'd tell you I've lost count of how many of Tatewood's fire scenes I've been to, but the truth is, I can tell you the exact number. And this is number twelve."

David saw that Peterson's face was slippery with sweat, his eyes red-rimmed.

"I go to sleep at night . . . I smell smoke and burnt hair. I close my eyes . . . I see people, incinerated people. They sit on the end of my bed. I been tracking this man so long I know what his farts smell like. I got a psychological profile on him that would fill your office, we printed it out."

David rocked back on the heels of his shoes. "A good hunter knows where the target is going, not where he's been."

Peterson shook his head. "We've tried that, I promise you. Problem is, there's so many targets he could go for."

"He ever fail before? Not finish a job?"

Peterson gave David a sideways look. "None I know of. Everything else has gone right down to the ground, except—"

"Except the Cajun Supper Club. Because we ignored the bomb threat and released the grids."

Peterson stuck his hands in his pockets, looked hard at David. "I think I get your drift, Detective, but give me some specifics."

"I think we set out bait. Make it irresistible. He likes the fire, Peterson. He likes the games. Let's throw the ball in his court, and be waiting by the hoop when he comes to play."

"Think it'll work, do you?"

"You tell me, Peterson. You're the one with the profile."

FORTY-NINE

DAVID PUT THE INTERROGATION VID INTO THE SLOT, THEN
settled next to Detectives Clements and Wart.

Wart rippled his fringe, getting comfortable. "The Calib-boy
should be present for this music event."

Clements shook her head. "Last one I took him to, Wart, he
just squirmed in his seat. Didn't pay the least bit of attention."

"It is the wrong music of choice. This is one to be different."

"I don't have time to fool with it," Clements said.

David looked at the two of them, then back to the monitor.
The static cleared, and he saw Mel in the interrogation room,
feet up on the table.

Clements went up to the VCR, turned up the volume.

Jordiki stood next to the wall, and looking at him made
David's heart beat harder, his palms sweat. He focused on
String, who skittered from one side of the room to the other,
deliberately trying to annoy the other Elaki.

Mel opened his arms, as if he wanted to take Jordiki in a
passionate embrace. "Hey, you're psychic, right? Take a look
at your future. Ain't too bright, you think?"

Jordiki stayed still, but David could see the signs of dis-
comfort, tension.

"Charges will be the murder conspiracy, multiple counts,"
String said.

Jordiki followed String's movements with both eye stalks.
"There is no murder."

Mel gave the alien a half smile and tapped the computer
printout with a finger.

"We got you six ways to Sunday on the financing, Jo."

The alien reared up on his back fringe. David decided that it
was the nickname that bothered him, more than the evidence.

"Tell me of the Tatewood," String said.

"I do not know of a Tatewood. Is human?"

String said something Elaki-to-Elaki that David did not understand.

"String. *String*." Mel was shaking his head. "String, you can't do that, DA will have your scales in a bag. Talk people-talk, come on."

Jordiki skittered sideways, and Mel slammed the file on the table. "Sir? Jordiki, sir? Have you been threatened? Coerced in any way? Let me assure you—"

"There has been no threat," Jordiki said.

"You sure?"

Jordiki looked at String. "Reassure the human."

String waved a fin. "Do not speak over the head of this partner, you Jo. We have the financial connectors of the Mind Institute and Tatewood human. You have the proven financial bridge with you and the fire murders of hate. You may talk to us of Tatewood, and—"

"There will be negotiations?" Jordiki asked.

String's belly turned a darker color. "Yesss."

"Make the arrangements." Jordiki looked up at the monitor, and David felt his stomach jump.

This was a video and Jordiki was dead, he reminded himself.

Wart turned to Clements. "Must make the time, Yo Free. Have already reserved tickets."

"Wart . . . hell. Okay. Thanks, I guess."

The door opened and Mel walked in. "Just heard from Peterson, David, and—"

"How can this human be in two places at time and the same?" Wart asked.

Mel turned sideways, facing the Elaki. He glanced at David over one shoulder. "This is unbelievable. *Two* funny Elaki in the same building. Is it the coffee around here, or what?"

Clements leaned back in her chair. "He used to be very tame. You guys are a terrible influence."

David rubbed the back of his neck, realized his hand was shaky. "What did Peterson say?"

Mel sat on the edge of the table. "Said we got the go-ahead."

"For what?" Clements asked.

"We're smoking Tatewood," David said.

Wart waved a fin. "I must understand making a cigarette roll of the—"

Clements grimaced. "Quit playing dumb blond Elaki, Wart, you know exactly what he means."

David frowned, wondered if Elaki made a habit of feigning misunderstanding. Another irritating manifestation of quirky Elaki humor? Had String been making fun of them all this time?

"What's be the plan?" Wart asked.

"Bait," Mel said. "Cajun Supper Club just had smoke damage, right? Other than the second floor and the roof, okay, but still a lot of it standing. It's Tatewood's one big failure, that we know of. Peterson thinks Tatewood's going to jump at the chance to go back and try again, so we're being accommodating, and giving him another shot."

"How?" Clements asked.

David rubbed the top of the table with his finger. "We're back to the Racial Harmony Awards. Going to hold a dinner, some kind of fund-raiser there."

"Be an open invitation to trouble," Clements said.

Mel grinned and swung one leg. "That's what we're hoping."

Wart skittered to one side. "Perhaps we will make the showing on the Elaki Channel."

Clements rolled her eyes. "That's your big goal, Wart? Cable?"

FIFTY

DAVID LOOKED AROUND THE SUPPER CLUB, AMAZED AT HOW much could be accomplished in a short amount of time with the right bankroll and the best in nano technology.

The club was wide open and airy—most of the second floor had been torn away, the nasty little rooms replaced by an open floor that went halfway across the first, then stopped at a new escalator, put in particularly for the party.

Officially it was a benefit dinner dance, honoring past and present winners of the Racial Harmony Awards, attended by the wealthy, the socially prominent, and anyone else with the price of a ticket.

Many of them cops.

It was a slap in the face to the Kahaners. It was a target.

The balloons were Peterson's idea, one for every state, with the name of that year's award-winner. The big tease, Peterson called it. There had been publicity shots of the balloons being hung the day before. The party was getting a lot of play. The PR people at the FBI were good enough to go into business.

David knew the Kahaners would not be happy. He wondered if Tatewood would play.

He saw Mel and String, by the food table. Peterson talking to a woman in a red dress. He looked down the escalator at the crowd below.

No clowns. No purple balloons.

Clements was on duty, talking to Mel, though she did not look a bit cop-like in a slate-blue sequined dress. David saw her frown, and he braced himself for the fight, then she and Mel laughed. Miraculous. He looked back at Peterson, thinking there was something familiar about the woman in the red dress, just as she turned and saw him.

Teddy.

Someone called his name, and he turned, saw Rose, stunning in black.

"Anything?" he asked.

She shook her head. He saw, over Rose's shoulder, Teddy coming close.

"Hello, David." Teddy's eyes were bright and full of a wise kind of pain.

"Teddy, this is my wife, Rose. Rose, this is Teddy Blake. She works with—"

"With the FBI, yes, David, you told me."

David did not remember telling her. Rose smiled her social smile, and the two women shook hands, and David watched them like a man with something on his mind. Rose looked from David to Teddy, frowning slightly.

David felt a weird unexpected pride—how do you do, my wife and my lover, or is it ex-lover now? We never did resolve that, did we? He had the strange and dangerous urge to laugh. David Silver, King of the Jungle.

Rose looked at him and the feeling went away. His hands were shaking. He put them behind his back.

Rose gave Teddy a dismissive smile. "I want a drink. David, can I get you something? Teddy?"

"No," David said. Surely Rose knew better than to ask.

Teddy shook her head.

David looked at Rose. He offered to get her drink, but she said no.

"I want to talk to Mel anyway." She walked away, and Teddy stared after her.

"Excuse me, David, but I think Peterson wants me."

David touched her arm. "You can't avoid me forever."

"Who's avoiding you? Why do you think I came tonight, if not to see you? Now I've seen you, and I'm going."

"I don't understand what happened between us, Teddy. Did I miss something?"

"Look, David, I'm in a relationship right now that's starting to go sour. And the main problem is this psychic thing."

"Is it back?"

She shook her head, looked very young, then angry. "This man of mine doesn't believe in it and he has . . . contempt for it, okay? And that means contempt for *me*, so how can that be good? I put up with that attitude from Mama the whole time I was growing up—to this day, she and I don't speak. I just think I'd be making the same mistake all over again, if I start something up with you."

"I wish you'd thought of that before."

"Before what?"

"*Before* you started it up."

"It was a joint effort, don't you think?"

"You're projecting your problems with one relationship onto ours. Can't you keep us separate from everything else?"

"Like your wife?"

"Yeah, like my wife."

"I'm just trying not to make the same mistake twice. I'm flattered—"

"*Flattered?*" David thought he must sound stupid.

"I'm hoping we can be friends, David."

"My friends don't treat me like this."

Teddy narrowed her eyes. "Maybe not. But probably you don't sleep with them either."

David wondered how women got so good at making men feel they were in the wrong, no matter what.

FIFTY-ONE

THE CLOWNS CAME AT MIDNIGHT, DISPENSING FLOATING BOU-
quets of glorious purple balloons. The first clown through the
door was slammed into a wall and frisked, but at least fifty
more poured into the supper club right behind the first, and
suddenly balloons were as thick in the air as pollen on a hot
summer day.

David caught sight of Peterson and Brevitt, who crooked
his finger and motioned him over. Captain Halliday's voice
was soft in David's headset.

"David. We've had a fire call come in. Pierre's Café Bar."

God, David thought. Not Pierre's. But it made sense—
a restaurant that welcomed Elaki and humans on an equal
footing. Peterson was right. They couldn't guard them all.

"It was . . . okay, just in, David, false alarm."

"What?"

The captain's voice droned in his ear. "Got half the emergency units in town responding, and it's snarled the grid."

A woman looked at David, and he knew he seemed foolish,
conversing with the air.

She snagged a purple balloon and looped the string around
her wrist, smiling shyly. "Taking it home to my daughter."

David took the woman's hand and unwound the string,
smiling gently. He was aware of motion, all around. Cops,
clowns, everyone chasing balloons. Did Tatewood actually
think he could get away with this? They'd just round up all
the clowns.

David found Peterson. "Why aren't you evacuating?"

"We are, but it's going slow. Speaker system never made
it off the ground, so we're escorting them in groups."

David looked over his shoulder, saw a woman with a radio
talking to a group of old men in tuxedos.

One of the men put a hand on the woman's arm. "My dear, you are so charming. Are you sure we have to leave?"

She said, yes, sir.

"Too slow," David said.

Brevitt looked around, wearing his watchful look. "We got all the clowns rounded up now. None of them Tatewood."

"He could be disguised," Peterson said. "He's done that before."

"We can hope."

Clements came around a corner, hair swinging, metal box in her hands. She joined the huddle.

"We're not picking up anything, all the balloons are clean. I don't like this."

David frowned. "Fake fire call, Pierre's Café Bar. Tied up half the emergency units in town."

Mel detached himself from the buffet, crammed half a stuffed mushroom in his mouth. "David, you hear about—"

"Pierre's?"

Mel chewed, swallowed. "I been thinking about this. We got fake bomb threats before, right? Now we got fake fire calls. You think he's flipped it?"

Peterson turned and looked at Mel. "Flipped it how?"

"Before, the bomb was a fake. Now the fire is. Which means maybe this time there is a bomb. I mean, it makes sense. Guy's got a sense of humor."

Brevitt was shaking his head. "We've had this place tight the last forty-eight hours, and then we swept it. No way he could have planted a bomb."

"He might if he's a guest," Peterson said.

"We have more surveillance here than a girls' dorm."

Peterson grimaced. "You're living in the dark ages, Brevitt. Girls' dorms don't—"

David cut him off. "I think Mel's hit it, Peterson. We can't chance it. Pull the bomb squad in. Captain Halliday?"

There was a moment of delay, then the captain's voice sounded in David's ears. "I'm with you, David, bomb squad's been alerted. They've been on standby, so they should be with you in less than a minute."

David looked up. The evacuation was going well, but it needed to move faster.

"Let's get these people out of here."

* * *

The men and women in blue jumpsuits with BOMB SQUAD on the back had the added benefit of speeding people from the club. David personally saw the woman who had wrapped the balloon around her wrist to the door. She tried to get his phone number, but he just smiled and waved her out.

He saw Rose leading a group of men down the back staircase. He hoped she would stay with them. The room was almost clear. String glided across the ground floor, nearly colliding with a woman in a blue jumpsuit.

"Please, sir, to excuse."

The woman nodded, looked amused, and began checking the panel of controls beneath the arch of the escalator. David looked up to the second floor, and caught sight of Teddy. He thought how beautiful she was, light catching the sequins of her dress, red high heels strapped over delicate ankles. Balloons drifted by, like flowers. Someone had released the black balloons that listed the fifty states and their contest winners. One of them caught on the top handle of the escalator—David saw the glowing silver letters.

NORTH CAROLINA.

And he was on the Ferris wheel again, wind in his hair, thinking how much he wanted to kiss Teddy Blake. I'm afraid of two things, she had said. Escalators and North Carolina.

Had she seen her own death, and not realized it?

David saw the woman in the jumpsuit walk away—she moved quickly, hurried but controlled, the stiff-legged gait of an ex-con. And String had said, "sir." String, an alien, who did not pick up on the same male/female cues humans did. Who looked at the woman in the blue jumpsuit and said, "sir."

Not a woman, David thought. Tatewood. Planting the bomb that would bring the place down.

The mind was an incredible thing. One part of his focus was on Tatewood, aware of loud chatter, loud air-conditioning, music in the background, and his own voice, frantic on the headset, alerting Peterson, the captain, and anyone else tuned in. Tatewood was here. He'd planted a bomb. He was dressed like a woman, in a bomb squad jumper, and heading northwest from the escalator, bottom level.

The other part of him watched Teddy, thinking that sometimes a choice is not really a choice. He bounded up the steps, knowing that if Tatewood's bomb was on a remote, it would go off when he reached the top.

He thought that if he could reach her and touch her before the explosion, he'd be content. He could see that she was frightened, face pale, eyes wide and confused. Something was wrong and she did not know what to do. Her sixth sense was deafened and she was off balance without it. He called her name as he made the final leap to the top of the escalator, moving toward Teddy, toward his heart, toward his death and hers.

As soon as he had her in his grasp he was no longer content. He wanted more time, time while he ran with her, away from the escalator, toward the back staircase, minimally aware he was passing people, people who would soon be dead.

He did not have the breath to call out, he did not have the breath to warn them. He saw Clements, he saw Brevitt, he saw a waiter who was no more than a boy.

He saw the sign that said EXIT and knew they would never make it. It was his last thought before the shock wave hit, and he and Teddy went down.

FIFTY-TWO

A SHAKY VOICE WARNED DAVID NOT TO MOVE. HE THOUGHT about it awhile. He was sore and his head hurt, but he could move if he wanted, no trouble. He opened his eyes, saw the blue-white glow of emergency lights in the darkness. He turned sideways, and the floor beneath him creaked.

"*Stop.*"

David rubbed his eyes, trying to focus. Found himself face-to-face with a young, towheaded boy in a hard hat. The boy's eyes were wide, his face pale, and a bead of sweat hung over his upper lip where he was trying to grow a mustache.

"*Please*, for God's sake, be still, sir."

David thought of Teddy, reached for her.

"If you're looking for the girl, we got her out, okay? The supports are shaky, you understand me? We're about ready to collapse here, and the foundation is so iffy that it'll go before we can shore it up. So we've got to move slow and careful. Are you hurt? Can you climb down with me, or—"

"I'm okay."

The boy sighed deeply. "Good. Now just—"

"How many dead?" David asked.

"I don't know, man. They're holding the count until they see if you and me make it down."

David thought of Yolanda Clements. He squinted. "Give me your light."

"*Sir.*"

"Give—"

A rustling noise made both of them turn—vague dark shapes, moving close.

The boy's mouth hung open. "What the hell are you guys *doing* up here?"

David saw String and Wart, awkward but lightweight, heading his way.

"Beat it, kid," David said.

"What?"

"Go on. We have people to look for up here. Other cops. We're not coming down without them."

String lifted a fin. "Detective David, you are alive?"

"Not for long," the kid said.

Wart moved close. "Yo Free is here?"

David swallowed. "Not that way. Over there."

Wart aimed the light. It did not look good. A fallen support beam, rubble, what might be a foot.

"It is quiet, this," Wart said.

The Elaki moved ahead, going up and over rubble like top-heavy snakes. David went behind them on all fours, listening. He heard creaks, muted voices outside, the soft slide of Elaki scales and his own awkward scrabbles.

No faint voice, calling for help.

They found Brevitt first. He was on his back, hand thrown across his face, and David thought at first he must be alive. He was uncovered, and even as David pulled the arm away from the face, he knew there had to have been a reason the rescue workers passed him by.

Brevitt's eyes were open, and a dried streak of blood and spittle stained his chin and the corner of his mouth. David remembered him in the pancake house, methodically explaining the hunt for Tatewood. Clean-cut, probably had been a good boy all of his life. David lifted the left hand, saw the wedding ring, wondered if there were kids and sufficient life insurance.

Teddy was okay. He held the thought, right at the edge of awareness, and selfish or not, it comforted him.

David looked sideways at the rubble. No movement, no noise, no sign of Yolanda. He saw her again as he ran with Teddy, leaving them all behind.

And then String froze, bottom fringe quivering. "This I believe. Here."

Wart slid sideways, and David reached out to steady him, their shadows crossing String's light. David heard a crack, felt the shift of rubble.

"*Slow*," he told the Elaki.

Wart twitched, and they moved carefully toward String.

It was David who pulled the boards and plaster away, making quick work of what would have taken the Elaki long precious minutes. He found her hand, streaked with blood and dirt, felt the flutter of pulse in her wrist.

"Is dead?" Wart's eye prongs were rigid, his voice a strained whisper.

"Alive," David said, though the pulse was lazy and faint. He moved a board away, saw her face safe and sound and beautiful in a dark pocket of space. Her eyes were closed, and her head rolled from side to side. Tears leaked down the soft cheeks, and she cried silently, unaware, trapped in some dark agony of her own.

Wart touched her forehead, fin shedding scales. "Yo Free?"

Something roused her—his voice, his touch, the three of them crouched close, afraid to breathe. David pulled another board away, and she winced and cried out.

"Calib," she said.

David saw blood in her mouth. He bent close, and she opened her eyes. Her voice was strained, but cranky.

"Don't know fuck-all about fire scenes, do you, Silver?"

He laughed softly. "No, ma'am."

"He's not safe. Help me. Help me find him. Not safe." She tried to sit up, and David took her shoulders, felt thick wet blood on the back of her beautiful, blue-sequined dress.

"Light," he muttered.

String arced the light. Wart stayed still, his own light useless by his fringe. David saw the thick and wicked splinters of wood driven deeply into Yolanda's back, and shuddered. He saw a black well of blood beneath her, and death in her eyes.

He held her in his arms, unwilling to let her fall back. Could he not have taken just one moment to warn her? Could he not have caught her sweet warm hand as he ran by and saved them all?

He looked at Wart, shook his head. The Elaki jerked, and String looked from David to Wart, left eye prong drooping.

Clements looked up, face contorted. "Silver, damn it, help me find . . . help me find—"

"We have him," David said. "He's in the car with String, playing with the radio."

Clements smiled.

"He's safe," David said.

"Safe," she echoed. "Got to take him to the concert. I can't find those tickets."

"I have tickets, Yo Free."

"Wart," she said. Just his name. And smiled.

The animation left her eyes, and David knew that she was dead. He put a gentle hand into the front of her dress, checked her heart, found it still. She had lost enormous amounts of blood, and her skin was cool to the touch.

"Is gone?" String said.

David nodded.

Wart pulled away, emitting the high-pitched whistle of an Elaki in distress.

FIFTY-THREE

DAVID MUTED THE SOUND ON THE TELEVISION, WATCHED AS Peterson mouthed the usual press conference platitudes and the Federal Bureau of Investigation took full credit for the arrest of one Eugene Tatewood, a serial arsonist responsible for a series of supper club fires and arson deaths across the country, including Saigo City.

A quick clip showed Tatewood in handcuffs and chains—all for show—hair slicked back, doing that stiff-legged ex-con walk with Agent Peterson at his side. Tatewood looked at the camera, ducked his head, smiled the secret smile. David clenched his fists. A picture of Agent John Brevitt flashed across the screen, and the view cut to a funeral procession down the streets of Washington, DC.

No mention, no picture, of Arson Detective Yolanda Free Clements.

David heard a flute. String glided into the bull pen, followed by Calib and Wart.

"Must watch this pouchling most of the careful," Wart said.

String waved a fin. "Have the experience of human pouchlings."

"You will be the meet arrangements with this female emergency medical? You are certain she has not already the chemaki?"

String skittered sideways. "Sure, this is the yes."

Calib wore jeans that were too long, bunching over the tops of his shoes, dragging at the heels. He looked at every desk, frowning.

Looking for his mother, David thought. It would take time for this child to understand.

He raised a finger at Wart. "How long are you looking after the boy?"

"But always. Is the legal pouchling. Yo Free and I the agreement makes times and times ago."

String cocked an eye prong. "Pouchling needs the chemaki, so I am to arrange."

David looked from one Elaki to the other, wondering what he should say. Congratulations?

"Is the time, you are the ready?" Wart asked.

David nodded.

"Be wary of Wart's command of the van," String muttered.

"We'll take my car," David said.

String found a pair of handcuffs, handed them to the boy. David looked away.

David walked through the Psychic Fair with Warden at his side. No one gave them a second look.

"I appreciate this a lot."

"Isss my small pleasure." Even for an Elaki, the voice was toneless. Warden was faraway.

The dead were buried, and David knew he had been lucky. Rose and Mel were long gone by the time the bomb exploded. He and String and Wart had gotten out minutes before what was left of the second floor had come crashing down.

Peterson had literally sat on Tatewood until he'd gotten help. Tatewood had only been able to plant one of the three bombs in his possession, and if the FBI could keep their hands on him, he'd go down forever. He might not fall for the murder of Theresa Jenks, but he'd fall hard enough so that it wouldn't matter.

David paused in front of the familiar glass door while Warden studied the building with an educated eye.

"It will be okay, this."

David nodded and led the Elaki up the stairs. They went slowly. Narrow staircases were not Elaki-friendly.

David knocked at the scratched wood door. It was early; it took a while to get a response.

The door opened slowly, at last, and a man started at them, eyes blurred with sleep, hair mussed, movements slow and zombie-like. Candy Andy had aged since David saw him last, and he looked vulnerable in soiled white boxer shorts.

"What is this, any—" He gave David a second look, leaned against the doorjamb, crossing his bare bony legs. "Haven't seen you in a while, Officer. It's a little early to call. Make an appointment and come back."

"We have the warrant of investigation," Warden said.

Andy froze. "Investigation of what?"

"Building fire code violations. Please to let us in. You may get dressed if you wish. You are in the process of being arrested."

"This is ridiculous. Come on, Silver, you know I can beat this with the grandfather clause. This is pure harassment."

David nodded. "Yes. It is."

"Pleasse to get dressed or come to arrestment in underwear. Which?"

"Silver—"

David's radio went off, and he picked up the headset.

"Silver? Captain Halliday. Meet me on Bonheur Street, on the corner, right by the bridge."

"Can it wait?"

"No, it can't."

"I'm sorry, sir, but—"

"You can get here in about fifteen minutes, if you hustle. I know where you are, and I'm timing it."

David cut the connection. Thought about it.

"Who?" Warden said.

"Halliday. Unbelievably bad timing."

"I will take the care of thisss for you. *She* should be here. Would find thîs most to amuse."

David thought of Clements and Brevitt. Another incidence of bad timing. Death in police work often came down to bad timing.

David looked at Candy Andy, shivering in the hallway in spite of the heat, and wished, just a little, that he was the kind of cop who hit.

Instead he put a heavy hand on the man's shoulder. "Be nice to my Elaki," he said.

FIFTY-FOUR

DAVID LOOKED DOWN INTO THE WATER BENEATH THE BRIDGE, the brown muddy rivulets that had kept the secret all these years. He heard footsteps, felt Halliday's hand on his shoulder, was vaguely aware of a woman in a wet suit, wiping her hair with a towel.

"David?"

He was mesmerized by the water, the flow, the hidden depths. He turned reluctantly, looked at the captain, saw pity in the man's lean, hungry face.

"Sorry to get tough with you earlier. I didn't want to explain on the radio, and I thought you'd want to be here when they brought up the car."

David nodded.

"I couldn't call till we were sure. Diver brought up the car's records. You want to know what happened now, or later on?"

"Tell me."

"Want some coffee?"

"Just . . . tell me."

"Sorry. Evidently your father was at a hamburger place, no more than a block away, on Clairmont."

"It was a doughnut place then."

The captain nodded. "Anyway. He came out to the parking lot. It gets a little garbled here, but evidently he saw a wreck. Sounds like nothing more than a fender bender, for Chrissake. Car says a Cadillac was at the stoplight and got rear-ended by a white van—knocked it all the way across the intersection.

"Man in the Cadillac got out. Guy in the van got out. Guy in the van was carrying what the car thinks was some kind of high-powered automatic pistol. Van guy aims the pistol at the

226

Cadillac man across the road. Your father was there, in the parking lot—"

David did not need to hear the rest, though naturally he listened. He knew his father was not the kind of man to sit quietly by.

David could see it, see how it would go. His father would try to talk the man out of the gun. A maniac with a gun, angry over nothing, looking from his father to the man in the Cadillac, trying to decide who to shoot.

David heard the groan of gears, saw the arm of the crane. The captain was looking at him. "David? You going to be okay?"

"Why now? How'd you know the car was down there?"

The captain pointed. "Her."

David looked to the other side of the bridge. Teddy came toward him, braid loose and messy. She wore the blue jeans with the knee worn through, one shoe was untied, and her shirt was too big, cuffs down to her knuckles.

He was so glad to see her he almost cried.

She took his arm and led him away from the others. Getting right to the point, as always.

"After that night, where you saved my butt? It came back, David. You know."

He touched a loose strand of her hair, aware that he should not do such things, not with his coworkers watching.

"And for some reason, I started thinking about your daddy, and one thing led to another. Your captain was really great about the whole thing. He thinks a lot of you."

He nodded.

"Is this okay, David? You wanted to know?"

"I wanted to know."

"That's what I figured. Oh God, I was so scared I'd be wrong, and it wouldn't be him."

"Not you, Teddy. I'm glad for you, you know that, don't you?"

She smiled at him. "I feel like I been put back together."

He wondered if he would feel that way, given time.

She gave him her sideways look. "So, David. We friends, or aren't we?"

"We're friends."

"I didn't want to go, the way we left it. I been thinking a lot, about things. I want to go home and take a few days off, fool around in my garden, which has probably gone to hell. Get centered, you know? And then, can I call you, David? To see you again, if you know what I mean?"

The sensible thing to say would be no. He had let her get close, and he had gotten hurt.

"Call me," he said.

She looked over his shoulder, took his hand, and squeezed it. "All your buddies are watching, so pretend I am giving you the most passionate kiss ever."

"Now you pretend."

"What?"

He bent close and whispered in her ear. She blushed, and so did he.

"She's coming up!" came a shout.

David heard the gurgle of water. He closed his eyes.

"David, should I stay or go?"

"Just come and stand beside me."

"I guess a friend could do that."

FIFTY-FIVE

WHEN HE WALKED INTO THE KITCHEN THAT NIGHT, FULL OF news he did not know how to tell, David found his daughters drinking hot chocolate—a treat, even at the end of July.

He felt their delight in his presence, and he looked at their young faces, thinking that if it came down to a choice between their happiness and his, it was really no choice at all.

"We weren't sure you were coming home tonight." Rose's tone was light, for the benefit of the girls.

David knew she had wondered if he was coming home at all. She was wearing blue jeans and a black sweatshirt with the sleeves ripped out. Working clothes.

"Got a job?" he asked.

"Tonight."

"Something big?"

She nodded. "Guy Haas and I have been after a long time. Kills show horses for insurance money. Hires out."

David thought of Candy Andy, and Tatewood, and a dozen others, and knew there were some things he and Rose still shared.

"Go get him," David said softly.

Rose stood up and clapped her hands at the girls. "*Baths.* And make them fast, it's way past your bedtimes." She herded the girls down the hall, then looked at him over her shoulder. "It's easier, you know, when there's two of us."

David waited till Rose was gone, then got the girls out of bed, gathering them together in the kitchen.

"Who's sleepy?" he asked.

"Not me." Mattie rubbed her eyes.

"*I* am," Kendra said, frowning. Lisa stayed silent.

David made a sad face that they knew was fake. "Tooooo

bad. I wanted to go to a carnival and ride some rides, but I would feel silly, going by myself."

Mattie's eyes got huge.

"*Tonight?*" Lisa said. She began to hop up and down on the soft pink pads of her feet.

"It's *past* our bedtime," Kendra said.

David hung his head. "You're right. We better not. Mommy might be mad."

"*Don't tell her*," Mattie said.

David looked shocked. "You mean *lie?*"

Kendra tapped her chin. "No, no, not lie. Just don't bring it up."

David thought for a long moment while his daughters watched him, Mattie barely able to breathe. Lisa and Kendra knew the carnival was a given, but Mattie quaked with tension. David decided to have mercy.

"Okay," he said. "But if she finds out, we face up to it together."

"Daddy!" Mattie grabbed his waist and hugged him. "You don't have to, of course, but if you were hungry, maybe we would like some cotton candy?"

"You *have* to eat cotton candy, if you go to the fair."

"And ride the Ferris wheel?"

David patted her head. "And ride the Ferris wheel. Now. *Get dressed*, and make it fast. That means you, Kendra. Shoes, *and* socks."

"*Socks?*"

"Socks!"

David's daughters ran down the hallway, squealing as one slid into the bathroom ahead of the others. He stepped out the back door so he would not have to listen.

It was noisy out, country noises. Cicadas, crickets, traffic in the distance. Hazy too, but he could see stars. He flipped the porch light off, to discourage the moths, and leaned against the grape arbor.

David closed his eyes, thinking that peace of heart would be a wonderful thing.

He had a sudden and odd sensation that he was being watched. He turned his head slowly, and found himself eye-to-eye with the fat green iguana, nearly invisible beneath the cover of leaves.